PRAISE FOR **GOOD AS GONE**

"It's Amy Gentry's realistic portrayals of victims and their families that set *Good as Gone* apart from other page-turning crime dramas . . . A book that's hard to put down not only because of our investment in the plot, but also because of our investment in the lives of the complicated characters."

— AUSTIN CHRONICLE

"Compelling and emotionally nuanced."

— SEATTLE TIMES

"This smart, crisply written thriller begins with a 'ripped from the headlines' premise, but broadens to explore themes ranging from the mothering of daughters to the inwardness of suburban life."

— MINNEAPOLIS STAR TRIBUNE

"If you love a measured and thought-provoking novel of suspense, with one eye on character study and one eye on a city's conflicted culture, this might just be the next book for you."

— CRIME BY THE BOOK

"You need to read this book. Like a literary James Patterson, this is a not-to-miss debut." — Steph Opitz, book reviewer, MARIE CLAIRE

Praise for

GOOD AS GONE

"Amy Gentry has burst out of the gate with a monumentally intelligent, wily thriller about identity, vengeance, and homecoming that introduces readers to some of the most badass female characters on the shelf. *Good as Gone* is a river that shoots the reader deftly through rapids, over cliffs, past eerie vistas to a shocking, elegant, and well-earned ending. Do yourself a favor: jump in." —Kelly Luce, author of *Pull Me Under*

"A mother, a daughter, a zealot, an investigator, a family, a stripper, and more than a few survivors lay the riveting groundwork, but it's Amy Gentry's realistic portrayals of victims and their families that set *Good as Gone* apart from other page-turning crime dramas . . . The end result is a true 'novel of suspense': a book that's hard to put down not only because of our investment in the plot, but also because of our investment in the lives of the complicated characters." —*Austin Chronicle*

"A bracing, scarily honest look at what it means to be female—and to be a daughter, sister, wife, mother—wrapped up in a vicious thriller. Gentry's ambitious debut will satisfy fans of *Gone Girl, The Girl with the Dragon Tattoo,* and *The Killing*."

—Merritt Tierce, author of *Love Me Back*

"Both a mother-daughter and a family-under-fire story, *Good as Gone* is laden with confused identities and a thrumming plot."

—*Bustle*

"[A] superb first novel . . . Before you've even finished the book, you'll know that you want to read it again."

—*Christianity Today*

"*Good as Gone* . . . confirms the entrance of a powerful new voice in the world of crime fiction—Gentry knows crime fiction as a critic and as a writer, and brings her experiences with her for a novel that is as playful and self-aware in its structure as it is responsible in its themes."

—MysteryPeople

"Debut novelist Gentry delivers on genre expectations with crisp, unobtrusive writing and well-executed plot twists."

—*Kirkus Reviews*

"Clever perspective changes give Gentry's debut building suspense . . . Fans of Paula Hawkins's *The Girl on the Train* will enjoy the shifting points of view and the complex female characters, and those who liked Samantha Hunt's *Mr. Splitfoot* will appreciate the seedy characters and haunting theme of childhood vulnerability . . . Gentry's depiction of a family working through immense suffering will connect with many readers."

—*Booklist*

"Gentry's treatment is effective, with a swift-moving narrative and an interesting backstory for Julie and engrossing insight into Anna's ambivalence and grief . . . A good pick for fans of mysteries, thrillers, and family drama."

—*Library Journal*

GOOD AS GONE

GOOD
AS
GONE

AMY GENTRY

Mariner Books
Houghton Mifflin Harcourt
Boston   New York

First Mariner Books edition 2017

Copyright © 2016 by Amy Gentry

For information about permission to reproduce selections from this book, write to trade.permissions@hmhco.com or to Permissions, Houghton Mifflin Harcourt Publishing Company, 3 Park Avenue, 19th Floor, New York, New York 10016.

www.hmhco.com

Library of Congress Cataloging-in-Publication Data

Names: Gentry, Amy, author.
Title: Good as gone / Amy Gentry.
Description: Boston : Houghton Mifflin Harcourt, 2016.
Identifiers: LCCN 2016023390 (print) | LCCN 2016031648 (ebook) |
ISBN 9780544920958 (hardback) | ISBN 9780544916074 (ebook) |
ISBN 9781328745552 (pbk)
Subjects: LCSH: Teenage girls—Fiction. | Kidnapping—Fiction. | Mothers and daughters—Fiction. | Identity (Psychology)—Fiction. | Houston (Tex.)—Fiction. | Psychological fiction. | BISAC: FICTION / Suspense. | FICTION / Mystery & Detective / General. | GSAFD: Mystery Fiction. | Suspense fiction.
Classification: LCC PS3607.E567 G66 2016 (print) | LCC PS3607.E567 (ebook) |
DDC 813/.6—dc23
LC record available at https://lccn.loc.gov/2016023390

Book design by Chloe Foster

Printed in the United States of America
DOC 10 9 8 7 6 5 4 3 2 1

For Curtis, the best living human

GOOD AS GONE

Prologue

Jane woke up and whispered, "Julie?"

The room yawned around her. After two years of sleeping alone in her own bedroom in the new house, Jane no longer dreamed of the ceiling fan dropping onto the bed and chopping her up. The spiders, too, had vanished from the shadows; ten-year-olds don't need to have the corners checked before bedtime. Only occasionally, when something woke her in the middle of the night, the silence around her ached for Julie's soft breathing. In the old house, she used to hoist one foot over the top bunk railing and giggle until Julie said, *Shhh, Janie, go back to sleep.* Now, she shut her eyes tightly before they could drift toward the dark seams where the walls and ceiling met.

The next noise definitely came from Julie's room.

Jane pulled back the covers and slid her bare feet down to the carpet. In the old house, a braided rug slipped over the smooth wooden floor when she got out of bed. Now her feet barely made a sound on thick carpet as she padded to the door and peered down the dark hallway. A faint rectangle of lighter darkness hovered at the end — a closed door.

They rarely slept with doors closed; Janie's room got too hot, Julie's too cold. Mom grumbled about the air circulation in two-story houses, but Mom and Dad's room downstairs on the first floor was always shut at night, because they were adults. Now Julie was too, or wanted to be. Ever since her thirteenth birthday, she seemed to be practicing for adulthood all the time, brushing her hair slowly in front of the bathroom mirror as if rehearsing for some secret play, sitting at her desk to write in her diary instead of flopping on the bed stomach-first, like Jane. And closing her bedroom door.

At the end of the hall, the pale rectangle shuddered, a crack of darkness opening up around one side. Julie's bedroom door receded inward, four large fingers hooked around its edge.

Before she had time to think, Jane ducked into her closet, crouched down, and pulled the door shut behind her. The fingers — they were too high up on the door to belong to Julie, too large to belong to her mother. They didn't belong to her father either, but she didn't know how she knew they didn't, and that was the most unsettling thing of all.

A tiny, sickening click reminded her that the closet door never stayed closed for long. She threw her hands forward, but the door was already floating slowly open.

Jane squeezed her eyes shut as a soft tread started down the hallway.

When she opened them a moment later, the closet door had come to rest three inches from the door frame. The slice of hallway visible from her hiding place almost glowed against the closet's deeper darkness; she could see every fiber in the beige carpet, every ripple in the wall paint, and, hanging on the wall, half of a framed studio portrait in which long-ago Jane sat on long-ago Julie's lap, wearing a baby dress with a sailboat on it. The sailboat shook on its embroidered waves. Everything else was shaking too. The steps continued toward Jane's room.

The noisy floorboard in the middle of the hall moaned. The owner of the hand was now halfway to her room. Could he hear the creak in her ears each time her thundering heart shook the little boat? Jane resisted the urge to shrink back into her clothes on their rattling hangers.

Just then, a skinny foot appeared against the carpet, a patch of pink polish clinging to the big toenail, and Jane let out her breath. It was only Julie. She'd crouched over her toes perfecting the pink for an hour before her birthday party, but by the middle of the summer, most of it had scraped off on the rough white bottom of the backyard pool, leaving only these little triangles around the edges. So Jane had been wrong about the fingers, seeing things again, like the spiders in the shadows. Sure enough, here came Julie, moving into the frame with her ordinary Mickey Mouse nightshirt flapping around her ordinary knees, heading toward the staircase by Jane's room, probably just going down for a midnight snack. Jane's matching Donald Duck nightshirt was in a brown bag waiting to be taken to Goodwill; she'd already outgrown it. Her mom said she'd be taller than Julie someday. Jane hugged her pajama'd knees in relief.

But the fingers were back, this time perched on Julie's shoulder, clutching at the fabric of her nightshirt, her long blond hair trapped between their knobby knuckles. Jane barely had time to notice Julie's stiff, straight posture, like that of a wide-eyed puppet, before she saw the tall man following close behind her. Julie and the strange man moved together in slow motion, as if his long arm and hairy hand were a chain binding them together.

Wake up, wake up, wake up, Jane told herself, but nothing happened. Everything was frozen, including her, like in a dream; only Julie and the man kept moving. Slow, but faster than frozen; slow, but they were almost to her room. Janie opened her mouth to scream.

Then Julie saw her.

Jane's scream slid back down into her stomach as Julie stared straight into her closet hiding place. Jane stared back, begging Julie to tell her what to do next, readying herself to obey, to yell or cry or maybe even laugh if it was all a joke. Surely Julie wouldn't leave her alone in this bad dream. If Julie would just tell her what to do, Jane promised silently, she would listen to her and never complain from now on.

Without moving her head, Julie lifted her eyebrows and glanced meaningfully toward the man behind her, then back to Jane, as if telling her to take a good look, but Jane didn't want to; she kept her eyes trained on Julie instead. Girl and man turned on the landing without pausing at her door, and Jane saw why Julie was walking so stiffly: the man held the tip of a long, sharp knife to her back. Jane felt a nasty sting like a bug bite between her own shoulder blades, and her eyes filled up with tears.

They were poised at the top of the stairs when a loud tick sounded from the attic. Jane knew it was only the house settling, but the man stopped and looked over his shoulder nervously. In the split second before he looked back, Julie, as if freed from a spell, turned her head to Jane, raised her left index finger to her lips, and formed them into a silent *O*.

Shhh.

Jane obeyed. Julie started down the stairs, followed by the man with the knife.

And that, according to the only witness, is the story of how I lost my daughter—both my daughters, everything, everything—in a single night.

1

Julie's been gone for eight years, but she's been dead much longer—centuries—when I step outside into the steaming air on my way to teach my last class of the spring semester. The middle of May is as hot as human breath in Houston. Before I've even locked the door behind me, a damp friction starts up between my skin and clothes; five more paces to the garage, and every hidden place slickens. By the time I get to the car, the crooks of my knuckles are sweating up the plastic sides of the insulated travel cup, and my grip slips as I climb into the SUV, throwing oily beads of black coffee onto the lid. A few on my hand, too, but I let them burn and turn on the air conditioning.

Summer comes a little earlier every year.

I back the car out past the driveway security gate we installed after it was too late, thread through the neighborhood to the feeder road, and then merge onto I-10, where concrete climbs the sky in massive on-ramps like the ribbed tails of dinosaurs. By 8:00

a.m., the clogged-artery-and-triple-bypassed heart of rush hour, I am pushing my way into fourteen lanes of gridlock, a landscape of flashing hoods and red taillights winking feebly in the dingy morning.

I need to see over the cars, so the gas-saving Prius sits in the garage while I drive Tom's hulking black Range Rover—it's not as if he's using it—down three different freeways to the university and back every day. Crawling along at a snail's pace, I can forget about the other commuters and focus on the chipped letters mounted on the concrete awnings of strip malls: BIG BOY DOLLAR STORE, CARTRIDGE WORLD, L-A HAIR. The neon-pink grin of a Mexican restaurant, the yellow-and-blue behemoth of an IKEA rearing up behind the toll road, the jaundiced brick of apartment complexes barely shielded from the freeway by straggling rows of crape myrtles—everything reminds me that the worst has already happened. I need them like my mother needed her rosary. *Hail, Mister Carwash, full of grace, the Lord is with thee. Pray for us, O Qwik-Fast Printing. Our Lady of Self-Storage, to thee do we send up our sighs.*

Even Julie's billboards are gone. There used to be one right here, at the intersection of I-10 and Loop 610, by the senior-living tower wedged between First Baptist and a concrete flyover, but the trustees decided the billboards should come down five years ago. Or has it been longer? I believe it was due to the expense, though I never had any idea how much they were costing—the Julie Fund was Tom's territory. These days, the giant, tooth-whitened smile of a megachurch pastor beams down from the billboard next to the words FAITH EVERY DAY, NOT EVERY-DAY FAITH. I wonder if they papered him right over her face or if they tore her off in strips first. Ridiculous thought; the billboard's advertised a lot of things since then. Dentists, vasectomy reversals.

A line of Wordsworth from today's lesson plan rattles through my head like a bad joke: *Whither is fled the visionary gleam? / Where is it now, the glory and the dream?*

I flip my blinker and merge onto the loop. Despite all the time I've spent reading and studying Wordsworth's poetry—despite the fact that I am going to teach it in a few hours to a class full of impressionable young students and plan to continue teaching it as long as my university allows me to cling to my position without publication, committee work, or any effort besides the not-insubstantial difficulty I have getting out of bed every morning to face a world where the worst thing has already happened and somehow I'm still alive—I don't believe in the glory and the dream. I believe in statistics.

The statistics say that most abducted children are taken by people they know; Julie was taken by a stranger. The statistics say that most child abductors attempt to lure their victims into a vehicle; Julie was taken from her own bedroom at knifepoint in the middle of the night while my other daughter, Jane, watched from a closet. And finally, the statistics say that three-quarters of abducted children who are murdered are dead within the first three hours of being taken. Three hours is just about how long we think Jane sat in her closet, rigid with fear, before rousing Tom and me with panicked crying.

By the time we knew Julie was gone, her fate was sealed.

The inevitability of it has spread like an infection or the smell of gasoline. To make myself know that Julie is dead, I tell myself she always was—before she was born, before I was born. Before Wordsworth was born. Passing the pines of Memorial Park,

I picture her staring upward with sightless eyes under a blanket of reddish-gold needles. Driving by Crestview Apartments, I see her buried in the azalea bed. The strip mall with the SunRay Nail Salon and Spa yields visions of the dumpster behind the SunRay Nail Salon and Spa. That's my visionary gleam.

I used to want the world for Julie. Now I just want something to bury.

My class—the last before summer break—passes in a blur. I could teach Wordsworth in my sleep, and although I'm not sleeping now, I am dreaming. I see the crystal blue of the pool, shining like a plastic gem, surrounded by a freshly sanded deck under the tall, spindly pines. The girls were so excited about the pool, and I remember asking Tom, the accountant, whether we could afford it. The Energy Corridor District, with its surplus of Starbucks and neighborhood country clubs, wasn't really our style—especially not mine. But the girls loved the pool even more than they loved having their own rooms. They didn't seem to notice that we were moving out of shabby university housing to a part of town with two-story houses and two-car garages and green lawns studded with signs supporting high-school football teams. There are several reasons why we did that, but the one you want to hear, of course, is that we thought it would be safer.

"Class dismissed. Don't forget, your final papers are due in my box on the twenty-eighth, no later than five o'clock." By the time I get to "Have a nice summer," most of them are out of the door already.

As I walk down the hall to my office, I feel a light *brr* against my hip. It's a text from Tom.

Can you pick up Jane? IAH 4:05, United 1093.

I put the phone down, turn to my computer, and look up the University of Washington academic calendar. Then I check the university directory and call up a University of Washington administrator I know from grad school. A brief conversation follows.

I text Tom back. *Should I get dinner too?*

A few minutes later: *Nope.* And that's apparently all Tom and I are going to say to each other about Jane coming home early from her freshman year of college.

It's tricky picking Jane out of a crowd these days. You never know what color her hair is going to be. I stand close to baggage carousel 9 and wait until a tall girl with burgundy-black hair emerges from the crowd of passengers, a lock of faded-out green dangling in front of her eyes, having survived yet another dye job intact.

"Hi, Mom," she says.

"Hi, Jane." We hug, her heavy satchel thwacking my hip as she leans over, and then the empty baggage carousel utters a shuddering shriek and we both turn to look at it while I decide how best not to ask about her unexpected arrival.

"You changed your hair again," I observe.

"Yep."

Everything Jane says and does is a variation on the slammed door that first became her calling card in middle school, a couple of years after Julie was taken. In high school, Jane added loud music, hair dye, and random piercings to her repertoire, but the slammed door remained the centerpiece of the performance. Tom used to follow her dutifully up the stairs, where he weathered the sobs and yells I heard only in muffled form. I figured she needed her privacy.

"Did you have a good flight?"

"It was okay."

It was long. I suspect Jane chose the University of Washington because of its distance from Houston. When she was a little girl she used to say she wanted to go to the university where I teach, but the pennants came down around the same time the door slamming began. She might have ended up in Alaska if she hadn't insisted on going to a school that had quarters instead of semesters—every possible difference a crucial one. All typical teenage behavior, no doubt, but with Jane, it made a particular kind of perverse sense—as does the fact that, according to the registrar, she took incompletes in all her spring-quarter classes.

This after she'd stayed in Seattle through the entire school year. I didn't think much about her not coming home for Thanksgiving; it's commonly skipped by students on the quarter system, since the fall quarter starts so late. But when she explained to us over the phone in mid-December that she was just settling in, that one of her professors had invited her to a holiday dinner, that our family never really celebrated Christmas anyway, did we?, and that she felt like it would be good for her sense of independence to stay, I could practically hear Tom's heart breaking over the extension. I covered for his silence by saying the sensible thing, the only possible thing, really: "We'll miss you, of course, but we understand."

Now it seems the whole holiday situation was yet another slammed door to which I'd failed to respond properly.

"So," I say, starting again. "You still enjoying U-Dub?"

"Go Huskies," she says with a limp fist-pump. "Yeah, Mom. Nothing's really changed since last time we talked." The bags start dropping onto the conveyor belt, and we both lean forward.

"Was that coat warm enough for January up there? Winter stuff is on clearance, we could go shopping."

She picks self-consciously at the army jacket she's worn since she was sixteen. "This is fine. I told you guys, it doesn't get that cold."

"Classes going okay?"

"Yeah," she says. "Why?"

"Just making small talk."

"Well, they're going really well," she says. "Actually, they're going so well, my professors are letting me turn in papers in lieu of exams."

In lieu of exams! That sounds official. I wonder how she got them to agree to give her incompletes rather than failing her. My students usually just say "Family emergency" and hope I don't press them for details.

Carefully, I ask, "Is that something they do a lot at U-Dub?"

"Mom," she says. "Just say 'University of Washington.'"

I give her shoulder a quick squeeze. "We're just glad you're home." I lower my arm and we stand there, side by side, staring at the shiny metal chute, until half the passengers on the flight have claimed their bags and wheeled them off, their absence making the juddering of the conveyor belt sound even louder. Finally, Jane's rolling suitcase somersaults down the chute and thunks onto the belt in front of us. It was a graduation present—apple green and already dingy from its maiden voyage to Seattle and back, it almost matches her dyed-green streak. She grabs the suitcase before I can make a move but lets me take her satchel when she stops to peel off her army jacket in the blast of humid air that hits us outside the automatic sliding doors.

"I see we're in swamp mode already."

"No place like home," I reply and am rewarded with a half smile of acknowledgment.

The ride home is rocky, though. I'm shooting blanks on college life despite spending most of my time in a university.

"How are the dorms?"

"Pretty good."

"You still like your roommate?"

"She's fine. We stay out of each other's way."

"Are you going to room with her next year?"

"Probably not."

Finally I resort to a subject I'm sure will get results, although it pains me. "So, tell me about this English professor you ate Christmas dinner with."

"Her name is Caitlyn, and actually she's a professor of semiotics."

Caitlyn. "I didn't know they still taught semiotics in English departments."

"The course is called Intersectionalities. It's an English class, but it's cross-listed with linguistics, gender studies, and anthro. There are supposed to be all these prerequisites, but I went to Caitlyn's office hours on the first day and convinced her to let me in."

I can't help but feel a glow of pride. A true professor's kid, Jane knows all the angles. Moreover, this is the longest string of consecutive words she's spoken to me without Tom around for ages. "Tell me more about it, what did you read?"

"I think I'd rather wait and talk about it with Dad too," she says.

"Of course," I say.

"I don't want to say it all twice."

"Sure, sweetie."

I turn on NPR, and the measured, comforting sound of rush-hour news commentary fills the car as we inch past a firing range and a gym where an Olympian gymnastics coach is probably even now yelling at ponytailed girls in formation. Jane stares out her window. I assume she is wondering why Tom didn't come to pick her up instead of me. I'm wondering too.

A few minutes later we both find out. Pulling into the driveway, the sky just starting to glow with dusk, I spot Tom through the kitchen window, making dinner. As I open the door and walk in, I smell Jane's favorite pasta dish: fettuccine Alfredo tossed with breaded shrimp and grilled asparagus, a ridiculously decadent recipe Tom got off the Food Network and makes only on special occasions. An expiatory salad of fresh greens is in a bowl next to the cutting board, ready to join the bright Fiestaware on the dining-room table.

"Janie!" Tom opens his arms and steps forward, and Jane throws her arms around him, squeezing her eyes shut against his chest. I slip off to the bathroom, then to the bedroom to change out of my teaching outfit into more comfortable jeans, loitering for a few minutes to put away some laundry that's been sitting, folded, in a basket at the foot of the bed. When I return, they are talking animatedly, Tom's back to me as he chops heirloom tomatoes for the salad, Jane resting the tips of her fingers on the butcher block as if playing a piano.

"Dad, you would not believe the names people were throwing around in this class," she says. "Derrida, stuff like that. Everyone was so much smarter than me."

"Hey, she let you in, and she's the MacArthur Genius lady."

"Every time I opened my mouth I sounded like an idiot."

"At least you opened your mouth," he says, resting the knife to the side of the cutting board for a moment while he looks her in the eye. "I bet there were some people who were too scared to talk."

Jane's grateful smile, just visible over Tom's shoulder, curdles me like milk. As if he can sense it, Tom turns around and sees me standing there. He throws a handful of chopped tomatoes onto the pile of greens and picks up the salad bowl.

"Everything's ready!" he says. "Grab the pasta, Jane. Let's sit down and eat our first family dinner in God knows how long."

And that, believe it or not, is when the doorbell rings.

2

The first thing I see is her pale hair, all lit up in the rosy, polluted glow of the Houston sunset.

Then her face—ashen skin stretched thin over wide cheekbones flushed red across the top so that the dark circles stand out under her sunken eyes. The face looks both young and old. She wears worn-out jeans with holes at the knees, a T-shirt. She opens her mouth to speak, and I see that her feet are bare.

There's something familiar about her, but it's like my entire body has become fused with my surroundings, my brain rewired to resemble blind hands fumbling, the sensory data bumping uselessly around in search of something to latch onto: *Hair. Eyes. Young. Bare.*

Her eyes widen, and the color drains from her face.

My hands stretch out in front of me, palms out, fingers spread wide, ready to shield me from the nuclear sunset or as if I'm about to fall down, but it's the girl on the porch who falls, her knees buckling so that she folds up neatly as she collapses onto the mat, blond hair catching lightly in the azalea bushes on her way down. I open my mouth and I think I must be yelling for Tom, although I can't hear it because my brain is still blinded by the sunset glancing off her face. He comes running up behind me, stops, and then thunders through the doorway. When I look again, the girl has all but vanished into his arms, the loops and tangles of her hair crushed between his fingers as he hugs her to his chest, rocking back and forth. "Julie, Julie, Julie," he is sobbing, like the chorus of the nightmares that I now know have never stopped but have been unreeling every night for eight years, and perhaps all day long as well, in a continuous stream I have simply chosen to deny.

The sight of Jane standing stock-still in the hallway flips the light switch back on in my head. "Call 911," I manage to say. "Tell them we need an ambulance." To Tom, who is making strange, animal sounds of grief I have also heard in my dreams, I say, "Bring her in."

And just like that, the worst unhappens. Julie is home.

The first twenty-four hours after Julie's reappearance are oddly similar to the first twenty-four hours after her disappearance, a mirror symmetry that lends extra significance to every detail. There's the humidity of the long, hot summer's beginning, the crape myrtles that were already dropping their flowers when she was taken in early fall just now starting to put out blossoms like crumpled scraps of tissue paper. There are the sirens blaring their way through the neighborhood up to our house, just like last time, but bringing EMS rather than the police and at sunset rather than sunrise, so the neighbors who open their front doors to see what's happening are wearing work clothes rather than bathrobes, holding oven mitts rather than newspapers. Everything is backward, like a photo negative of tragedy.

Only one of us can ride in the ambulance with Julie, and Tom immediately steps forward, so Jane and I climb into the SUV and follow behind. When we pull up to the ED, they are unloading her gurney, now connected to a rolling IV, and she is wheeled inside and installed in a curtained-off room with that excruciating combination of slowness and urgency native to emergency departments.

The next thirty minutes pass like hours under the fluorescent lights. Julie wakes, mumbles, sleeps again. Tom sits by the bedside, holding Julie's hand and murmuring something unintelligible; I pace; Jane leans; nurses come in at odd intervals, never telling us anything but instead asking for details about insurance or Julie's medical history, questions that seem so useless and redundant that I become convinced some of these people just want to see the famous Whitaker girl in the flesh. One nurse comes in to draw blood, and Julie starts awake at the cold wet cotton swab on her inner forearm, keeps her eyes open just long enough to nod vaguely at the nurse's bright questions, then fades as soon as the needle is in. The curtain that separates us from the hall flutters as people rush by and does nothing to block out the cacophony of squeaking wheels, indecipherable PA announcements, and hallway conferences punctuated with loud sighs and occasional laughter.

When the doctor finally comes, she sends everyone out of the room over Tom's and my objections.

"I just need her for two seconds," she says. "You — Mom, Dad — don't go anywhere."

Needless to say, we don't, but Jane takes the opportunity to find a restroom. The doctor emerges from the curtained room after a hushed conversation I strain unsuccessfully to hear, and I glimpse Julie in the background, awake but flushed and disoriented, before she pulls the curtain shut behind her. Julie is dehydrated, the doctor tells us, suffering from exhaustion and exposure, and hasn't eaten for a few days, but there don't seem to be any injuries or illnesses, no substances in her bloodstream. "After the fluids take effect, most likely she'll be right as rain," she finishes, her use of the expression *right as rain* proving she cannot possibly have read the chart, or she has never watched the news, or she is so calloused by her job that she lacks the power to think past a stock phrase indelibly associated in her mind with the word *fluids*. "Just get her to the clinic for a follow-up after a few weeks. They'll schedule her when she's discharged."

As we file back into Julie's room, there's a knock on the wall, and a police detective steps in after us. Fortyish, with dark hair, looking not unlike a police detective from a TV show but far less attractive, he leaves the curtain open a foot and stares at Julie from the improvised doorway.

"Julie Whitaker," he says. "Unbelievable."

Julie doesn't take any notice of him, but on seeing Tom and me again, she collapses back onto the pillow, crying tearlessly. Tom rushes to enfold her in his arms. Noting my expression, the doctor says they'll move Julie to a room with a door as soon as one opens up, and then she hustles out. The cop introduces himself as Detective Overbey and starts asking me questions about the circumstances of Julie's arrival, which I answer as best I can considering that, for all I know, she could have come straight out of the glowing orange sunset or a god's forehead or the side of a man opened up while he was sleeping. The question of how she was delivered to us seems that unimportant.

In the background, I hear Tom repeating the words "You're safe now. It's okay. The doctor says you're going to be okay." He is talking to himself as much as to her, and though the words aren't meant for me, they're so comforting that I let my attention drift toward them and away from Detective Overbey's questions.

He notices. "I'd like to talk to Julie alone for just a few minutes."

"No," Julie says, clutching Tom's arm but looking at me. "Don't go."

"This won't take long."

Tom stands directly in front of Julie's bed. He's a tall, broad man, imposing even with a gut. "Absolutely not. We left her alone once tonight, for the doctor. We're not leaving her again."

Tom and the detective begin to argue back and forth, and the tiny curtained room shrinks. The same words keep coming up, and at first I think Detective Overbey is questioning our mental health or Julie's; he is talking about the *sane*, the *safe*. Finally, he addresses Julie directly, speaking right through Tom. "I know you're not feeling well, ma'am, and I hate to bother you right now," he says. "But I need to ask: Were you sexually assaulted?"

Julie just looks at the detective and nods. Tom sets his jaw, and I find a moment to be glad Jane is still not back from the restroom.

Detective Overbey explains about the forensic exam, and I realize SANE and SAFE are acronyms. "The sexual assault nurse examiner has already been dispatched," he says. "She should be here soon to set up the exam room. The minute you're off the IV, she can get started."

Julie shakes her head no, and Tom steps forward, looking ready for a fistfight.

Detective Overbey, equally imposing, stands his ground. "If there's any evidence of sexual assault, it's best to collect it—"

"Listen," Tom says, pointing his finger at the detective for emphasis. "We've done everything the police told us to since day one and never asked a single question we weren't supposed to. Eight years later, after we've—" He chokes. "Years since we've heard any news, and our missing daughter shows up on our doorstep, no thanks to you. And now you want to keep her up all night asking her questions, treating her like a crime scene?" He snorts. "We'll come in tomorrow."

Detective Overbey starts to answer but a faint noise from Julie's bed stops him.

"The last time was—a long time ago," she says quietly. "At least six months."

Detective Overbey sighs as if the news that our daughter hasn't been raped in six months is disappointing but acceptable. "Okay, then. We still recommend you come back for the exam, but from a forensic perspective there's no rush. Rest up, and we'll get a full statement from you folks at the station tomorrow."

Julie nods weakly. Tom slumps forward, hands on knees.

Jane comes in, a juice box in her hand. She must have gotten it from the nurses' station. When she sees Julie awake, she smiles shyly and says, "Welcome back."

Six hours later, in the middle of the night, Julie is discharged, fully hydrated and wearing hospital scrubs to replace the scruffy T-shirt and jeans the police took for evidence. She leans on Tom's arm while I sweep everything into my purse: prophylactic antibiotics for chlamydia and gonorrhea, a prescription for Valium in case she has trouble sleeping, and a folder stuffed to bursting with pamphlets on sexual assault and Xeroxed phone lists for HPD Victim Services and various women's shelters. It also holds Detective Overbey's card, tucked into four slits in the front of the folder so it won't get lost. I remove it and slip it into the back pocket of my jeans.

Tom drives us home, Julie sleeping in the back seat of the SUV on the disposable pillow they let her keep. Jane, who slept quite a bit in the hospital, now stares at Julie silently. Nobody talks—in part because we don't want to wake Julie, but also because we ourselves do not want to wake up. Or maybe that's just me.

It's 3:00 a.m. when we open the back door and walk into the kitchen through the laundry room. It looks like some other family's house preserved on a perfectly normal day, a museum of ordinariness: over the washing machine, a blouse drips dry; on the cutting board, a heap of glistening red chopped tomatoes lies next to a knife in a puddle of red juice. Through the doorway to the dining room, Jane's elaborate homecoming meal sits forgotten on the dining-room table, the salad wilted, the breading on the fried shrimp gone soggy, the sauce jelled on the cold, gummy pasta. As the others pass through the kitchen into the living room, I head into the dining room and start picking up the dishes full of pasta. It takes only a moment for me to stack the evidence that we were surviving in the kitchen sink.

When I join them in the living room, Jane and Tom are standing awkwardly by the sofa with Julie, like people putting up a distant relative for the night. Tom is shaking his head, red-faced, and when I realize what they are discussing, my efforts in the dining room seem futile.

Tom moved his office into Julie's room seven years ago. He did not discuss it with me first; nor did he let me know he was quitting his accounting job, the job we moved to the Energy Corridor for in the first place, to go into private practice as a tax consultant. One day I passed her room and saw it had been transformed from bedroom to carefully tended shrine, a desk and file cabinet where her bed used to be, posters replaced with framed pictures of Julie. I understood without being told that this new office was to be his command center for the search, that he was turning his longing for her into a full-time job. Only now, with Julie standing in front of us, does it look like an exorcism.

"I don't mind the sofa," Julie is saying.

"She can have my room," Jane says, still hanging back, like she's afraid to stand too close. Clutching her elbow awkwardly, she looks more like her ten-year-old self than I would have thought possible, though I notice with a pang that she's taller than Julie by quite a few inches. Jane stares at Julie, not hungrily, like Tom, who looks as if he'll never let her out of his sight again, but with a wary expression. "I don't mind."

"No, please," Julie says. "I don't want to take anyone's room."

I have a sudden longing to bed her down between Tom and me, like we did when she was a seven-year-old with a fever and couldn't stop shivering. This, however, is not practical, and meanwhile, the living room yawns open like a mouth around us, the windows dark behind the curtains.

"Tom, the air mattress?" I offer. "She could be in her room until we can move your desk out."

"A door that closes would be nice," she says, and it's decided. She has no toiletries or luggage, and no one wants to ask why, so Jane gives her a T-shirt and shorts to sleep in and I scrounge up a spare toothbrush still in its package. After the bustle is over, Julie disappears behind the door of Tom's office like the sun behind a cloud. I wonder if she is comforted or disturbed by all the pictures of her in there.

By the time we have seen Jane to bed as well, with reassurances that she can decide if she wants to come to the station when she wakes up, it's almost dawn. The bedroom door closes and my legs want to buckle under me, but I also feel more awake than I have for years. My mind is racing, or rather somersaulting, tumbling over itself as I go through my bathroom routine.

Tom says, "Anna?" in a way that suggests it is the second or third time. I come out of the bathroom and see him lying on his side of the bed, looking up expectantly.

Instead of finding out what he wants, I surprise myself by saying exactly what I'm thinking: "What are we going to do?"

"She's back," he says. "We don't have to do anything anymore."

I slide out of my jeans, keeping my T-shirt on to sleep in.

"She's back," he repeats, like a stubborn child.

"We don't know what she's been through." I think of the detective's card tucked into the pocket of my jeans as I hang them on the back of the closet door. "We have to be careful."

"We should have been more careful then." His voice breaks a little.

I emerge from the closet. "She may not be—the same."

"None of us are," Tom says. There's a long pause. "You didn't believe she would ever come home."

I sit down on the edge of the bed. I can feel his eyes burrowing into the back of my head, and I close my own, tasting the accusation.

After a moment I turn to face him. "I didn't believe we would *find* her," I say, trusting him to know the difference.

He doesn't answer. But as I lean over to turn off the light on my nightstand, I feel something shift, just a little piece of the night air between us moving aside, like a breeze wafting through a chink in a wall. He turns onto his side, facing away from me, but there's something about this argument that reminds me of the marriage we used to have, the arguments that bubbled up only when we were in bed together. How gamely we entered every fight back then, knowing we'd still wake up next to each other in the morning.

Now, staring at Tom's back, I think, *Julie is home. Anything can happen.*

I see her face again the way I saw it on the front porch, just barely familiar, the flesh melted away from her cheekbones and jaw, leaving a butterfly of bone.

"Good night," I say.

I sleep until noon and wake to the noise of pans clattering downstairs, voices in the kitchen.

I know this dream. It's the one where Julie shows up, and I say, "I've dreamed about you so many times, but this time you're really home." Now I get up and splash water on my face in the bathroom and look at myself in the mirror, waiting for the features to distort, to drift. Everything stays put. This one is real.

A chill runs through me and a faint headache alights in my frontal lobe. I pull on my jeans from last night and head downstairs.

The kitchen table is bathed in light. My radiantly blond daughter sits on the side nearest the window, still wearing Jane's T-shirt, which is too big on her. Tom beams at her from the head of the table as they talk—about nothing, it seems: orange juice, the weather, does anybody want more eggs. For a moment it looks almost normal. Then Jane comes in with a glass in her hand and sits across from Julie, and a shiver walks down my spine as I observe the odd regularity that has returned to our family: a girl for each side of the table, four sides for four people. The words *fearful symmetry* pop into my head.

"Good morning," I say from the doorway.

"You slept forever," Jane says, but Julie is already getting up and in three long strides she has embraced me. It takes me aback. How long has it been since a daughter of mine came rushing into *my* arms from across the room? Just as I am starting to notice the scent of her hair, she pulls back and looks at me, her hands sliding down my arms to grasp my hands. "Hi, Mom," she says, a little awkwardly, and for a moment we are looking straight into each other's eyes.

I have become accustomed to looking at Jane, who shares my distinctive features, my sharp nose and deep-set eyes. As I stare into Julie's woman's face, I realize there are no moles, no bumps or blemishes or wrinkles.

She's *perfect*.

She breaks away, embarrassed, and I realize I have been staring.

"I'm sorry," I say. "I haven't seen your face in so long."

"I know," Tom says.

"Sit down, I'm just getting some coffee," I say. "Did you sleep okay?" There's a big pan on the stove with some scrambled eggs left in it, and I put some on a plate, suddenly ravenous.

"I slept very well," she says, like a polite guest. "The air mattress was comfortable."

"She's only been up for a few minutes," Tom says. "I've been fielding phone calls from the police department all morning. *Come in whenever you want* apparently means 'If you're not here by nine you'll be hearing from us.'" His face darkens. "I suppose it makes sense. They're worried about the press. I'm sure that'll be starting anytime now."

Julie's smile fades. "I guess we should probably go, now that Mom's awake."

Tom puts a hand over hers on the table. "You take as much time as you need."

"The sooner we go, the sooner it'll be over," I say.

Tom's eyes tear up, and I realize he doesn't want to know what she went through. At the same time, it occurs to me that I do.

Julie is studying my face with an almost grateful expression. "Yes," she says. "I want to get it over with." I can tell by the way she's looking at me that Julie needs me there, and no one else. I can't keep Tom away from the police station, but I decide I'm going to persuade him to stay out in the hall, which means Jane will have to come too, to give him someone to look after.

"Come on, Julie," I say. "I'll find you something in my closet to wear." A skirt, I think, looking at her dwindled frame. And I'll need some safety pins.

"He said he would kill me if I struggled. Kill my family."

"You believed him?" says Overbey.

We are sitting in the police station—me, Julie, Overbey, and a younger female detective, Detective Harris—in a private room with frosted-glass windows and a single table. Tom is outside waiting in the lobby with Jane, per Julie's request. Overbey wanted to question Julie alone, but she looked from his face to my face and then back, and he sighed and invited me in. I'm holding but not drinking a cup of black coffee so weak you can see air bubbles clinging to the inside of the Styrofoam, read the imprint of the serial number on the bottom. It was brought to me by Detective Harris—*Typical,* I think—while Overbey asked the questions.

"Of course I believed him," Julie says now. "He had a knife at my throat."

"A kitchen knife," Overbey says, consulting his notes, as if he doesn't already know everything in the case file. "Taken from the household. Any other weapons?"

"She was thirteen," I break in, but Overbey holds up his hand and nods for Julie to go on, and it's true she doesn't seem upset.

"Not that I saw. But I believed him. And if it was happening to me again now, knowing what I know about him, I would still believe him." She takes a breath. "Once we were out of the house, we got on a bus just by the CVS, there on Memorial Drive, and went to the bus station downtown."

"Did anyone see you?"

"The bus driver, maybe, but I was too scared to say anything. At the bus station he bought two tickets. We got off in El Paso." She pauses, and her eyes go dead. "That's where he raped me for the first time."

"Do you remember where you were?"

"Some motel. I don't remember which one."

"Motel Six? Econo Lodge?"

She glares at him icily. "Sorry. We stayed there for only a couple days and then we were gone again. We moved all the time. He stole a car in El Paso"—Overbey makes a subtle gesture without looking at Harris, who writes something down—"and for a while we drove that, but he sold it somehow, I guess. He just came back without it one day."

"He left you alone?"

"Yes. He left me tied up and gagged when he had to go out. We were in Mexico when he sold the car, I think, but I'm not sure because I was blindfolded, and then I was in the back of a van for a long time." The duct-taped-in-a-van dream floats before my eyes. "It took me a while to find out he'd sold me."

"He what?" Overbey looks up sharply.

"He sold me," she says. "Five men, maybe six."

Harris nods and returns to writing.

"Did those men—"

"Oh yes." She gives a cold, brittle smile. "Yes, they did."

My eyes close.

"Mrs. Whitaker, are you all right?" It's Harris's voice. I am sinking, eyes shut, into a cold black vapor that prickles at my extremities. I hear Overbey correct his partner—"Mrs. *Davalos* goes by her maiden name"—and snap my eyes back open, but the black dots take a moment to clear.

"I'm fine," I whisper. I want to reach for Julie's hand, but her arms are folded tightly across her chest.

"Could you identify any of the men?"

"I was blindfolded," she repeats patiently.

"Any accents?"

She thinks. "Some of them spoke Spanish to each other, but none of them talked very much. Anyway, that was a couple of days

—I think? I can't remember it very well. Then they sold me again. To someone important this time."

The detectives look meaningfully at each other. "Who?"

"I never knew his name. The other men called him El Jefe when they were talking about him, *señor* to his face."

"Go on," Overbey says calmly while Harris scribbles furiously. "How did you know he was important?"

"He had a giant house, like a compound, with bodyguards and a household staff and a lot of men with big guns coming to him for orders." She stops and takes a breath. "Please don't ask me where, I don't know. I didn't go outside."

"For how long?"

"For eight years."

Later, I tell Tom as little as I can get away with, enough to explain the pages of thumbnail photos Julie looked through at the station, pictures of Mexican men in their fifties with high foreheads and thick chins. I narrate the various stages of her captivity, but not the cigarette burns she got when she tried to escape; the years of rape, but not the way she spoke of them, as if describing the plot of a not particularly interesting television show. I tell him that her captor tired of her, but not that she was too old for him once out of her teens; I tell him that she was blindfolded and taken in a helicopter to a rooftop in Juárez, but not that the guard was most likely supposed to kill her rather than let her go. I tell him that she hid in the back of a truck to get across the border, but not that she was afraid of the U.S. Border Patrol because she wasn't sure she could still speak English, or anything at all, after so long; that she jumped out of the truck at a stoplight and ran, but not that she dragged herself foot after foot along the I-10 feeder road for miles, invisible from the freeway, like the people you learn not to see stumbling through gas-station parking lots, clutching their possessions in plastic bags.

"My God," he says under his breath. We are at the kitchen table and the girls are upstairs in bed, a peculiar throwback to the quiet discussions we used to have long ago, about topics so trivial I can't imagine why we bothered hiding them. "So she was sold to a human-trafficking ring, then to some drug lord?"

It's strange how hearing him say those phrases out loud makes it into a story more than the jumbled words in the interview room did. "That's what it sounds like, yes."

Tom is leaning forward on his elbows on the kitchen table, holding on to himself, every muscle tensed. "Well, is that what the detectives say?"

"They didn't say much at all, really. They were just taking her statement, asking questions."

"Right. They don't want to say anything that might upset us, like, you know, *human trafficking* or *forced prostitution.* That might imply they know about it and can't do anything to stop it!" Tom's voice breaks on this last exclamation. He's not bothering to lower his voice anymore.

"I think they may know something. Harris mentioned a task force—"

"Yes, there's a statewide task force on human trafficking," Tom surprises me by saying. I am reminded of how much work he has done, how many search organizations he's joined, the support group for parents of missing children, the Facebook pages, and wonder what else he knows that I don't. "They formed it a couple of years ago, after a big report came out. Obviously it came too late to help Julie. But I guess we should be thrilled that she can help them." He sighs heavily. "How was she in there?"

"She seemed—fine," I say. "All things considered. One of the detectives told me she's in shock and needs to see a therapist."

"Of course," Tom says. "I'll find someone. I'll call tonight."

3

To get through the first week, I take her shopping. What else am I going to do with this twenty-one-year-old woman who has shown up to replace my missing thirteen-year-old daughter? Besides, she doesn't have any clothes. The first few days, I lend her things of mine to wear—she's closer to my size than Jane's—but it gives me the strangest feeling to see her draped in one of my severe black tunics, her blond hair swallowed up in its oversize cowl, like a paper doll dressed for a funeral.

"I have some errands to run at Target," I lie. "Want to come? We can get you some clothes."

Julie used to love back-to-school shopping with me, especially picking out all the notebooks and pens and pencils in purple and pink and glittery green. On top of buying her the usual jeans and T-shirts and underwear, I always got her one completely new first-day-of-school outfit, and she would keep it hanging on her doorknob for weeks, counting down the days. I still go to the same Target, which has, of course, barely changed at all in eight years, and I wonder whether the memories it brings back of one of our few mother-daughter activities are as pleasant to her as they are to me.

But once we're there, the red walls seem too aggressive somehow, the fluorescent lights glaring on the white linoleum walkways headache-inducing. Julie follows me obediently around the store as if it's her first time in there, or indeed in any store, and I can't help but wince at the racks of neon bikinis all tangled up on their hangers, the viscose minidresses lying on the floor under the sale rack, the red-and-white bull's-eye logo suspended over bins of brightly colored underwear. If the clothes in my closet seem too dour for a twenty-one-year-old, everything here seems too flimsy and disposable for someone with a face like Julie's. Hurrying us past the clothing department, I grab a cheese grater at random from the kitchen section and we stand, a little absurdly, in the express lane, waiting to check out.

Julie stares fixedly at the rows of candy bars in their bright boxes, and I am struck by how much this is like standing at the baggage carousel with Jane, the silence of two people trying to pretend it's ordinary how little they're talking. Except with Jane, I know she doesn't want to talk, not to me anyway. With Julie — who knows. But whatever conversation I am waiting to have with her, we are not going to have it in the express lane of Target, not even with the extra two minutes gained from the woman in front of us arguing over a sale price. I've heard the story, but who really knows what she's been through or how she feels about it? *Look at her now,* I think, *staring at nothing.*

But she's not. Once we get through the line and out into the car, she says, "I used to love that movie."

"What movie?"

"*A Little Princess.*"

Now I recall seeing it on the display stand near the register. I don't remember much about the movie aside from its exceptionally lurid color palette. It's one of those boarding-school stories, I know, where they're mean to the orphan girl. They keep her up in the attic. I feel a hint of panic.

"You should have said something. We could have bought it."

"It's okay, I don't want it."

"We can go back."

"Mom. I was just remembering."

But I'm almost crying in the silence that follows. She turns her head toward the window and says, "The Indian Gentleman searches everywhere for her so he can pass on her father's fortune, but it turns out she's been next door to him the whole time."

I try to speak, but nothing comes out.

"I used to think about that sometimes," she says shortly, by way of explanation, turning her head back to me. The veil of kindness has dropped back over her eyes. Outside, it starts to rain.

We speed toward Nordstrom, where I buy her heaping armfuls of silk tank tops, designer jeans, cashmere sweaters on ultra-sale, collared shirts and peasant blouses and plain, tissue-thin T-shirts at fifty bucks a pop. I buy her a purse, a wallet, a belt. A pair of brown calfskin loafers and some white sandals and three pairs of flats in different colors, all designer, but with the logo-print fabric tucked away on the inside, so you can't tell how expensive they are. I'll know, though.

Julie will know too, although I do my best to keep the price tags away from her after I catch her checking the tag on a blouse and then trying unobtrusively to hang it back on the rack. "Julie," I say firmly. She nods with a small smile, and I feel a rush of elation, strong, like the first sip of coffee after a good night's rest.

For the next two hours I stand outside the dressing room and hand her sizes and shades and styles of everything: bras, blazers, even swimsuits. While I am pondering which fancy restaurant we will take her out to first, she cracks the door open and holds out her hand for a smaller size of a fitted, knee-length dress in royal blue. Handing it to her, I glimpse, through the gaping sleeve openings of the too-big dress, a coin-size blob on her rib cage in a bluish-greenish shade of black that seems somehow wrong for a bruise. The door closes before I can ask her about it, and the dress doesn't suit her, so we don't end up buying it. We have plenty of other options.

We walk out with four giant shopping bags stuffed to their tops, two bags apiece, like a scene in a movie about rich and powerful women. And I *do* feel powerful, almost if we've gotten away with something, though the four-figure total on the receipt shows otherwise. Julie is smiling too, unabashedly, wearing a knit top and jeans that we ripped the tags off, right at the register, while the long receipt was still whirring its way out of the printer. The sun came out from behind clouds while we were inside and is now steaming away the new puddles in the parking lot, high and bright. Everything sparkles. I think with a sharp thrill of Tom, at his computer, seeing the transaction come up in his linked accounting software. It's more than our monthly house payment.

Only late at night, just as I'm drifting off, does that precise shade of bluish-greenish black on her rib cage evoke the word *tattoo*.

The next day, I drive her to a pebbled-concrete office complex off Memorial Drive, Tom's phone call having yielded a referral to the dark and slightly down-at-heel office of Carol Morse, PsyD. Julie goes in, and in the waiting area, where the ficus trees are mysteriously flourishing in the absence of natural light, I pull out a book on Byron and landscape, then put it down and spend ninety minutes paging through magazines instead. I think about the many appointments in my future, all the waiting rooms in store for me, and hope they update the magazines regularly.

On the way home, Julie asks if she can drive herself to her therapy appointments.

Tom and I argue about it for three days straight.

"She can't drive without a license," he says. "End of story."

"The therapist's office isn't that far away. She won't have to go on the highway—"

"Then we'll get her a bike."

But in a city without sidewalks, a bike feels more dangerous to me than a car. "And have her get honked at, even hit? People get abducted off bikes, Tom. And the bus is just as bad." *Unprotected,* I want to say. I think of Julie walking along the feeder road. "Of course she'll get a license, but it takes months, and there are all those tests and forms and documents. What does she do until then? She'll have to get a vision test—"

"She should! There are reasons for those things," Tom says, but I can tell he's wavering, and so I keep fighting. It's the first thing Julie has really asked me for, and she asked *me,* not Tom. I assume she wants to be alone in the car for the same reason I do: that sheltered, armored feeling of sitting high up behind the tinted windows in the recycled, air-conditioned air, the total privacy. It's something I can give her that's better than clothes.

In the end, we compromise. I sign her up for the midsummer session of driver's ed at the community college near our house, and Tom agrees to take Julie out for driving lessons now so she can get herself to therapy and back, carefully, using the neighborhood roads. The private lessons are what clinches it; his resolve crumbles in the face of her obvious delight at the prospect, and for the next week they wake up conspiratorially early and head off to various parking structures around town for a few hours. When they come back, we eat lunch together, and then Tom goes to work while Julie and I swim in the pool. In the afternoons, I take her out shopping—we buy all her bedroom furniture in one trip to IKEA, as if she's a college student—or to her therapy appointment, when she has one, or, a few times, to an afternoon movie. After a family dinner, we watch TV with Jane curled up nearby, absorbed in her notebook. It's a cozy routine, one where Julie is always accounted for and our time together is comfortably filled with tasks so no one has to reach far for things to talk about that aren't Julie's eight-year absence or find reasons to gently touch her forearm that aren't, at least not obviously, about checking to make sure she's still there.

For the first few weeks, this routine feels like it could last forever, in spite of minor disturbances. Tom answers the phone sharply when he doesn't recognize the caller ID, telling the reporters that we're not interested in talking; "I don't know when," he snaps, "our family needs privacy right now." Eventually he turns the ringer off, and I sink back into the bliss of knowing he is taking care of things, as he did in the days after it happened. In the back of my mind are certain topics I avoid thinking about—my job, Jane's incompletes, the SANE, the SAFE—but then I send my department chair an e-mail telling him my grades will be late and decide that Jane, who has grown quieter in Julie's presence, must be making progress on her late papers. What else could she be writing about in her notebook all the time? And when Julie starts driving after a few weeks of early-morning lessons with Tom, she gets to her appointments and back just fine, as I knew she would. This is our new normal, and it feels like something we are all learning together, as a family.

Tom and I even start having sex again, something that hasn't happened regularly for years. He touches me gingerly, as if he can sense that my skin feels almost raw. Julie has been in the house for a few weeks, and though I'm getting used to it, it still feels like someone has rubbed me all over with a rasp. Every pore seems to be open, every hair a fine filament ready to shoot me full of sensation at the slightest breeze. I have been fighting for so long to stifle sensation. I remember when the grief was so potent I would lie on the sofa with the television on drinking vodka gimlets, one after the other, just waiting to pass out, staying as still as possible, teaching myself the art of numbness. And now it is as if I've been dropped into scalding water and the numbness has peeled away and the skin underneath is affronted by air.

If there is something missing—if I am afraid to love her quite as much as before—it is only because the potential for love feels so big and so intense that I fear I will disappear in the expression of it, that it will blow my skin away like clouds and I will be nothing.

• • •

I wake up one morning with Jane standing over me, shaking my elbow. For a moment, caught in dreams I can't remember, I think we're doing the whole thing over again.

"Mom," she whispers urgently. "Mom, can you wake up?"

I reach a hand instinctively over to Tom.

"Don't wake Dad. Just come quick, okay?"

I'm naked under the covers, I realize in time to keep from pushing them off me. Jane sees. "I'll wait outside. It's Julie," she adds unnecessarily, since even as I wake up completely I'm still reliving that day.

I skip the bathrobe and pull on jeans and yesterday's shirt in case we need to get right into the car. "Gone?" I ask when I'm out of the bedroom, my skin clamping shut under the air conditioning.

Jane looks at me oddly and shakes her head. "No, nothing like that. I think she's sick."

We're still whispering as she leads me upstairs. Jane peers down the hall at the closed bathroom door.

"It's locked," she says helplessly.

"How long?"

"I don't know," she says. "Since before I got up, half an hour ago. I thought she was taking a bath but then I heard her—moaning, or something. I knocked, but she won't answer." Her voice is quavering.

I walk to the bathroom door, knock softly. "Julie?"

There is no moaning now, only a rhythmic click and shuffle that I associate immediately with a night spent doubled over on the toilet.

"Baby, are you okay in there? Are you hurting?"

Two words sent explosively outward on an expulsion of breath, barely audible.

"What?"

"Go away." Followed by a gasp of pain.

I turn to Jane. "Get a blanket from the hall closet and put it in the car. My keys are on the table. I'll be down in a few minutes." She leaves immediately to follow my orders.

Facing the bathroom door, I say, "Julie. You're going to have to let me in. You're going to unlock the door, okay?"

Nothing but a moan and the rhythm of the clicking toilet seat.

The next thing I know, I am in the bathroom. I don't remember this part, but Tom tells me later that he woke up to pounding (mine) and screaming (Julie's), and that by the time he made it to the hall in his boxers, my arm had already disappeared up to the shoulder in a ragged hole in the bathroom door, and then I was turning the doorknob from the inside, pulling my arm out, and opening the door. Between my bloody fist and the blood on the bathroom floor, there was blood everywhere, and he turned around and around looking for the intruder who had laid waste to the household.

But however I got in, when I see Julie, I know what's happening to her right away. I had one myself, after Jane. It's a painful, bloody thing, though I remember wishing during the worst times that I had lost Julie that way instead of the other.

Tears are streaming down her face, and I wrap a towel around her shoulders and help her to her feet. "I'll call you from the hospital," I tell Tom, who is still shaking as he follows us down the stairs and into the kitchen. The last thing I say to him, as he stands by the island in his boxers, is "I didn't know we even had a gun." More to remind him he's holding it than anything else. He stares down at it in his hand as if he hadn't known either.

"She's okay," I tell Tom over the phone from my chair in the waiting area. "Ovarian cysts can be very painful when they rupture. Tell Jane it's okay." He protests. "Yes, they're concerned about the blood too, but they don't think it's anything serious. It was mostly mine, from the door. The ultrasound—"

The ultrasound showed a tiny, irregular smudge, already half disintegrating, washed out in the early morning, tiny bits of tissue in a thick red exodus. When she saw what was on the monitor, she went pale and silent, dropped my hand, and said, "Get out." I got out, but before I did, I saw her face.

She knew.

I end the call with Tom, put the phone back in my purse, and sit. If any of the staff in the emergency department heard me and knew I was lying, they didn't care enough to give me even a glance. I bet they've heard plenty of miscarriages become ovarian cysts on the phone with Dad.

I reach for a magazine and wince at the pain in my bandaged knuckles. Thinking of the clothes I bought her, I grimace. Have the snug jeans become more snug in the past few weeks? Have I failed to notice? I remember the tattoo, remember, above all, what she told the police: "Six months." Now seven. And hate myself for thinking, *She lied, she lied, she lied*.

But omissions aren't necessarily lies, are they? This is what the therapy is for, telling the horrible details that don't add up but make all the difference. Surely that's what she does in the therapist's office for ninety minutes twice a week: talks to a surrogate me—isn't that the theory? A trained professional onto whom she can project a version of me that, unlike the real me, will be able to handle everything, hold everything, make it all make sense?

The therapist, Carol Morse, suddenly seems like the answer. She can't tell me anything confidential, of course, but maybe under the circumstances—a pregnancy, a miscarriage, Julie's health at stake—she'll find a way to give me some insights into what's going on with my daughter. There's so much more to her than I know, but I can handle Julie's truth. I've already had the worst thing happen to me that can ever happen to a parent. And now, in a sense, Julie has too. It's something we share.

When she's finally discharged, we walk to the car. Another late night has turned into early morning during our time in the hospital. The sun is coming up, the freeway still clear, the heat just a soft shimmer that promises more to come. We drive for a few minutes in silence.

"It was the guard," she says. "In the helicopter. I don't know why I didn't want to say. I guess because—" She struggles. "It wasn't really rape."

Pause. I take in this detail, try to make it fit.

"What I mean is, I offered. I thought he'd be less likely to kill me. I—I didn't want to tell you. Because I was ashamed. Anyway I thought—" She gasps a little. "I thought I couldn't get pregnant. My period has never been regular since—" She stops when a tear rolls down my cheek. "Well, ever."

I nod. This woman is older than twenty-one. I am not as old as she is, and I am forty-six, with lines of mourning etched all over my face that will never go away. But she knew. I saw her face when she looked at the ultrasound screen.

"I love you," I say, and it's the truth, the absolute truth. But in this new world, after the miscarriage, it sounds like a lie.

"Mom," she says, despairingly.

"I won't tell your father or Jane. This is between us."

A warm wave of relief radiates from her as she settles back in her seat. This is what she has wanted all along. She looks out the window, and I look at the road ahead, and we are closer in our secret than we have ever been.

Julie

woke up to a fresh round of cramps with a strangled cry.

The television was on, but muted; was it the same movie she fell asleep to or a different one? While she was still half asleep, Tom came running down the stairs from her bedroom, which he was using as an office during the daytime while they figured out where to move his desk. This made her nervous, but she didn't want to say anything about it.

Looking at him now, standing at the bottom of the stairs, she briefly remembered him from last night, holding a gun. She wondered where it was now.

"Did I hear you calling? Are you okay?"

"I'm fine. Just a bad dream." At first she'd dreamed of Cal, but it got bad near the end, when the cramps started rocketing through her body louder and louder. She couldn't remember the worst of it with Tom standing there, just a feeling of dirt all around her mouth and the colors yellow and red—the shades of the afghan, she noted with disgust, throwing it off her. Now that she was awake, the sharp pain in her abdomen was already subsiding to a dull, empty ache.

"Can I make you some tea?"

"I'd like to get out of the house." The air in here was somehow both cold and stifling, and the big windows made her feel like some kind of specimen under glass. Or maybe it was the way they all watched her. "Can I take the car?"

"You mother left a few minutes ago. Jane's got mine," he said swiftly. She could tell the idea of her driving without a license still made him uncomfortable. "Your mom should be back soon. She was just going by her office for some late term papers. Why don't you keep resting for a while? You could watch another movie."

She swiveled her feet to the ground. "It's okay. I'll just take a walk."

He watched her doubtfully as she pushed herself to standing. Her legs felt quivery, as if her feet were still in the stirrups. "I'll be fine, Dad," she forced herself to say. "I just need some head space. Let me go get dressed, okay?"

He nodded. "I'll be in the kitchen."

She went up to her room, opened the closet door, and stared at the rows of brand-new flats and boots, some she hadn't worn yet that were still in their boxes. She could see, down the hall in Jane's room, a pair of beat-up Converse high-top sneakers slouching toe to heel by the side of Jane's bed, where it was her habit to kick them off. On an impulse, she walked down the hall and grabbed them. They gaped a little, so she added a second pair of socks, and, instead of wrapping the laces around the ankles like Jane, she laced them all the way to the top and double-tied the knot.

She wanted something that wouldn't come off if she had to start running.

The thought made her legs feel wobblier than ever. She grabbed a hoodie out of Jane's closet, then thought better of it—Tom might notice—and hung it back up. There was nothing like a hoodie in her own closet, just cardigans and blazers and other things she'd never worn before. They'd excited her in the store for that reason, but now their unfaded pastels looked like candy to her. Too visible. She grabbed the most subdued cardigan, a soft gray one, and put it on. Then she reached under her brand-new and punishingly stiff mattress, slid the phone out from between it and the box spring, and tucked it into her front pocket, hoping the cardigan would mostly cover it.

Downstairs, she breezed past Tom, grabbed her new purse, and yelled, "I'll be back before dinner," over her shoulder as the door swung shut behind her. The outside air hit her face like steam off a bowl of soup; sitting in Tom and Anna's freezing house, you forgot the sweltering heat waiting on the other side of the window. She peeled her cardigan off at the bottom of the driveway and stuffed it into her purse.

At the end of the block, she slipped the phone out of her pocket and turned it on, grateful for her last-minute inspiration to ditch it with her IDs in the front bushes before ringing the door-bell. Losing consciousness had not been part of the plan. Maybe it was the heat and all the walking, but when Jane stepped into the hallway, Julie had thought she was seeing Charlotte's ghost. The hospital had not been part of the plan either, but at least the doctor had shed light on certain particulars.

Particulars that, of course, Anna now knew too.

No wonder she'd felt so weak. This whole time she'd thought it was love she was fighting against, or tearing herself away from, that feeling of warm belonging that threatened to betray her whenever Cal looked at her. Now she knew the betrayal ran deeper, down into her blood, bones, and tissue. No wonder she'd felt violated. No wonder she'd felt possessed.

It was a lucky thing he never found out what was inside her.

Recovering the phone had been tricky, since they watched her so closely those first few days. But on the third day she'd slipped out for the mail and picked it up on the way back in. Thank God the phone had stayed dry under the awning, and the IDs were all still there, rubber-banded to its back. When she'd powered it up, the screen flashed on, and there was Cal, smiling at her with that infuriating expression of faith and love she'd drunk in so deeply and grown so strong on—strong enough to remember who she really was and why he couldn't find out. By the time she saw the article in the library that day—Cal had dropped her off there to study the GED books—she was strong enough to tear herself away.

She'd scrubbed everything else off her phone before she was out of Seattle, but she couldn't quite bring herself to get rid of Cal. She felt as if he were with her still in some indefinable way. When, at the hospital, she'd learned what it was, she'd thought, maybe, somehow, when she was finished here, she could go back.

She knew it was a stupid idea, and her body agreed. It had made the decision for her.

She took one last, long look at the face on the screen, and for a moment she was lying next to him again, her fingers tracing his chest lightly, his fingers twined in her hair, listening as he described his mother's white face, one eye swollen shut, framed in the rear window of his aunt's Volkswagen. Sending one last, blank look in the direction of the small black boy crying at the kitchen window before twisting her blond head away and turning her back on him forever.

She got the point, and it wasn't just that she, too, was a blond. Sometimes people had to leave, she'd thought to herself. She took a deep breath and pressed delete.

Then she noticed the new voicemail message. Not recognizing the number, she pushed play and listened but a moment later jerked the phone away from her ear like it had bitten her. How many times would she have to delete him before he was gone? And how many times would it still hurt? She'd never picked up, and she'd stopped listening to the messages after the first few; they all said the same thing. Now he was trying her from different numbers, hoping to catch her off guard. She glanced once more at the unknown number, and then with a jolt recognized the area code: Portland, Oregon. It might be a coincidence, a cell phone borrowed from a friend. But what if he actually had gone to Portland? It might mean he was trying to find her, following her trail, starting with Will. Of course that's where he would start. He'd always wanted an excuse to confront Will and get her stuff back; he'd said facing the past was important, as if he'd know the first thing about it. He could be finding out, though, right now. And once he started in that direction, how long would it be until he found her?

Looking around at Tom and Anna's neighborhood, she could barely believe she was here, much less picture Cal turning up. Empty of pedestrians in the heat of the afternoon, the neighborhood had high white curbs but no sidewalks, and she walked in the street, stepping around straggling ropes of soft tar. She passed house after house, all of them huge to her after Cal's pinched Seattle apartment, their plush lawns trimmed with fat shrubs and clumps of begonias so perfect and motionless in the dead air, they looked like silk flowers. Some of the porches had columns, like plantation houses.

Following the noise of traffic, she stepped out of the subdivision and started walking along a busy thoroughfare. Cars spat hot breath and gravel at her ankles as they raced by. There was no sidewalk here either, no curb even, just a narrow trail worn in the crabgrass near the greasy roadside before it plunged into runoff ditches padded at the bottom with tangled weeds. She walked past a rambling strip mall: Kroger, Qwik Klean, Jenny's Gifts, the streaky glass box of a Dairy Queen. The only logical destination of this ragged path was the bus stop. She cast a glance toward the kiosk and saw three women waiting for the bus in service uniforms, each with a rolling cart full of bottles. Cleaning ladies. Her back hurt just looking at them.

As she passed a McDonald's, she saw a long blue awning peeking out from the strip center behind it: BOBBY'S POOL HALL, in dingy white block letters. She walked toward it in relief. So there were hiding places here, after all. Although the other stores in the strip center had glass fronts, she noted that Bobby's windows were covered with weather-beaten plywood and wondered if there was any business in the back. Not that she needed any, she hurriedly told herself; she was going to be here only a few weeks. But it wasn't a bad idea to find out what was around. Besides, she had money in her wallet, and maybe what she really wanted was to sit for a few hours away from the roadside, drinking away the pain in her gut.

At this time of the afternoon, there were only a few barflies. They sat close to the entrance, talking with a curly-haired woman behind the bar who laughed loudly as she wedged limes on a cutting board. None of them paid any attention to her until she leaned against the bar. Then the bartender stopped laughing abruptly.

"What do you want, honey?" She squinted. "Job? You gotta be eighteen."

"Corona, please."

The woman laughed. "You're going to have to show me some ID, hon."

Julie dug through her new wallet and pulled out one that said she was twenty-four. Even as she handed it over, she felt a moment of panic. It was a California driver's license, a real one, the kind you can get in a lot of trouble for stealing.

The bartender gave it a long, hard look, then glanced at her, then back down at the ID. "Mercedes Rodriguez?" she said, drawing out the syllables like it was an impossible name for anyone to have.

"Mercy," she said automatically. The last time she'd used Mercy, she'd had short brown hair, but it was dark in Bobby's Pool Hall, and the wide-cheekboned face and blue eyes looked close enough. *Mercy, Mercy,* she told her face, *look like Mercy.*

It almost worked. She could feel the woman struggling to care. Then someone called "Bev!" from the end of the bar, and the bartender glanced anxiously over her shoulder, and by the time she looked back at Mercy, she was having none of it. "Sorry, señorita," she said, all the patience draining from her voice. "You don't look twenty-four, and it's an out-of-state ID. I gotta be careful in this neighborhood. For all I know, you wandered over from the high school." Bev threw the ID down on the counter and hustled off.

This goddamn city. She wasn't planning to be here long, but she'd already flashed a fake ID within ten blocks of Tom and Anna's house and been turned down. *Don't shit where you eat* meant something different when she was working at the Black Rose, but it applied here too. She grabbed the ID off the counter and shoved it back into her pocket.

Now the two men at the bar were staring at her. One of them said, "Come on, Bev, have a heart!"

The other chimed in, "She's old enough. I can always tell, like rings on a tree." He guffawed.

Now she really had to get away. On a sudden instinct, she pulled the phone out and dialed one of the numbers Tom and Anna had made her write down on a scrap of paper and keep in her new wallet.

"Hello?" The voice had the doubtful tone of someone picking up an unknown number.

"Hey, Jane," she said. "It's Julie."

"Where are you? What number is this?"

She looked out the window and saw a sign across the street. "I'm at the Starbucks by our house. I borrowed a phone off someone. Listen, I had to get out of there, Mom and Dad were hovering. Can you pick me up?"

"Are you at the Starbucks on Memorial?"

"Yeah. I have to go, this lady needs her phone back."

"Just hang on, I'm at a friend's house. I'll be there in a few minutes." Jane hung up.

She slammed the bar door behind her as hard as she dared, but it bounced on a cushion of air six inches from the frame and she could still hear the voices inside laughing at her as she hurriedly crossed the street.

Fifteen minutes later, Jane pulled into the Starbucks parking lot in Tom's SUV, rolled down the window, and said, "Nice shoes."

"Thanks." Julie looked down and saw Jane's Converse on her feet. "I mean, I'm sorry."

"It's okay." Despite the dark hair and bangs, Jane didn't look much like Charlotte at all. Jane was taller, stronger, Julie told herself.

"Mom got me all these flats," she apologized. "I just wanted something I could walk in." She pulled the heavy passenger-side door open and climbed in.

"I said it was okay." Looking closely at Jane's face, especially when she smiled, Julie could tell she had never been very far from home. College didn't count, even if it was halfway across the country—it was still closer to home than a single bus ride could take you. If you looked past Jane's piercings (two: nose and eyebrow), tattoos (two small ones, one on her shoulder and one on her hip, and Anna didn't know about either), and hair (the bleach-and-green was clearly a home job, but the black dye was from a salon), you saw a girl who'd never had to take the bus all that much.

Julie regretted putting her own hair through this last round of bleach. It had looked smooth enough at first, but now the ends were getting ragged, the part below her shoulders breaking off and poofing out. Worst of all, darker hair was creeping in at her hairline. If she hadn't needed to look the part so desperately, she could probably have gotten away with dirty blond.

But she hadn't wanted to be a dirty blond. She'd wanted to be Julie.

Jane clicked her keys against the wheel impatiently. "So where are we going?"

"I want to chop all this off," Julie said, holding out a handful of split ends.

"Like, right now?"

"Yeah, right now. And dye it, maybe. I figured you'd know a good place for that."

Jane looked impressed. "I can take you to the place I go. It's in Montrose. What color are you going to dye it?" She squinted shrewdly. "Better not be black."

"I don't know, maybe red," she said without thinking. At the Rose, she'd always made bank with red hair. Besides, white-blond Julie was starting to get to her. She'd stared at the pictures of the missing girl and at herself in the mirror beforehand, but when she started playing Julie for Anna and Tom and Jane, something shifted. She saw Julie's innocence in the way all three of them looked at her, and it was unnerving. Anna, in particular, watched her as if she might break.

Jane was already pulling out of the parking lot, her strong jaw set under its sprinkling of covered-up acne, saying, "Cool, let's get out of here." If Julie was worried about Anna, she should have started with Jane in the first place. Shutting Anna out was Jane's superpower.

Tom's Range Rover was a smooth ride, just more ease and luxury so built into Jane's existence she didn't even know it was there. Jane wove in and out of the four-lane traffic on Westheimer as she drove toward the city, the SUV soon dwarfed by hulking black Suburbans with tinted windows, shiny trucks that were all tire and no flatbed, a Hummer that looked like it could transform into a robot. A few lanes away, a silver convertible idled like a half-melted bullet in the sun. The apartments gave way to spar-kling-white office buildings set on lots kissed around their edges with manicured shrubs and palm trees. Everything gleamed, even the street signs, which were mounted on giant chrome arcs.

"Can you believe how much the Galleria has changed?"

She caught the small dip in Jane's voice and immediately felt a prickling on the back of her neck, alerting her to a shared mem-ory she was in no position to ignore.

"Yeah, I know," she said.

"Do you remember that time Mom dropped us off at the Gal-leria to do our Christmas shopping?"

"That's what I was thinking about too."

"I thought we were so cool," Jane went on, her eyes on the taillights ahead of them. The traffic light had changed and they were inching sluggishly forward, but they weren't going to make it past the danger zone on this green. "It felt like we were so grown up. You must have been in, what, sixth or seventh grade? Because —" She broke off. "And I would have been in fourth or fifth. We bought lunch at that one fancy food-court place with the crepes. Do you remember splitting up for an hour to buy each other's presents? That was my favorite part. We, like, synchronized our watches and met at the bakery afterward." She laughed. "I even doubled back and hid which direction I was coming from so you wouldn't guess where I bought your present. I think it was Claire's or something."

Jane's voice tugged at her ear, but Julie was distracted by a boy of around twelve or thirteen in a T-shirt and saggy, wide-legged blue jeans weighed down with a heavy wallet chain who was striding through the still-sidewalk-less guts of the drainage ditch parallel to the road. His tangled hair was long and brown and very deliberately shielding his face as he marched, hands in pockets, visibly sweating. He reached the base of one of the chrome arcs, which proved to be a formidable obstacle at ground level. Trapped between an evergreen shrub and the curved chrome, he hiked up his billowing, half-shredded pants leg with one hand and stepped over it, like a cartoon lady pulling up her skirts to step over a puddle.

"Julie?" Jane's voice came back to her, and she realized she'd missed a question. The music was quieter; Jane must have just turned it down. "Do you remember? What you did that time when we split up?"

"Tried on prom dresses," she said. "Pretended I was a princess."

"Oh," Jane said, and laughed. "Well, that definitely explains why I ended up getting a gift certificate from Waldenbooks that year."

She knew better than to let this moment pass because of some stupid kid. "I thought you loved reading!"

"You could have picked out a book, though." Impossibly, Jane sounded hurt, although she was still laughing. "You know, I don't think I ever used the gift certificate. I mean, after everything happened."

The light changed, and they barely made it through the intersection this time, moving at a snail's pace. She watched the boy swim through the weeds by the side of the road until they gained on him, pulled ahead, and finally passed him. In the rearview mirror he looked almost motionless.

She turned back to Jane. "Look, pull the car over. Do you want

me to get you the newest Baby-Sitters Club book? They're probably on number ten thousand by now."

It worked. Jane laughed and turned the music up.

In Montrose, they parked the car outside a hair salon that had a
tattoo parlor upstairs. They got out, and Jane took a deep breath.
This must be where Jane went to feel like Houston was her city,
not just some place she accidentally wound up because her parents
lived there. The sad part was Jane's pride in her insider knowledge,
as if it were hard-won. As if anyone couldn't walk into any city and
find the artists and gays and addicts and tattoo parlors within half
an hour by bumming a couple of cigarettes and picking up the free
papers on the street corner.

The salon was full of clients, but the woman behind the counter
eyed Julie and said she could get her color started and then cut her
next customer's hair while the dye was processing. Julie eased into
the chair, felt the woman's fingers in her hair, and saw her look
down critically; she said, "Short and red," fast, before the woman
could comment on her roots. The woman met her eyes in the mirror and said, "Okay, hon, let me get the book." She left and came
back with a floppy binder full of inch-long swatches like the silken
manes of tiny horses or trophies of all the girls she'd ever been.
Julie pointed to one, and the woman nodded. "Oh, sure, number
eight, that'll look good on you," and she disappeared into the back
to mix the dye.

Jane stood behind her, looking at her face in the mirror. "Mom'll
freak," she said. "But I think it's going to look amazing."

"What do you want to do while I'm cooking?"

"Look at magazines, I guess." Jane shrugged. Julie could see the realization dawning in Jane's eyes that there was nothing particularly special about this place. Anywhere must seem hip when you're getting your hair dyed to piss off your mom.

That gave Julie an idea. "You could go upstairs," she said. "Get a tattoo while you're waiting."

"Think I'm made of money?"

"Don't you have a credit card?"

"Mom cosigned. It'll show up on her bill."

A wave of generosity, accompanied by the need to get Jane out of the room before it became obvious she had roots, made Julie point at her Anna-bought purse on the floor. "She gave me a couple hundred bucks. Why don't you pay for my hair with your card, and I'll give you the cash? You can spend it upstairs."

Jane hesitated.

"Don't tell me you don't have your next one already picked out." Julie predicted something small and discreet, but visible.

"I was thinking of a little outline of Texas on my left ring finger," Jane admitted.

"So get one!"

"Mom will see," Jane said. "I figured I'd wait—"

"Until what? Until you're thirty? Come on, quit hiding who you really are."

She could tell Jane was eating this up. "You'll be okay down here?" she said, reaching for the purse.

"Yeah. I don't mind magazines." It was true. She used to ogle them in their plastic folders at the library when Cal dropped her off to study for the GED. Once she'd even smuggled a *Better Homes and Gardens* into the restroom and ripped out a picture of a fluffy white cake surrounded by silver and gold Christmas ornaments

—not for the recipe, just the picture. Now the magazine cake was crumpled in a dumpster somewhere in Jersey Village, where the bus had dropped her off, along with her shoes, a cheap gold necklace with a dangling horse charm, and her backpack full of souvenirs. All her earthly possessions. Except—

She lurched forward, but it was too late; Jane was already digging through the floppy bag. Before she could even form the words *Give it to me, I'll find it,* Jane had the wallet in her hand and was fanning the ATM-fresh twenties out of its pocket. Julie sat back quickly, willing Jane not to notice the IDs in the wallet, the phone in the inner pocket of the purse, or her own momentary panic.

But Jane just beamed at the stack of bills. "Thanks!" she said and headed for the stairs.

Just in time. The hairstylist was back in a black apron holding a bowl full of glowing red paste in one hand and a brush in the other. "This is going to be gorgeous," she said, "trust me," and Julie did, she really did. She leaned back and felt the cold goop applied to her part. "We're getting rid of those nasty roots first," the stylist said and continued to chatter, the way good hairdressers do when they can tell you don't want to say much. At one point she said, "My sister and I are like y'all—we look so different, people never believe we're related."

She let the stylist tilt her chin down toward the floor and finally figured out something that had been bothering her since her arrival in Houston. It had been nagging at the corners of her vision everywhere she went, from Target to the therapist to Bobby's Pool Hall to the weathered-brick coffee shop where Jane had insisted on stopping for pastries on the way to the hair place.

Something not quite right, some quality that made the whole city feel like a stage set. Now, surrounded by other clients and with her head pointed floorward, looking under the table with its big mirror, she could see them propped up on footrests on the other side, all in a row: the shoes.

They were pristine. The patent-leather flats so shiny, the soles of the Reebok sneakers fluorescent yellow, the miraculously white leather sandals with gold lions on them framing brightly polished toenails without a single chip. Staring at the floor, she cast her mind back through the past few weeks and saw a parade of flip-flops and leather boots looking as unscuffed as if they'd just come out of the box. She could see, framed by the black plastic smock, her own feet perched on the silver bar in Jane's Converse, which had felt comfortably worn. Now she noticed that the tiny holes in the canvas—one near the right toe, another on the side, another near the heel—were too perfectly placed. She'd worn through shoes before; the canvas should have been frayed under the laces, the holes should have bloomed unattractively along the seam of the heel, not in neat little ovals in the middle of the fabric, and the rubber should have been thin enough under the soles for her to feel every pebble on the sidewalk. These weren't worn; they were distressed.

She imagined a city divided between those like herself and the kid with the oversize pants—people whose shoes endured a constant pounding, scuffing, sweating, straining, and staining with grass and mud and soft, oozing tar—and those who whooshed past them in SUVs, the ones who never walked more than twenty steps outside each day, much less to a bus stop or convenience store, and whose shoes, therefore, *never wore out*.

She wished for a moment she could tell Cal.

Not Jane, though. Jane had never walked anywhere. She would have found ways to rebel against Anna and Tom without ever having to rebel against that.

The hairdresser tilted Julie's head back up, and she glanced at the ceiling, hoping, for Jane's sake, that the needle upstairs wasn't hurting her too much.

4

If Tom suspects the ovarian cyst is not an ovarian cyst, he doesn't say anything about it, and I, in return, say nothing about the gun that appeared in his hand last night. After we settle Julie on the sofa Monday morning with hot tea and the remote control, she turns on a cable movie that's already halfway over, one of those holiday-themed romantic comedies with six different plots so isolated from one another that most of the stars probably never shared a soundstage. I notice *A Little Princess,* which I went back and got her that first week, still lying in its plastic wrapping on top of the Blu-ray player.

I sit next to her with her feet in my lap under the afghan, rubbing them absently. She looks incredibly weary, and within fifteen minutes she has fallen asleep, her night in pain having caught up with her.

I move her bundled feet gently off my lap, slip the remote from under her arm, and mute the television just as some stockbroker in a natty suit looks up, realizes it's five minutes until midnight, and tears out of his office to propose to the actress on the other side of the movie. Tom is in the kitchen, putting the breakfast dishes away before he goes upstairs to work.

The thought of Tom's presence in Julie's room is not the only reason I don't want to go back to bed. The tiredness nags at me, but something else does too.

"I have to pick up some papers from my office," I say. "I hate to leave just now, but she'll sleep for a while." I glance at Julie. "And I need to get it over with so I can start working on grades." Tom doesn't need to know that I've successfully lobbied the chair of my department to let me turn in final grades at the end of the summer. It's amazing how sensitive department heads are to my particular brand of family emergency—the kind that involves knives and young daughters and the national news.

Tom looks at me mutely from the kitchen, and I admit to myself that I'd feel better if I knew how long I've been living in a house with a loaded gun. "Will you be around in case she wakes up?" I ask instead.

"Of course," he says. "Is she—"

"I told you, she's fine," I snap. Then soften. "I just don't want her to wake up all alone."

He nods.

On the phone with Carol Morse in the car, I must sound a little off, although I feel my request to see her is perfectly reasonable. After all, she's invited me to make an appointment with her before. "Do you want to come in with Julie this afternoon?" she asks.

I know Julie won't be coming this afternoon—she'll be sleeping. But I can tell Carol about that when I see her.

"No, I thought this time I would just—I want to see you by myself."

"All right," she says, and then, "I have a cancellation this morning at eleven. Can you make that?"

It's probably her lunch break. Maybe I sound worse than I think I do.

I kill an hour at the paperback bookstore next to her office, thumbing through romances and mysteries. When I walk in, I'm somewhat surprised to find her younger than I remembered, no older than me, and wearing chino capris. For some reason, this bothers me.

"Come in, come in," she says and gestures me over to a sofa with a woven blanket draped over one arm. I notice a box of tissues sitting on the side table by a lamp with an artfully lumpy ceramic base, and I wonder if Julie ever cries here. Carol Morse closes the door and sits opposite me in a low-backed chair.

"Thanks for fitting me in," I say, suddenly nervous. "I hope this is—it's a little strange. It's about Julie."

"How is Julie?" she asks with an appropriate degree of concern.

"Fine. Well, not fine," I say. "She's sick today, so she won't be coming in." Carol just looks at me, but for some reason I don't want to tell her about the hospital. Right now it's the only secret Julie and I share; perhaps I'm afraid to find out Carol already knows. I continue, probing to see whether she'll volunteer the information on her own. "I was sort of hoping you could help me out with Julie a little. I feel like—I feel like she's keeping things from me. And I know you can't talk about what she says to you, but I have some things to tell you that might change your mind on that."

"On patient confidentiality? That's impossible."

"Even for a parent?"

"Especially for a parent." She looks at me levelly. "Anna, are you aware that your daughter hasn't come to her sessions for the past two weeks?"

After a stunned pause, I manage to say, "Carol, how could I be aware of that, since nobody bothered to tell me?" She stays silent for long enough that I become uncomfortably conscious of my hostile tone. "I mean, no, no, I had no idea. She's been saying she's coming here, I just assumed—I mean, wouldn't you think we would want to know that?"

"Julie is an adult," the woman says coolly. "Her appointments are completely confidential." I have a sudden picture of Carol Morse at home with her husband, listening to Fleetwood Mac in the Jacuzzi she surely has on the back deck of the house she purchased by taking strangers' money for reassurances that their lives are okay, that everything will work out.

With difficulty, I control my urge to get up. "She was here for the first two sessions, I know she was," I say. "Can you tell me anything about what she said? Can you tell me—anything at all?" I have to get something out of this woman. "Please. She hasn't told us anything beyond what's in the police report. Which—" I can't bring myself to say that what she told the police isn't true. Not all of it anyway.

While I am searching for the words to tell her about the hospital and the ultrasound, Carol Morse says, "Have you asked Julie?"

Have I asked Julie? Have I—something shorts out in my brain. I want to stand and shriek; I want to knock over the artful ceramic lamp and fling the woven throw to the ground and stomp on it.

Instead I ask, "Do you have children?"

"No, I don't," she says evenly.

"I can tell," I say. I grab my purse, standing up.

"Mrs. Whitaker," she says.

"Dr.," I snap.

"Dr. —"

"Davalos."

"Dr. Dava—"

"Oh, you can call me Anna."

"Anna," she says, refusing to take the bait. She's not even standing, and although I want to storm out, somehow the fact that she is still sitting in her low-backed chair keeps me from doing so for a moment longer. "Anna, Julie has had an incredibly difficult time. I can tell you that much. The trauma of what she's been through is not something most people can imagine."

She wants to talk about trauma.

"Many survivors of sexual abuse feel an overwhelming sense of shame," she says. "Especially when the abuse is prolonged and combined with other trauma. She needs to feel that she's safe talking to you."

"Of course she's safe," I say. Angry tears have started streaming down my face despite my efforts.

"She's not sure how to relate to her family anymore, or to anyone who hasn't been through what she has. She might protect you from the details because she doesn't want to make you sad or upset."

"Just tell me," I beg.

"Your job is to let her know you love her, no matter what happened."

"Please."

"Anna, don't you want to come sit down? We have thirty more

minutes in this appointment. I feel like it would be good for you to talk to someone as well. Don't you think that's true?"

I get out of there and into my car so fast I'm almost halfway home before it occurs to me to swing by the university. Both to substantiate my lie—there might really be student papers, after all—and to sit behind a closed door with a lock on it and think. I don't want to see or talk to anyone right now, not even Julie. When I get to my office, I notice a flashing red light on the phone, indicating that I have messages. It takes me a second to figure out how to retrieve them; hardly anybody calls office phones these days. The first three messages are from reporters, and I delete them without listening past the introduction.

After the fourth beep: "Uh, Dr. Davalos, this is Alex Mercado. I'm a private investigator. I know you aren't talking to the press right now, and I don't need to ask you any questions. Actually, I have some information to share with you—some things I think you'll be interested in knowing. So, uh, give me a call back." He leaves a phone number. "Again, it's Alex Mercado, and I'd like to meet somewhere and talk face to face, if that's okay."

"End of message," says the female voice recording. "To repeat this message, press—"

I copy the number down on the second listening. Then I listen to the message two or three more times before deleting it, just to make sure I'm really hearing someone self-identify as a "private investigator" on my voicemail. I am.

We never hired a PI to find Julie. We had so much faith in the police then—a thought that presses a burst of angry laughter out of me now. I suppose I thought of private eyes as a solution only for people in movies. But then, I wasn't the one in charge of the solutions, or much of anything, for a while. The first thing I do now is turn on my desktop computer and Google *Alex Mercado private investigator*. He comes up right away under a link for AMI Inc., which leads to a website so corny I think, *There's no way this isn't fake.* There's actually a fedora in the logo. What next, a magnifying glass? I open a new tab and start looking around for websites where PIs are registered, searching for credentials.

Back when Julie disappeared, there were crackpots. We didn't want to change our number because we still believed she might try to contact us, and even though the police had a special tip line set aside for Julie, we still got the calls: *I have information you'll want to know,* they always said, or *I saw her, I swear to God it was her, she's in Tucson,* or *She's in Jacksonville,* or *She's in Missouri City.* One or two of them refused to be referred to the police. *It has to be you, and it has to be in person.* Needless to say, the police were listening in on our line, which I assume had as much to do with their suspicion of Tom and me as anything else—God, what a time—and the calls must have all been traced to lonely middle-aged men living with their ailing mothers or teenagers playing games of truth or dare because none of them turned up any leads.

At the time, I found it hard to believe that so many people would want to be a part of such a horrible circumstance, but in the years since, the years of forgotten nightmares and long commutes past her hundreds of imaginary graves, I have almost felt I understood them. It's so easy to forget how terrible the world is. Tragedy reminds us. It is purifying in that way. But when it starts to fade, you have to return to the source, over and over.

When I find a reliable-looking registration site searchable by ZIP code, I'm surprised to find that Alex Mercado Investigations is the second name to come up. On the AMI website, I click the

About Us link and am treated to Alex Mercado's credentials: Almost three years as a police detective in the special victims unit of the Houston Police Department. Six years as a private detective. A few links to news stories about crimes that the agency claims to have helped solve; one of the links mentions his name.

I pick up the phone and dial. A male voice answers after the second ring.

"Alex Mercado Investigations. Is this Anna Davalos?"

"Yes," I say, a bit startled, although of course he would have caller ID. "You left a message earlier."

"Thanks for getting back to me," he says. "Look, I realize this is a little odd, but I would really like to meet with you and talk about some things."

"About Julie?"

"Of course. I don't feel comfortable saying more on the phone. Would you be able to meet me somewhere?"

"Yes, but it has to be today. It has to be now." It's remarkable how easy it is to finish this conversation: I suggest a diner, not the cutesy retro kind you find around my neighborhood, but a Waffle House near the freeway. I feel my pulse racing, but my voice stays absolutely cool and untroubled as I say, "I'll meet you there in half an hour." It's like I set up things like this every day.

Just before I'm about to hang up, he asks one last question, as if he can't resist. "Have you ever heard of Gretchen Farber?"

"No," I say. "Who's that?"

"Don't worry about it," he says. "I'll see you in half an hour."

Gretchen

made one mistake, and the mistake's name was Cal. He was supposed to be another rung on the ladder out of the dark hole she had come from. It was her fault he'd become more.

At the time, she'd been planning her next move for so long it felt inevitable. As soon as the set was over, she smiled, murmured "Thank you" into the mic, and slipped offstage fast. She headed toward the ladies' room but swerved past it fluidly at the last second, slipping out the back door instead and then pounding through the alleyway and around to the front entrance. Then she waited. One minute, two minutes, three minutes, heart throbbing painfully from the sprint and her skin prickling in the chill. Coatless, her black Salvation Army trench still slouched up alibi-style next to her purse backstage. At least it wasn't raining, for once, aside from a little halo of mist around the neon club sign.

And then he was there, pulling his collar up as he emerged onto the sidewalk, the neon light shining pink on his shaved head. She steeled herself to make his dreams come true, trying to look as if she'd been waiting for someone else when he happened to step into her path. "Hey, do you have a cigarette? I'm dying."

He just looked at her, blinked for a moment, then broke into a helpless smile. "I don't smoke," he said. "I'm sorry."

"Don't be. It's a nasty habit. I'm not supposed to be doing it. If my band sees me, they'll kill me." She gestured toward her throat, opened her mouth, pointing into it as if he could see the damage that cigarettes had already done to her vocal cords. Then she remembered Will's hands at her neck, how she'd worn a turtleneck but couldn't sing for two days afterward. Will had told Dave and Len she had laryngitis.

"Are you okay?" he asked suddenly, his smile going out.

She had only thirty more seconds to get this settled, so she let herself come a little unsewn, just enough to throw a natural wobble into her voice. "Rough night," she admitted. "Honestly, I kind of need a break from those guys. Where are you headed?"

"Nowhere," he said. "Home. Do you need a ride?"

"Yeah," she said. "If you're okay swinging by a drugstore or something for smokes." She laughed. "I'm sorry, I feel like a complete weirdo."

"No, it's okay," he said, and she knew it was far more than that. She was still watching the door just behind him out of the corner of her eye. Plenty of people were smoking under the sign, but there was no one out here she didn't want to see — yet. The door flapped open incessantly, burping out a few more plaid-flannel shirts each time. He noticed her noticing and twitched to look over his shoulder, and she willed her eyes to become china plates fixed on his until he stopped.

"I'm Cal," he said, extending a hand. "And it's right around midnight, so you"—he gestured toward the dingy marquee—"must be Gretchen."

She wasn't, but he was so proud of that line she knew immediately he didn't have any others. So she just nodded yes and grasped his warm hand, cracking open a little at the thought of all the things he was taking on faith. When she said, "Thanks, Cal," her voice broke again, not on purpose this time, and she pulled her hand back fast; he took a step forward, like you do when you see something just beginning to topple off a shelf.

She righted herself and said, "So, where are you parked?"

"That way." He pointed, and she let him march past her with just the faintest brush of shoulders, falling in a little behind. Giving him some time without her in his sightline so that he could reflect on his unbelievable good luck. That idea was so sad she almost laughed. She hoped he would forget about the cigarettes, because although she could hold a lungful of pot for a minute and a half before letting it out, cigarettes made her cough and cough.

He didn't forget. The car slowed down five blocks from the club and he prepared to turn into a gas station.

"What I really am is hungry," she said suddenly, like a confession. "Are you hungry?"

"I could eat."

"Do you know anywhere that's open? I've only been to Seattle for gigs, I don't know anything around here."

"Sure, yeah." Cal seemed unfazed by the sudden switch. "Do you have to get back anytime soon?"

"I'm just hungry," she repeated.

She wondered if they'd found her purse sitting under the stool yet, then realized Cal was saying something she'd missed. "I'm sorry, what? I'm—"

"You're tired too," he said. "I was just saying it was a great set. Are you always this worn out after a performance?"

"No," she said, leaning back into the passenger seat as the warm, familiar exhaustion of being borne away washed over her. The feeling of leaving: a perfect feeling, better than any safety in the world.

She was glad when the diner turned out to be fifteen minutes out along a highway between tall traffic barriers and taller trees. It was dark, but she could barely see the Space Needle poking up over a hill; that was how far away downtown was, with the club, and the van, and Will, who would by now be looking around impatiently, maybe sending someone into the ladies' room to check on her.

Cal opened the door for her. The diner had steam on the insides of its windows and smelled wonderful.

"This is perfect," she said as they slid onto the curved benches of wood-grain Formica. She ordered a burger and fries. Cal got a tuna melt with a salad.

"So you come up here for gigs a lot?" Cal asked.

"You should know."

He blushed. *Very pretty,* she thought.

"Yeah, I've seen you a few times," he said carefully. "You guys play a lot in Portland?"

"A couple times a week," she said.

"How long have you been singing?"

She looked for something on the table to play with, found the ridged white saltshaker. "I've been with the band six months."

"Do you like it?"

"I like being good at it," she said.

"That's not really the same," he said. "Do you like the *feeling?*"

"I like the *feeling* of being good at it."

"I mean, do you need to sing to live? Because when I see you up there, you look like you do."

"Well, I don't," she said, annoyed by the idea. "I'm just trying to do a good job."

"Well, that's what you look like. It's amazing to see. It's—like nobody else should see it, you know?"

"Yeah, that's what Will thinks too," she said with a short laugh. "I'm the only reason we're getting booked or he'd lock me up and make me sing just for him."

"I didn't mean that," Cal said.

"I know you didn't. But that's what it's like."

Cal furrowed his brow, obviously trying to think of something to say. She decided to save him the effort.

"He hits me," she said levelly. "I'm running away from him."

"He hits you."

"And I'm running away from him."

He took the saltshaker out of her hands and set it upright in front of her. She could feel him taking in, for the first time, her lack of a coat, her lack of a purse. Now was the moment when he would also surmise, correctly, that he was buying her dinner. She tried not to hold her breath waiting for his next question.

"How can I help?"

She looked into his eyes, which were dark brown with watery blue rings around the irises, and made her voice soft. "You're helping right now. Didn't you know?" She took the shaker back and laid it on its side, spun it around so that a few tiny salt grains flew out onto the table with every whirl. She let the salt lie, knowing instinctively how much he wanted to sweep it away. He didn't.

The food came. She picked up the burger and crammed in a

bite. Out of the corner of her eye, she noticed Cal giving a thank-you nod to the waitress, and only after she walked away did he unroll his fork and knife and spread the paper napkin in his lap. Then he picked up the knife and cut the sandwich in half diagonally.

"Wow," she said.

"What?" He picked up one triangle and bit off the corner.

Her mouth full, she gestured toward his sandwich with the hamburger in her hands.

"I like to eat one half at a time, in case I want to take the rest home," he said. "And I find triangles aesthetically pleasing."

"That's creepy." She laughed. "Like a serial killer."

"How old are you?" he asked.

"What an impolite question!"

"Forget it," he said. "You're obviously not old enough to want to hide your age, so you must be too young."

"Twenty-seven."

"Bullshit," he said.

"How old are you?" She put a French fry in her mouth, left it between her teeth for a moment too long before biting down.

He raised an eyebrow at her. "Too old for you."

"Forty?"

"Thanks." He laughed. "Thirty, actually."

"I'm twenty-five."

"Yeah, I bet," he said. "Christ. Shouldn't you be in college or something?"

"I graduated early," she said. "I'm a fast learner."

"How about that," Cal said.

"You're not, though."

"How do you know?"

She aimed a French fry at his nose and fired. "Because you didn't see that coming."

She hadn't seen it coming either. This flirtatious buoyancy was new to her. She'd never been anything but sultry or sweet with Will, as the situation demanded; with Lina, silent and compliant. She wondered in a detached way how much of this was an act, how much a real response to the warm diner, the food hitting her stomach, her muscles relaxing. The absence of fear, for the first time in months.

Meanwhile, Cal was studying her with a serious expression. "Listen, Gretchen," he said. "I can find you a place to stay for a while."

"Can I stay with you?"

He hesitated. "Do you have anyone else you can call?"

"Do I look like I have anyone else I can call?" she said with a gesture that took in the two of them, alone, and the midnight diner.

"Well . . ." He paused, then sighed. "I guess you can crash at my place tonight."

"You do this often? Offer strangers a bed?"

"I knew someone else who had to leave a bad situation in a hurry once," he said, ignoring her provocation.

She'd stopped listening, though, after the word *tonight*. The rest would come. Once she was inside his house, she knew well enough how to make it stick. She just didn't know it would stick for her too. That was her mistake.

5

Alex Mercado looks about ten years younger than any private investigator I've ever seen in a movie or TV show. He has a round, boyish face, tan and clean-shaven. To my relief, he's not wearing a fedora—I realize now that I've been picturing him in one because of the website, but of course he's dressed unobtrusively, in jeans and an untucked polo shirt. Nevertheless, in a Waffle House sparsely populated with single men drinking coffee alone in booths, I can tell right away which one is looking for me, and he confirms it by standing and leaning over to shake my hand across the booth.

"I'm Alex. Thanks for coming," he says and gestures for me to sit across from him. The brown plastic of the booth squeaks as I slide toward the wall with its frosted-glass partition on top. It's been a long time since I've been in a Waffle House. Looking around, I wonder if this is the type of place where my students hang out when they're hung over. Its smell—cinnamon apples and slightly rancid cooking oil—is strangely pleasant.

"You come here often?" I ask. "I think I've seen you here before."

He looks slightly taken aback, and I think, *That's for the caller ID, buddy.*

"I just wanted somewhere we could talk without being interrupted," he says. His voice is a little raspy, but instead of making him seem older, it makes him sound almost adolescent, like his voice is breaking. He looks around and laughs. "There's only one waitress working the floor right now, and believe me, she's not all that attentive."

"Just so you're aware, my husband knows I'm here."

"Okay," he says. I can tell he doesn't believe me.

"Shoot," I say to get the pleasantries over with.

"I know this is a delicate subject," he says, pronouncing the word *delicate* with more attention to each syllable than is usual. "I know you're probably feeling very—"

"Yes, I am," I say. "So what's this all about?"

"Have you talked to your daughter about what happened?"

"The police report—"

"I know what's in the police report."

"You do?" I have, of course, seen news footage from the press conference the police gave, but without the family there as a central attraction, it went fast, just someone speaking the words *safe and sound* and *human-trafficking task force* and then *safe and sound* one more time amid flashing cameras while Julie's seventh-grade picture floated in one corner and a banner scrolled across the bottom of the screen: KIDNAPPED 13-YEAR-OLD HOME SAFE EIGHT

YEARS LATER. Certainly no details from the police report have been released to the public. "How do you know?"

"I read it," he says.

"How?"

"I'm a PI, I have my ways. But I didn't ask about the report. Have you talked to your daughter about what happened?"

"I was there when she gave her statement."

He just looks at me.

"We don't spend every waking minute talking about it," I say. "If that's what you mean."

"You don't want to know?"

"I don't want to pry."

"Mrs. Davalos."

"Dr.," I say without thinking, but he presses on.

"Have you noticed any inconsistencies in Julie's story?"

Four missed therapy appointments. A tattoo. The look on her face when she saw the ultrasound screen. Her voice: *Get out.*

"Has it ever occurred to you to wonder—" He breaks off and drops his voice, putting on a serious face, not quite apologetic, but concerned. "Look, Mrs.—*Dr.* Davalos. There have been cases of—it's unusual, but frankly, so is a missing child showing up on her own eight years later, out of nowhere. Even after just three days, when no ransom has been set and there's a weapon involved, the likelihood of recovery—"

"I'm aware."

"Now, the cops aren't going to question it. She's home, she's safe, and she's not their problem anymore."

"They're still looking for—"

He cuts me off. "Sure, it would look great for them to pull in the bad guy after all this time, expose a human-trafficking ring. Terrific headline. But I have to tell you, Doc, from what I read, that is one bizarre trafficking ring. You don't kidnap a kid in Texas and drag her across three states if you're trying to get her to Mexico. The border's right there."

"Maybe the kidnapper didn't have a plan," I say.

"Sure," Alex says. "Maybe he's a garden-variety psychopath—I mean, they're not that common, but maybe. And he sees her somewhere, who knows where, and takes her opportunistically, on an impulse, and then he needs to get rid of her fast after—okay. And he happens to bump into this trafficking ring, and she winds up in Mexico with El Jefe the drug lord who lives on a compound right out of a movie." He pauses, shakes his head. "That was a gutsy move, but smart."

"What do you mean, smart?" I say. "What move?"

"Because now the FBI is involved." He's starting to talk more to himself than to me, the concern yielding to an expression I find almost unbearable—one of *interest*. "Then there's the statewide task force, HPD, and the county, all these levels trying to work together. Everything gets complicated, and it gets slow. The investigation could drag on for months and months. And in the meantime, do you think the cops *want* her face in the media, reminding everyone how they dropped the ball for eight years? Why do you think that press conference went by in such a hurry? You think they want to remind everyone that America's kidnapping sweetheart just wandered back on her own?" Alex has been talking rapidly, and now he pauses, so I know I am in for it. "Especially when she was probably right under their noses the whole time, and they didn't do anything to save her?"

"Under their—" *But she's safe,* I think.

He pushes a large manila envelope across the table to me, and although I feel a warning signal going off somewhere in my head —*Don't open it, don't open it*— I pry open the metal fastener and lift the flap. I lay it flat on the table, put two fingers in, and slide out some articles and a photograph. The photograph doesn't make sense to me at first, and then it does, for a brief sickening instant —scraps of rotting fabric, and something worse—and I look away and catch a glimpse of the headlines: *River Oaks. Houston Neighborhood.*

Remains Found.

I push everything back into the envelope and press the flap over the fastener as my stomach heaves into my throat.

"Who hired you?" My voice is shaking.

"I was just starting out on the force when your daughter disappeared," Alex says conversationally, without answering or touching the envelope, as if suddenly we've been lifted out of this nightmarish Waffle House and dropped into the getting-to-know-you phase of an awkward first date. "I hated it. I was out in a couple of years. Believe me, to walk away from those benefits just gets harder, so if you find out it's not for you, you have to leave fast." He laughs once. "My wife evidently thought the same thing."

"Who hired you?" I repeat.

"Nobody—"

"Then what the hell are you trying to do here?"

A waitress walks up with a tall plastic carafe in hand, and, unbelievably, Alex gestures toward his cup and lets her fill it up. He gives her a little nod of thanks and watches as she walks away, then turns back to me. As he opens his mouth, I feel a buzz at my hip. Tom must be wondering where I am. What time is it anyway?

"Anna, I was there. Don't you want to know why they never found your daughter?"

"I assume gross incompetence was an issue." The sound of my first name in his scraping voice makes me so angry I can barely contain myself. It's time to end this farcical conversation. "I have to go," I say, standing up. Distantly, I feel my phone vibrate in my purse a second time.

"You want the truth. So do I. Well, I have reason to believe the truth is . . . worse than we thought. What's in that envelope" —he's talking faster and faster, jabbing his pointer finger at the unspeakable thing burning a yellow rectangle on the bottom of my cornea—"they're not even going to compare it with your daughter's dental records. Julie Whitaker's been removed from the missing-persons database. I checked."

"Because she's home," I whisper. Lying on the sofa under an afghan.

Brr. Another text.

"They think the remains are eight to ten years old, Anna. They think it's a thirteen-year-old girl. But Julie's name won't come up at all—"

"Why should it?"

"—unless you introduce a reasonable doubt that the woman living in your house is not who she says she is."

"The woman living in my house?" I repeat, like an idiot.

"Could you just do me a favor? Could you get me a sample of her DNA? Some hair off a brush, ideally."

Brr. Brr. I pull the phone out of my purse, look down briefly, read Tom's latest text, and feel suddenly dizzy.

But Alex goes on. "I have a friend in the crime lab who'll run a hair sample and see if it's a match. We don't go to anyone, and no one finds out, not even her, until you're—until we have an answer."

"I'm sorry." I push the envelope back across the table, like an entrée I can't finish.

"Put it this way. You're sure it's her? Okay. So this is just confirmation, peace of mind." He looks at me shrewdly.

Brr.

"But you're not sure, are you? Not entirely."

He's still seated with his hands folded in front of him on the table, but it feels like he's looming over me, reaching into the innermost recesses of my mind, putting his fingers all over everything. It's the kind of violation that implicates you through and through, like failing to set the alarm or leaving the door unlocked or simply living in a world where anyone can walk into your kitchen and take your daughter away at knifepoint. A world where that can happen is a world where I can fail at every act of faith and trust, a world where the best thing that ever happened to me is just another mask for the worst thing, and the worst thing that ever happened to me fits inside a manila envelope, fits into two words, really: *Remains Found.*

"I'm sure," I say.

"You have my number," he says. He doesn't offer me the envelope again. "Call me if you want to talk more."

My phone is buzzing continuously now. I have to get home to Tom and face the punishments already raining down on us for my doubts. I start toward the door. It feels like I've been gone forever, impossible to believe I stormed out of Carol Morse's office just a few hours ago. But the thought of the missed therapy appointments suddenly gives me a use for the wrecking ball in the booth behind me. I turn and take a couple of quick steps back toward the table.

"I don't give a damn about *that*," I say, refusing to look at the envelope again. "But if you really want to help me, find out where she goes on Tuesday and Thursday afternoons. She leaves the house at one thirty. Follow her."

"I thought you'd never ask."

"This is not pro bono," I say. "This is for me. I'll pay."

"Okay." He nods. "But you do something for me too, Anna. Search for a band called Gretchen at Midnight. Look for a video on YouTube. Tell me whose face you see. And if it changes your mind, call me."

Vi

woke up at seven in the morning with a stiff jaw and sticky yellow stars behind her eyes. Will was still passed out beside her, snoring and rasping.

For a moment she didn't remember why her jaw hurt. Then she stepped into the bathroom and saw the shower curtain half pulled down and the shampoo bottles arrested mid-roll in the tub, remembered his hands holding her neck against the wall under a rain of water. When he'd released her, she'd grabbed at the curtain blindly to keep from falling, with predictable results. She'd stayed huddled there, listening to the sound the water made hitting the plastic curtain over her head, waiting for him to come back and yell at her for the mess she'd made. He never came.

It was the first time Will had hit her, but not the first time she'd thought he was going to. She was already intimately familiar with the song he'd sing when he woke up after a night like last night. How could he trust her, with her past? Dancing for all those men — women too — more than dancing. That was the first verse. Then came the chorus, in which he avoided last night's sour names, just cried and swore he'd never believe he was enough for her. Second verse, same as the first. Then, best of all, the bridge: Didn't she understand he'd been betrayed before? He was a virgin until he was twenty-two because his college girlfriend said she wasn't ready, but then it turned out she was sleeping with someone else. He'd been a perfect gentleman, and she'd *betrayed* him.

Vi always pretended she was hearing it for the first time. He'd cry and cry and beg for forgiveness, but somehow, it would still be her fault. And his memory of having apologized and groveled and told her the humiliating story once again would only make the next time worse.

She went back to the bedroom and looked at him. Will was beautiful in repose. He had a jaw like a statue's, hard and rounded at the same time, and his bluish whisker shadow made his skin look like marble. She imagined putting her hand on him where his had been on her, just under the jaw, then leaning down and squeezing hard.

His eyelids, almost translucent, fluttered, and she suddenly put a hand to her own tender jaw. The bruises were forming just under the jawline, where they could be swaddled in a scarf or turtleneck. No one would have to see.

Almost as if he knew just where to grab. Almost as if he'd done this before.

The bathroom took only a few minutes to clean up. He would cry, yes, and apologize, but he wouldn't want to see any reminders. He'd want to have sex first thing, when her breasts were still slick with his tears, and she would accommodate him gently, lovingly; there was, even now, a calculating little twitch in her groin at the thought. She lay back down in her underwear and carefully arranged herself in bed next to his still form, draping the sheet over them both, tucking them in. She closed her eyes. She wasn't going to be able to go back to sleep, but that was fine. She used the time behind her eyelids to make a plan.

The plan involved Seattle. Will had been booking gigs there to get her out of town. He was worried she'd fall in with her old crowd again, Lina's crowd, even though none of them would talk to her after the breakup. Most of them she hadn't known well in the first place, so when she was out playing gigs with Will and saw them once in a while, it wasn't strange for them to pretend they didn't recognize her. She did the same.

It didn't happen much, though, because they weren't playing lesbian dive bars anymore. Will had called up two of his old band mates and said, "I have a girl singer." Vi's haunting vocals were laid over electric guitar, and she was singing lead, not backup. The lyrics sounded to her like badly written suicide notes, but you couldn't hear them all that well, so it didn't matter much. Will was right; people liked to see a girl fronting a band. It didn't seem to matter what kind of ripped-up clothes she was wearing; their faces turned up toward her like flowers, like she was an angel of light. And sometimes she really felt like one. The stage lights bleached out her eyeballs under the lids so she felt like she was staring straight up into heaven, and if the lights left dark splotches in her vision after she opened them, it just meant she had to look at the world around her a little less.

The band was called, depressingly, Midnight. But after a while it became clear that people were showing up for Vi, and in a moment of inspiration, Will suggested they change the name of the band to Gretchen at Midnight, after some children's story his mom had read to him when he was little. She was ready to say goodbye to Vi by this time anyway, and, just as she suspected, people started calling her Gretchen. She liked it. Gretchen was a healthier name than Violet, and Gretchen was a healthier girl, not a night bloomer but a bright yellow flower. Her hair grew longer and she started bleaching streaks into it, and the blonder it got, the better it looked with the dark T-shirts and jeans she wore on-stage, and everything was more or less fine.

At least, it was in a holding pattern until she slipped and said something stupid that exposed her, lethally, two different ways at once. Dave and Len were talking about hitting up strip clubs after a gig, and they mentioned the Black Rose. A little high off the crowd that night, she cracked a dumb joke about the dykes who went there for fresh fish, and Will, with his occasional radar for such things, looked at her with a sudden, uncanny flicker of recognition and said, "How do you know?"

She didn't bother denying it; he'd kissed the tiny black rose on her rib cage a hundred times without knowing what it stood for. Now he stared at her and she felt the tattoo burning under her T-shirt, its meaning suddenly unmistakable.

It was over, a fact that she knew right away and he, danger-ously, didn't. From that point on, whenever she stood on the stage glowing like a street sign, he didn't see Vi anymore, he saw Starr dancing under the hot lights, Starr who should have been long gone. After shows, no matter how happy he seemed with the band's share of the door, he said, "Every single person in that room wanted you."

She just shrugged, because wasn't that kind of the point?

At first it turned him on. When they got home, he'd grab her hard, lift her shirt and rub his thumb over the tattoo until the skin under her left breast was bruised and raw, fuck her like he was trying to own her from the inside out. Useless, she could have told him; nobody owned what was in there, not even her. But it wasn't long before disgust eclipsed desire, and then his eyes went black, and fucking her wasn't enough, he had to get in some other way.

The shower rod had broken, and she could feel more breakage on the way. It was time to get out, but her next situation had to be something different. No more Linas, no more Wills. She was done playing a rag doll, whether she got tucked in at night or thrown against the wall.

Anyway, the band was starting to get too popular. At almost every show now, she saw a few glowing rectangles held aloft to record, and she didn't like it. She knew she'd have to plan tight and move fast, because these days Will never let her out of his sight for long. When they were all on the road together, he played her guardian angel, meaning she and Will had a cheap motel room while the rest of the band crashed on sofas. One day soon he'd start making her crack the door open while she peed, and she'd never be alone again, not even in the john.

She started drinking a beer with the band before the show, in the round on the house that took the sting out of dismal pay. Will liked her taking part in this pre-show ritual; he'd warned her enough times, crushing his fifth or sixth empty while she kept herself sharp, not to act any better than she was. The tide would eventually turn, of course, but she thought she knew approximately how much longer she could drink with the guys before that happened. She snuggled up closer to Will to buy herself a little more time, ignoring Dave and Len as much as she could with them all crammed into a booth together, and made sure everyone saw her hit the ladies' room just before they all went onstage together. Will laughed and said it was stage fright, but when the time was right, missing this step would give her an excuse to disappear immediately after the set.

Every time they played Seattle she felt like a kid on a swing, scanning the ground as she whooshed forward, looking for the perfect moment to jump off. She didn't know exactly who she was looking for until she saw him: a man in the audience at the Ploughman she'd seen before, always alone. Just a man, but that night onstage, as the hot red lights lay on her face like a mask she could slip out from under, she sensed him like a wet stain on the front of a blouse, felt him watching her, and when she saw his dark face ringed by lighter faces, a hole in the pale crowd, she knew. She closed her eyes, let her voice hover in the alto register for a few lines, and then reached out for him with her soprano, scaling the stage lights with her voice and bursting upward into the quiet dark at their center like a surfacing diver.

That night in October, with the mantle of drizzle descending again, a curtain that wouldn't lift for the next seven months, she jumped.

6

By the time I get home, I've forgotten all about the video and Gretchen Farber, because she's gone, Julie is gone.

I want to scream at Tom for letting her leave the house. Of course, he doesn't know about the miscarriage, he doesn't know she's supposed to stay off her feet for twenty-four hours. He doesn't know she might be bleeding, she might be hurting. But still—when I get home, she has been gone for five hours with no word, and he is frantic. We drive up and down Memorial, stopping in coffee shops and stores, asking if anyone has seen her. One barista at Starbucks says he thinks he saw her get into an SUV outside.

We aren't so crazed that we don't think of Jane, out somewhere in Tom's SUV. When Jane's phone goes straight to voicemail, the way it does when it's dead, that's when the scenarios begin to spiral out of control. Some men from Mexico have been looking for Julie and have finally found her, perhaps when the girls were together, and they've taken both of them, or it was Jane who picked Julie up, but they were T-boned at an intersection and are now lying comatose in a hospital; catastrophic scenes tantalizing because they're impossible, like lightning striking twice in the same spot. I yell at Tom and Tom yells back and then we hug each other tightly, and Tom calls the police. He's on hold with them when the two girls finally stumble into our kitchen after dark, sopping wet and giggling like mad.

It's the laughter that unhinges me. For the past four hours, since I came home to find both girls gone, I have been sitting at this kitchen table believing with a morbid certainty that this is my fault. That going to Julie's therapist and, worse, meeting with that Mercado person, some crank who got my work number off the faculty website, was a betrayal that meant I was unworthy of having Julie back. As I made my way through the list of Jane's friends —Bella, April, then further, to friends she probably doesn't hang out with anymore but whose parents' numbers we have—and Tom shouted between hold times at Detectives Harris and Overbey and anyone else who would listen, I knew, deep down, that they were gone because of me.

And now they are here, and they are laughing.

"Where have you been?" I ask quietly.

They're still in their sister bubble—Julie and Janie, Janie and Julie, just like old times, though Julie, already detecting something wrong, has started to sober up a little.

"Oh my God, so many places!" Jane puts a hand on Julie's shoulder to steady herself.

"You could start by explaining why you're soaking wet."

"Oh," she says. "Yes. That was mostly an accident." There's something a little hectic in Jane's voice, but I'm in no mood to listen to it. She can see my expression, though. "You tell her, Julie. She likes you." She explodes into nervous titters.

Julie starts to explain. "The traffic was bad on the way home, so we stopped to eat. And then Jane wanted to show me the sculpture garden, but it was already closed—"

"We jumped the wall," Jane says. "I've done it a lot, but this is the first time I've ever been chased off by a security guard!" She's giggling again. "So then we went to that big fountain in the middle of the roundabout in Hermann Park—"

"We wanted to make a wish."

"—and things got a little out of hand. And we went swimming."

"She was taking money out of the fountain!" says Julie, starting to laugh a little again.

"Well, I didn't have any change. I didn't think the wishes would mind being recycled."

They've already forgotten the expression on my face that stopped them in their tracks a moment before. In their minds they're still tumbling together into the broad bowl of the giant fountain, chasing each other through the arcing spray while cars honk all around.

It's too much to bear. I get up from the kitchen table. I don't even know what I'm doing or which one of them I'm moving toward, but Julie sees me coming and melts into the door frame. Without breaking stride, I slap Jane's cheek.

"Anna!" Tom shouts.

"What were you thinking?" I demand. "We must have left two dozen messages. What the hell happened?"

Tom crosses over to where Julie is hugging the door frame and puts one arm around her. He is not standing between Jane and me, but he looks like he is ready to be in an instant.

Jane holds her hand to her face, stunned. "You hit me."

Baby, I'm sorry is what I mean to say, but harsher words come out: "You owe your father and me an apology."

"You hit me," says Jane. "You fucking *bitch*."

"Jane." Tom steps in with a warning tone.

"My phone must have died! Jeez, I'll look if you want." She fumbles through her bag until she finds the phone, pushes the "on" button, and waves it around. "See? Dead!"

"It's your responsibility to keep it charged, always. You know that."

"Since when do you care?" Jane drops the phone back in her purse. "This isn't even about me. I've been five minutes late before and you haven't even noticed."

"You're five hours late, not five minutes," says Tom. "We had no idea where you were."

"I miss dinner all the time," Jane says. "Nobody's ever hit me before. Hell, nothing I do around here raises an eyebrow." She laughs. "Why is it different when she's with me? Is it because you're afraid something will happen to the one who matters?"

"You can take care of yourself," I spit.

"What's that supposed to mean?"

"You let her go once!" I'm yelling now. "You watched her walk out the door!"

Jane's eyes widen. She comes over to me, close enough for me to feel how much taller than me she is. She raises a hand, and for a moment, I think she's going to slap me. Instead, she points to Julie.

"Blame me if you want to, but don't forget, she's standing right over there. You can ask her whatever questions you want."

My eyes follow the pointing finger, and for the first time, I notice Julie's hair, which is wet and plastered to her head like Jane's but starting to dry. I see the short, feathery red cap, fluffed upward at the hairline by a cowlick, and for a moment, I can't even speak.

"I told you she would freak out," Jane says, but nobody pays attention now.

"I'm sorry," Julie whispers.

"Why—" I take a step toward Julie, reach out a hand, and tentatively touch the place over her ears where her long, silvery-pale hair used to be. I ruffle the side hair, pull it forward, check that it's real.

Then I start crying. I can't help it.

"I can't believe this," says Jane. "She's the one who left the house today without telling anyone where she was going. She's the one who disappeared. Not me. Not me!" There's a bandage on Jane's left ring finger that has come loose and is flapping around. When she sees that no one will try to stop her, she doesn't bother stomping, just rushes upstairs and slams the door to her room.

Julie follows, but slowly, one foot in front of the other, wading through my grief like it's a current in a flood, like she might lose her footing and be swept away. She looks as if she has lost more children than I can possibly imagine.

My mother slapped me once.

The summer after fifth grade, Angie Pugh invited me to spend part of my summer vacation with her family in Northeast Harbor. My mother, who had strong ideas about raising girls, reluctantly agreed, but I had outgrown my swimsuit, and shopping for a new one was torture. She stood behind me in the corner of the dressing room, watching with a frown as I tugged each suit over my newly widened hips. The suit we finally picked out had polka dots and a full, ruffled skirt that hung halfway to my knees—I had maxed out my growth spurt the year before and would never be an inch over five feet.

The first day of my vacation with Angie, she made a face at the polka-dotted suit and said, "Here, take one of mine." She opened up a drawer full of bikinis from the juniors' department, bathing suits my mom would never even let me take off the rack. I tried a crocheted bikini with a halter top and beaded hip ties that clicked when I walked. Angie looked at me appraisingly and said, "Now I get what it's *supposed* to look like." She sounded jealous, but only a little; after all, she was the one with the vacation home in Northeast Harbor, and I was the one with the Catholic mother.

For ten days we played tetherball and Ping-Pong, walked to the old-fashioned soda fountain for Coke floats, told each other ghost stories under the covers with a flashlight. At the end of the vacation I gave Angie her suit back, but I hadn't thought about the tan lines. My mother, who did not believe in knocking, came in while I was changing.

As I cried from the sting, she yelled, "Do you know what the men who saw you were thinking? Do you?"

I didn't believe her. To me, it was just a body. But when summer ended I found out that to the boys in my school, the men in the streets, to anyone who looked, it was more than that; it was an open book full of horrible secrets, a dirty magazine anyone could paw through. My mother never hit me again, but I hated her for being right.

My mother died before Julie's hips ever filled out a skirt. She never saw me get my first heart-stop—that moment when you look at your girl in a certain light and see that she'll eventually become a woman, and it reminds you of every boy who put a pencil up your skirt when you walked ahead of him on the stairs, every man who stared at you at the bus stop, every honk on the street, every leering comment. You remember being alone, gloriously alone, reading a book in a sundress, feeling the grass prickling your thighs and the sun on your forearms, and then realizing that you weren't alone at all as a man you were ashamed to feel afraid of walked up and asked if he could put sunscreen on your back. You look at your daughter and it all comes back, every microsecond when you felt that twin surge of shame and fear, but this time it's outside of you, happening to a body that feels like yours but doesn't belong to you, so there's no way to protect it.

It stopped my heart back then. I was scared for her, scared *of* her. I held my breath and thought, *This will be over soon enough. By the time she's a teenager, she'll wise up. Like I did.*

She didn't make it.

"How dare you." Tom is angrier at me than I've ever seen him, leaning down to force eye contact but still looking every inch of the foot taller than me he is. "We do not do that, Anna. We don't do that to our kids."

"You were as scared as I was."

"I don't care how scared you were," he says, his frame growing larger every second. "We agreed: Never in our house. I saw too much of it in mine."

"And how are your sisters doing, Tom?" I say, raising my eyes to his suddenly.

"Scared shitless of their father!" he snaps back. "And probably their husbands too! Is that what you want?"

"*And how many of them were kidnapped and sold to the highest bid-*

der?" I yell. "*And how many of them were raped every day for eight years?*"

"Anna—"

"They were *safe,* Tom! They were *kept* safe!"

He puts his finger right up in my face and bites off every word with a growl. "If you think that's how it felt growing up with my father, you don't know the first goddamn *thing* about safe."

But I'm beyond reason now. The screaming has unleashed something too big to make a sound. I think I am sobbing, but then I realize I am only gasping, again and again, struggling for air. I feel dizzy, and my vision clouds. The next minute I come to, still standing in the same place, crushed against Tom's chest. It is as if he's pushing the air back into my lungs, and the big black thing in me dissolves into ordinary tears.

"Why did she do it," I say, sobbing against him. "Why?"

"You know Jane," he says. "She lost track of time. And Julie, I think she was just feeling cooped up, trapped. You know what she's been through." He shudders and gives a deep sigh. "I was as worried as you—and as angry. But now that we know they're okay, honestly, I think it was probably good for the girls to get some bonding time."

"I meant—her hair."

Tom releases me, takes a step backward, and stares. "You can't be serious."

I know he's kept up with Jane all these years, fighting through the traps she set to keep us away, while I was too happy to believe she didn't want my interference. But Julie—how has he kept up with her too? How does he still have that connection from before? How did he know to move straight to Julie and hold her close when I went straight to Jane and did what I did?

"They're like strangers."

He looks at me with disbelief. "Anna. That's how all mothers of teenage girls feel."

But Julie, as Carol Morse reminded me, is an adult. Tom doesn't know about Carol Morse and the miscarriage, Alex Mercado and the envelope. He doesn't look into those eyes and wonder if they're the right shade of blue and then think to himself, *Would I even know the difference?*

I could tell Tom everything, but I'm the one who let the poison in, and we're already being punished for it. What better proof of my sacrilege than this horrible feeling of not recognizing my own children, kicking them out of the nest for having the wrong scent, striking them when I want to hold them, all because they disappear at odd times of the day and night and I never know what they will look like when they return?

"You're right," I say. "I know you're right."

Tom and I can afford only one fight a night. We are too newly repaired for more. I allow myself to be taken to bed. When he is asleep, I slip into the bathroom with my phone, mute the volume, and search until I find a YouTube video called "Gretchen at Midnight @ Chapel Pub—10/2/14." I push the triangle to play the clip and watch as Julie's face, no bigger than a smudged white thumbprint on the screen, opens its mouth under stage lights and silently sings.

Violet

sang for the first time in Lina's backyard.

Violet never thought of it as *her* backyard, although she'd lived there almost a year, long enough to dye her hair blue and then bleach it and clip it short and start growing it out all over again as a ripe strawberry blond. Short hair was nothing special in this company, of course, but she could tell Lina liked it better show-pony-long, no matter the color.

Lina had friends over, and they'd all been drinking. It had gotten dark and a little chilly, so they lit up the fire pit out back and dragged chairs from the kitchen around it. Lina never smoked pot, so Violet usually avoided it too. It should have been a sign to her that she was ready for a change when, this time, she took the joint that appeared on her left as if by magic, held in Susan's hand. "Vee," said Lina, but she turned and shrugged almost immediately as Violet took a long pull.

Violet relished the small opportunity to remind Lina she was not a knickknack picked up somewhere exotic for a song. Nobody except Lina operated on the assumption that getting Violet off the pole was the same as having bought and paid for her, but it lingered on the air like the smell of fireworks, the scent of a dangerous excitement that was over before anyone else could enjoy it. Expelling a lungful of pot smoke without a sound, Violet handed the joint back to Susan, who grinned handsomely and passed it on.

Once rid of the joint, Susan pulled a guitar from behind her seat.

"Troubadour time already?" said Susan's girlfriend, Beck, from across the circle, where she was wrapped in a woven blanket.

But Susan didn't sing a love song. She began by strumming the guitar with her bare knuckles, and then started up a picking pattern that reminded Violet of running water, dissolving the chords into individual notes. The joint was loosening the knots in Violet's limbs one by one, and the tension of her status as a trophy girlfriend who should be seen and not heard began unfurling like cream in coffee. Susan's fingers on the strings plucked at her arm hairs, her leg hairs, the hairs on the back of her neck.

Then Susan started singing in a throaty alto, a folk song. *She walks these hills in a long, black veil. She visits my grave when the night winds wail.* The song was strangely familiar—or maybe she was just stoned—and Violet's mind raced to grab the tail of each line, never quite catching up. Then the guitar's rounded edge bumped against her bare knee, sending its shiver up her thigh to her cunt, and for the first time, she was attracted to a woman, really attracted. And it wasn't Lina.

Beck was looking over at Susan with an expression in which patience and paranoia mingled—she was high too—but most of the others were still chatting and laughing and clinking beer bottles and wineglasses onto the ground or scraping sandaled feet across the concrete to grab another bottle from inside.

Then Violet started to sing.

At first she sang along with Susan, and then she started to split on the rhyming words—*veil, wail, sees, me*—soaring upward in response to Susan's emphasis, following the bumps of her voice the way she used to follow John David's. And then, finally, she peeled her voice off the back of Susan's, as if she'd been riding along on the back of a bird, and, catching the feeling of flight, spread her own wings. After that it was like dancing. She and Susan breathed in together and spent their breath together, vibrating like two strings on the same instrument.

Outside the pocket of air where they were singing, wineglasses dangled and beer bottles hung in the air, suspended halfway to parted lips.

When the notes knit themselves back into chords, Violet knew it was done, and the high flew out of her just like that, leaving a sleepy vacancy.

The women in the circle clapped and exclaimed over Violet as if she were a precocious child or an animal that could talk. Someone said, "Lina, where have you been hiding this one?" As though she hadn't been to all their poetry readings and dinner parties this summer, not to mention the Black Rose, where she'd watched them get lap dances from her former coworkers.

While Lina lapped up the praise, Susan put a hand on her arm and asked, "Where did you learn to sing like that?"

"Church," she answered truthfully, and because she was still a little high, the word seemed to encompass everything she meant by it, which was John David and the darkness at the center of light and the things both ugly and sweet she would offer anyone if it meant survival. Susan nodded, and Violet thought for a moment she really understood. What could have happened to Susan that she did?

"If you ever want to join me for an open mic sometime," Susan said and patted her arm twice with a wink.

Violet knew by the prickling in her skin, and by Lina's eyes on her, that the circle had become charged with a dangerous energy. She imagined herself transforming into the sputtering, sparkling catherine wheel that would burn down Susan and Beck's life together, forcing them to decide who would keep the condo in Northwest and the restaurant they co-owned and their four-year-old son. She weighed all that against the pot-fueled flickering in her cunt that she could exhaust in a single evening or at most a few weeks.

It was tempting.

She snuffed out the tiny flame. "I don't think I could," she said. Susan was too complicated.

Anyway, saying no to Susan had an upside. Lina was so grateful that when the next chance came around, as Violet had known it would, Lina said yes. And then Violet was singing folk music with trios in little cafés, filling out harmonies here and there with other kinds of bands too, and she felt the satisfaction of belatedly scrubbing away the last of Starr the stripper with the red waterfall of hair down her back, and flipping into her new identity, Violet the singer with the strawberry-blond bob that was growing out, little by little. She drifted from gig to gig, band to band, until she ran into a male drummer.

Will was single, so all she had to break up was a band.

7

When I wake up the next morning, Tom is outside cleaning the pool.

I watch him through the bedroom window as he stands at the pool's pebbled ledge, sweeping the long pole of the vacuum slowly across the bottom like a gondolier. With each measured stroke, last night feels farther away. The tingle in my palm from slapping Jane, Tom's yelling, and, most of all, the face on my cell-phone screen cradled in my palm as I crouched in the bathroom—it's all gone now, washed clean by sleep and early-morning showers. A mistake. A misunderstanding. A blond girl in a blurry video. I grab a pair of fresh jeans out of the laundry basket and pull them on, then feel a lump in the back pocket and find Detective Overbey's card, pulped in the washing machine and fuzzed from the dryer, unreadable. I throw it in the trash.

I take my coffee outside and settle into a deck chair to watch Tom's rhythmic movements. It's one of those rare, sparkling, rain-cooled mornings that occasionally graces Houston in June, a throwback to March, a day you could almost mistake for an ordinary summer day in a more hospitable climate. The shadows of the tall pine trees move on the deck; the breezes that languidly stir their tops back and forth barely reach me. A yellow worm of late-season oak pollen drops into my mug, and I fish it out. We may have our problems, but after all, we are a family again, husband and wife and two beautiful daughters, together at last.

The door opens and Jane comes out, rolling a suitcase behind her.

"Sweetie?" Tom calls as she wheels the suitcase to the car, ignoring us. I hear a car door open, then close again with a thump. As she passes by the deck without her suitcase, Tom says, "Jane?"

"I'm going back. I bought my ticket last night. I'm staying with April tonight, and she's taking me to the airport tomorrow morning."

Tom turns off the vacuum and leans the handle against a tree. "Sweetie—we talked about this. Maybe you need some time to—"

"I want to go back. Now." Tom doesn't ask why. Neither of us do. "Will you take me to April's house?"

"Sure, sure," he says. She disappears back inside. He turns to me.

It's my cue. "I'll apologize," I say. And then, when he looks down at his sandaled feet: "I'm sorry." He doesn't look up as I walk past, but his anger is palpable.

I go upstairs and knock on Jane's door and, when there is no reply, open it an inch at a time, softly saying, "Hey."

Jane is rummaging through her closet. She looks at me over her shoulder and then returns immediately to what she is doing, which is stuffing an open duffle bag full of things she is apparently choosing more or less at random.

Behind me, the shower starts running, and I think of Julie's new hair. I wonder how much of the excess dye will wash down the drain, whether the red will stain the tub. Then I snap back to Jane standing in front of me, back turned.

"I'm so sorry, Jane. There was no excuse for that. We were just —I was so worried."

Jane yanks a sweater off a hanger and throws it into the bag. "Be worried," she says. "You can do it without me around."

I take a step inside the door and close it behind me. She whirls.

"Did I say you could come in?"

"Jane, please."

"Please what? Please stay out of the way so you can be with your other daughter, your real daughter, the one you care about? Please be fine, so you don't have to give me any of your precious time or listen to what I say?"

"Please stay." She looks at me with such longing, her jaw set and quivering, like she used to when she was a child. "Your father needs you."

Her eyes drop to the floor, and when they come up her chin isn't shaking anymore. "I'll go out for breakfast with him on the way to April's. Would that make him happy?"

"I think he would like that, yes."

"I'll miss him. I'll miss both of you—all of you." She wipes her eyes with her flannel shirtsleeve. "I just—can't be here right now. It's making me crazy. She's my sister too, you know. I missed her too. I was frightened too all these years." She looks around at the room, at her closet. "I hate this room. Sleeping here still gives me nightmares."

"We couldn't move," I say. "We—"

"I know, I know, you wanted her to be able to find you. And she did. So that's all that matters. I get it." She goes back to stuffing more things into the bag. "I don't even mind that you've barely asked me about my school situation at all—"

"Jane—"

"Don't. I'll figure it out on my own. I always do." She finishes her job and grabs the bag off the floor, throws it on her bed. "Just don't take it out on me because she found you, not the other way around."

There's a gentle knock at the door, and Jane pushes past me to open it.

Julie is standing in the doorway holding a pair of black high-top tennis shoes in her hands. With her short hair plastered wetly to her skull, she looks older and smaller, almost birdlike.

"You'll need these," she says, holding out the shoes.

"You can keep them," Jane says, her voice roughening around the edges. "I need a new pair anyway."

"Are you sure?" says Julie.

"Yeah," Jane says. "I want you to have them."

"Thanks," says Julie.

"You have my e-mail address, right?" Jane asks. I feel like I should be leaving the girls alone to say goodbye, but they are directly blocking the door, so I just stand, hands in jean pockets, waiting.

"Yeah," Julie says. "Thanks for hanging out. I had a nice time."

"Me too," says Jane. She lunges forward and gives Julie a quick hug. "I love you. I'm glad you're home."

Then she turns to zip up the bag on the bed. She grabs a stack of notebooks from her desk and loops her book bag over one shoulder. By the time she turns back to the door, Julie is gone, the door to her room shut.

I reach out my hand for a bag, but Jane shakes her head, grabs the duffle, and moves out the door. She makes it all the way down the stairs at a brisk march, *thump-thump-thump,* the heavy, purposeful Jane step, as if she's shipping out; I follow in her footsteps more softly and slowly. Tom gets up from the kitchen table when he sees her and steps toward her, reaching out for the bags. She surrenders everything to him, even the notebooks, and he silently carries them out to the car. I keep shadowing her until we reach the back door, where Julie must have hovered long ago, a knife at her back, before taking her last step over the threshold of childhood and into whatever was waiting for her on the other side.

My hands still in my pockets, I want to reach out for Jane's shoulder. I don't, but maybe some invisible part of me does, like a phantom limb, because she turns around anyway.

"Mom," she says, and she buries her head in my shoulder for a second, her arms pinning mine down, almost hurting me.

When she pulls away, I've got tears in my eyes, but I let them stand and subside and pull my hands out of my pockets at last, rest one on her elbow. "I love you," I say.

Her face is serious and a little sad. "Mom," she says. "I think you should know something. Julie has a cell phone. She told me she borrowed one to call me yesterday, but then I saw it in her purse." She reaches into her pocket and pulls out a slip of paper. "I wrote the number down." She gently takes my hand away from her elbow, and the last bit of Jane I feel is her fingers pressing the paper into my palm.

Then she's gone. The car growls down the driveway, and I stand there a bit too long before putting the paper in my pocket, still feeling Jane's touch and wondering absently why she has a white bandage around one of her fingers.

When I turn, Julie is standing by the kitchen island, looking at me. I wonder how long she's been there, what she heard and what she saw.

Starr

learned how to lie at the Black Rose in Portland, Oregon. Not that she'd never lied before — to police officers, to foster parents, to anyone who looked like he or she might use the truth to hurt her. But those were lies she told with words, and anyone who was really paying attention could see through words. At the Black Rose, she learned to lie with her whole body.

She'd washed up in Pioneer Courthouse Square as Mercy with brown, shoulder-length, under-the-radar hair, and walked due east over the river until she was through with walking. She'd passed two other clubs, but the Rose was the first one with a picture on the dingy sign, and the swirls of dark petals surrounded by a spiky halo appealed to her. She didn't even have to take her clothes off to get the job, just show Gary, a tall, skinny guy with a hipster mustache, proof that she was over twenty-one. He explained that she'd be renting her mandatory stage time with watery ten-dollar drinks the customers bought her, ten drinks for one stage dance, twenty for two, and so on. If she didn't make her drink quota, she'd be buying the rest herself at the end of the night, out of the cash she made from lap dances and stage dollars—*after* tipping out the bar, the door, the waitresses, and the security staff. So it would *behoove* her, Gary said, enjoying the use of the word, to hustle as many drinks off her lap dances as she could.

As for rules—well, since deregulation, anything went. No no-touch rule, no three-foot rule, and nothing had to be covered. He gestured over to one of the armchairs that lined the walls, where a dancer was sitting naked in a customer's lap, her legs open, his fingers sunk inside her up to the third joint. The customer's head leaned back against the wall while the dancer rolled on him absently. "Thank you, Oregon Supreme Court," Gary said, with a smile implied but none on his face.

She didn't have to do that stuff, of course. The point was, she could do just about whatever she wanted. She could light her pubes on fire for all he cared. There was just one thing.

"You can't be Mercy. We've got one already."

Starr's first stage dance was on a Thursday afternoon, too early, though you couldn't tell what time it was inside the windowless club, where the fog machine churned day and night. She gyrated awkwardly to the music, slithering out of the makeshift girl-next-door costume she'd cobbled together with a stolen G-string from a mall store, and awaited the exposed and endangered feeling. But the closer she got to peeling the G-string down around her ankles, the more clothed she felt. Naked on the stage save for neon-yellow platform heels, she was unassailable, stripped down to armor that could never be taken off.

When she got down from the stage and walked among her prey, the feeling faded—they were sad daytime customers, and since there was a club on every block, it was nothing they hadn't seen before. The newly eviscerated vice laws meant the strippers could use their bodies to wrest money from wallets with brazen aggression. Some of the girls ended every dance lying on their backs, arms pasted to the floor, waving their legs like strange underwater plants around naked genitals elevated to customer-face level. Their pussies were as dry as mouths left open too long and as impersonal as rubber chickens, but it didn't matter; men stood transfixed, peering into the permanent gooseflesh as if they could will its transformation into warm, wet intimacy. Starr tried the helicopter move at home once, but her abdominal muscles were pathetic. She could barely manage the most basic pole moves, though she was learning from her roommates, most of whom were dancers too.

Gary had pointed her toward the dilapidated Victorian off Hawthorne with half the front steps rotted out and black-taped windows that beaded up and sweated in the never-ending drizzle. She didn't leave anything there; her backpack full of trophies and her slowly growing collection of outfits were safer in a locker at the Rose, and she wore her only jewelry, the gold chain with the little horse charm, around her ankle while she danced.

For all she was addicted to the hot lights on her sweaty skin and the bitter taste of the fog machine in the back of her throat, there was no doubt Starr was a terrible stage dancer. Her lap dances were more successful. She hated being down on the floor amid the stares and gropes and was distant and sullen. But sullen had its own appeal for some, and she had her customers just like the girls who giggled and flirted had theirs. Enthusiasm was not required so long as she got the script right, and the lines were almost painfully easy to memorize; it didn't matter whether or not they believed her, it was all part of the transaction. She learned which customers to tell it was only her first or second time doing this, which to tell that she was saving money for college or some new toys for her kid. With others, she didn't say anything about herself at all, just made a kind of purring noise, as if she felt lucky to be grinding on their crotches.

Still, there were too many strippers and not enough customers. Some of the girls rolled their eyes about the "de-reg" and bitched that a worse thing had never happened. Some nights Starr barely took home anything after tip-out. Plus, there were a million ways you could slip and fall in the newly permissive atmosphere, a million ways you could ruin everything in the split second between a smile and a nod. She had seen girls followed out back on their cigarette breaks by their favorite customers after an offer to make a little extra money and then come back that same night with a black eye or a broken strap, or not at all.

Starr, remembering the Petes, had no interest in these side transactions. But if she said no too many times, she risked losing herself a regular, which meant losing the club a regular, and that wasn't good either. So her job was to say nothing at all, to communicate neither yes nor no but keep looking as if she might say yes someday, as if she were just waiting for the right moment. It was an education in disappearing.

Graduation came when another dancer handed her a plastic tub half full of Manic Panic hair dye in an unmissable shade of red and said, "Trust me. It'll show up under the lights." Advice of this nature didn't come often, so Starr took it and found that being brighter on the outside meant, paradoxically, making an even darker hiding place for herself on the inside.

Over the next eight months she learned it didn't have to be just hair; it could be an accent, or a strange last name, or a fake tattoo on the back of her neck. It could be bright blue eyeliner, a pair of cowboy boots, or something outlandish she made up on the spot when customers asked where she was from: a farm she had grown up on, a famous ballerina she had studied with. When you looked like she did, with wide cheekbones and smooth, white skin and big, blank kewpie-doll eyes, people would accept anything about you but the truth. Whether she told them she'd been a porn star or a prizefighter, they believed her, in a way they'd never believed or cared about her invented baby sister or community college courses. She started making real cash, buying four stage dances a night and entertaining tables of a dozen customers or more who came in just for her. Moreover, they bought drinks for any girls she brought over, and that made the other dancers friendly.

After one particularly full shift, she and a few other girls went down the street and got matching tattoos of the spiky-haloed rose on the club's sign. She didn't know what else she could spend cash on that wouldn't weigh her down.

But the other law of being highly visible was you had to leave while the shine was still on. So when a group of women started frequenting the Black Rose during her shifts, Starr took note.

Lina, short for Carolina, was a fifty-five-year-old El Salvadorian with a short, grizzled mane, a thick neck, and a body that was round and pleasant. Lina came in all the time with her girlfriend, Heidi, who looked a bit like Starr without her makeup. Then one time Lina came in without Heidi, and Starr, who was ready to quit the club and move out of the Hawthorne house, got the message. She left with Lina at the end of her shift.

Lina lived in a huge Victorian in Northeast so high up it was practically on stilts. A beard of ground cover spilled down over a mossy concrete wall that looked barely adequate to keep the front yard from tumbling into the street. A stone staircase studded with clumps of tiny violets pinched shut in the predawn chill led from sidewalk to front door. Starr climbed up first, past gnarled Japanese maples with spidery leaves and bleeding-heart bushes whose hot-pink blossoms looked frozen in the act of ripping themselves open. The rough steps seemed endless after a long shift, but when Starr got to the top, she could see it was going to be worth it. The oval of stained glass in the door was just catching the first rays of sunlight.

Lina opened the door and let Starr in. The floor was made of cool, silky wood, covered with a big, soft rug of yellowish-white fur.

"Alpaca," Lina said, watching Starr's face as she wiggled her toes in the shag. "From home. They're very cheap there. I got that for three hundred bucks."

That didn't sound cheap to Starr, but she just said, "It's nice." The ceiling was vaulted over the living room, and there was a large abstract painting hanging on the wall. It looked like fruit dropped from a great height. "Did you paint that?" she asked.

"As a matter of fact, I did," Lina said. Her voice toughened up and she looked around the room casually. "You like it?"

"It makes me feel a little dizzy," Starr said truthfully. "Can I lie down?"

"Of course," said Lina, and she ushered her out of the vaulted living room and into a side room lined with raw wood where there was a tall bed covered by a shimmering, reddish-orange comforter. The wooden blinds were drawn, and it was blessedly dark. Without hesitation, Starr pulled off her shoes and climbed up on the mattress, which sank under her weight. She slid to the center and flipped over onto her back, exhausted, staring at the motionless ceiling fan of dark wood. She wondered what used to go through Heidi's head when she stared at the ceiling fan. Where had Heidi worked before Lina came along? Had she fallen in love with Lina?

"Why don't you tell me your real name? I don't think it's Starr."

She could feel the tiny beads embroidered on the comforter biting into her spine, like the princess and the pea. "Violet," she said, thinking of the purple flowers outside on the steep lawn. It wasn't the most convincing name she'd ever come up with, but she needed something as good as Heidi—who'd surely made up her name, too, before she'd been extracted as neatly as a tooth so that Starr could occupy her dent in the bed. Wouldn't it be easier if she could just use Heidi's name? She imagined herself saying, *Heidi*, and Lina saying, *What a coincidence*.

But the bed was the softest place she'd been in months, and she accidentally said the second part out loud. Just as Lina said, "What is?" Starr let go of the ceiling fan with her eyes and fell backward into slumber.

8

As the door closes behind her, the superficial layer of animation Jane brings to the house falls away, and the uneasy secrets Julie and I share swell up to fill the kitchen like a scent.

"How are you feeling today?" I ask.

"Okay," she says, placing a hand on her stomach. "Like a bad period."

I nod, remembering my miscarriage. "Did you tell Jane?"

She shakes her head. "No. We were having a nice time. I didn't want to make her feel bad."

"You know, you could have called me to pick you up. If you wanted to get out of the house." She's silent. "We could have gotten lunch or something. Gone shopping."

"More shopping?" she says with a quick laugh. Then she puts on an appreciative face. "I just wanted my sister."

. . . *and now she's gone.* The second half of the statement trails along in its wake like a ghost.

"I'm glad you girls got to spend a little time together. And I'm so sorry for the way I behaved. I just wish we had known where you were." I'm choosing my words carefully, giving her plenty of space, like she's a deer behind a tree instead of a girl behind a butcher block.

"I'm really sorry about that," she says. "I guess I started feeling a little — trapped."

I can't even think about what that word must mean for her. Hearing her say it is different from when Tom said it last night. It makes me feel trapped too, suffocated by grief. Like she's keeping me in a room with all the lights off. I scramble at the evidence of her lies, the paper folded up in the pocket of my jeans, but I am so afraid of confronting her with it that what I end up saying instead is "Julie, I think it's time we get you a cell phone."

She doesn't blink. I let a beat go by before I continue. "For Tom and me, really. So we can reach you, and you can reach us, if you need to."

Should I have waited a moment longer? Was her mouth opening to tell me the truth when I cut her off? *I have one already, it's in my bag, here's a plausible explanation of how I came to have it, along with my very good reasons for not mentioning it.*

At any rate, what she says now is "Thanks, Mom." And I feel a strange relief that I don't yet have to hear the plausible explanation, the very good reasons. She goes on: "Can I ask you something I've been worried about?"

"Of course." *Maybe it is coming, right now, after all.*

"I'm kind of worried about . . . money."

It's so unexpected, so unlike something Jane, for instance, would say, that I just repeat the word blankly. "Money?"

"Well, I know I'll have to get a job at some point."

"Oh, honey, you don't need to think about—"

"But I do need to think about it. I do," she insists. "We haven't talked about what it was like for you guys after it happened, but I know you must have spent a lot of—I mean, I know it's expensive. I've—seen the billboards."

"You have?"

"I looked up some stuff about my case on the Internet," she says.

Has she been on Tom's computer? Or did she use the secret phone?

"I just—I know Dad left his job. And Jane's in college—"

"Your father does fine, and so do I. We're fine, Julie."

"—and now I'm here."

"Which is the best and luckiest and most wonderful thing that could ever have happened to us."

"I know. I know. I just—" She throws up her hands. "I have to figure out what I'm going to do with my life." And then, in a slightly different tone: "I've been applying for jobs, you know."

I'm caught off guard. "What kind of jobs?"

"Oh, anything," she says evasively. "Baristas, cashiers. I even went inside that bar around the corner yesterday—I forget the name—to ask if they needed a dishwasher."

It takes me a moment to realize what bar she's talking about. That squalid, sad little bar in the strip center? Billy's or Bobby's or something? She went in *there?* She's watching my face, hanging on my flickering expressions, so I try to look expectant, like I'm waiting without judgment for her to finish.

"I tried Starbucks too," she goes on quickly, "but I didn't end up applying there. I was too tired. And kind of addled, I guess from the painkillers. That's when I called Jane."

"On a borrowed phone," I add. I can't help it.

"Yeah. I don't know why I didn't call Dad, except I knew Jane had the car and that he would have to walk in the heat to come get me. I didn't want to be too much of a bother. And I was kind of—not thinking too straight."

This whole conversation is a lie.

"Anyway, so I wanted to tell you—I feel really bad about this, but I want you to know where I've been." She takes a breath, steeling herself for the big revelation. "For the past few weeks, I haven't been going to therapy."

I brace myself. She's going to tell me everything. And it will make sense. It will make perfect sense.

"I've just been driving around," she says, and so it's to be another lie after all, I think, and then immediately afterward I'm not sure. "I can't bear to think of all that money it's costing, so I just cancel, and then I drive around trying to figure out what I'm going to do. If I get a job, like as a waitress or something, I can study for my GED at night, and then—maybe I'll go to college too, someday. Like Jane." She looks up on that last phrase with an absurd kind of hope, daring me to disbelieve the emotion underneath those words. It works; the thought of all the opportunities Jane's had, all the opportunities Julie missed out on and that can never be made up, is paralyzing.

My head hurts from trying to separate what's real from what's not. "That's—I'm glad you're thinking about your future," I manage. "I mean, I want those things for you too, if that's what you want. But for now, you have to see a therapist. Someone else, if you don't like her. Money doesn't come into it. We'll be fine, we'll manage."

GOOD AS GONE

"You've spent so much on me already," she presses on. "All those clothes, new furniture, and now a phone. And if I ever do catch up enough to get into college—I don't know what college costs, but I doubt there are special scholarships for kidnapped girls."

The word *scholarships* makes me think of something. "The Julie Fund," I say.

"What's that?" she asks.

"The public donation fund in your name. It's how we paid for the billboards and the reward money and—everything else." *We* did? Tom, the accountant, did. He handled everything, while I —who knows what I was doing. I can barely remember the days, weeks, months. "There was a sum put aside for ransom. We were going to use it to set up a scholarship in your name if—" I can't finish.

"Can't we use it now?" she says. "I mean, I'm back."

"It doesn't work like that," I say, groping through hazy memories for the details. "There are restrictions to what public donations can be used for, and somebody who's not in the family has to be in charge of it. Tom and I can't even make a withdrawal without getting in touch with the fund administrator."

Just as I realize I don't know the answer to the next question she's going to ask, she asks it: "Who's the fund administrator?"

"Oh, I'd have to find out from your dad," I reply lamely. "But you're the sole beneficiary."

I look up and realize she's staring at me.

I can almost see the next words forming on her lips, so before she can ask, I say, "Somewhere in the neighborhood of fifty thousand dollars."

She doesn't even try to conceal how much larger the number

is than she was expecting. "Wow," she says. And then tears start wobbling in her blue eyes; her chin shakes. "You must have really wanted to find me."

It's only after she goes upstairs to take a bath, and I hear her sobs coming from the bathroom, that I wonder how she could have read enough to find out about the billboards without coming across anything about the Julie Fund.

The New Girl

was thinking about her next name as she watched Mercedes gather the sheet taut with one hand, lift the mattress corner with the other, flip up a folded white triangle, smooth the crease, and tuck it in. Before she could catch the trick of the fold, Mercedes had already finished and moved over to her side of the bed. It took the more experienced woman fifteen seconds to pull out the new girl's lousy attempt at a hospital corner and refold it.

"It looks like putting on a diaper," the new girl said.

Mercedes paused what she was doing—scooting on one knee from corner to corner as she tucked in the bottom edge of the sheet—and rolled her unusual blue eyes. "Guess you've never done that before either, huh?"

The new girl felt herself flush.

Later, when they were in the supply closet together loading the cart with wrapped rolls of toilet paper, Mercedes said, "Maybe you do have a little one?" The new girl didn't answer right away. "I shouldn't have assumed."

The new girl shrugged and ran the palm of her hand lightly over the spray tops hooked on the cart, feeling for the empties. "Do you have kids?" she asked.

"*Dos,* and that's it for me," Mercedes said, crossing herself with a laugh. "It's all I can handle."

"I couldn't even handle one."

"You're too young," Mercedes said. "Better wait until you're my age."

"How old are you?"

"Twenty-four."

It did seem old to the new girl, enviably so. She'd gotten a nasty shock when she ran out of bus money in Eugene and found out at the first strip club she tried that you had to be twenty-one to work there. Her fake IDs were good enough to get her waved into bars, but she knew they'd never survive close inspection in the back office of a club where alcohol was served. Still, she'd given it one shot with Jessica Morgenstern, her twenty-two-year-old Texas blond-blue, at a second club.

The guy barely glanced at it under the black light before tossing it back to her. "Try across the parking lot," he said. "They hire illegals over there."

She snatched the fake ID back and crossed over to the Budget Village Inn and Suites. Maids made tips, didn't they? She wasn't entirely convinced, but the motel staff was overwhelmed that morning because of some college football game. She hardly had time to think about it, much less drop a fake, before the desk manager, balancing the telephone receiver on one shoulder, shoved a uniform at her across the counter and pointed her toward Mercedes's cart down the hall. "Just do what she tells you, *comprende?*" he said with his hand over the mouthpiece, barely glancing at her.

At the back of the motel, a large storage room full of broken furniture culled from the suites hosted a rotating circle of undocumented workers who didn't have family members in town. The young woman with whom she shared a sprung mattress mumbled in her sleep, but at least it was a bed. The work seemed all right too, at first, and she congratulated herself on her sturdy back and legs, strong from riding horses in Red Bluff.

More troubling to her were the crowds of college-age kids and their parents all decked out in green-and-yellow T-shirts with duck mascots on them, loud and patronizing and always annoyed when they had to cross over to the other side of the hall to accommodate the squealing housekeeping carts. She stared hardest at the blond, ponytailed girls. When she entered their rooms, she touched charm bracelets left carelessly on dressers, expensive-looking bottles of hair conditioner in showers, logoed duffles spilling sandals and pink pajamas onto the floor.

On the third day, searing pains started up in the new girl's shoulders, lower back, neck, and upper arms. She could barely roll out of the storage-room bed, and vacuuming sent shooting pains up through her skull in rhythm with the roar of the machine. That morning, while Mercedes was cleaning a bathroom, the new girl stole a moment to rub her shoulders while the vacuum idled. She spotted a long green-and-yellow ribbon on the dresser, lifted it up, and tied it around her own ponytail, wincing at the burn in her triceps, then stared at herself in the mirror and pursed her lips up in a tight, rosebud smile. When she heard the toilet flush, distant and faint behind the vacuum noise, she yanked the ribbon off. Mercedes emerged from the bathroom holding a dwindled roll of toilet paper and exaggeratedly mouthing the word *Restock*.

After they finished up in the supply closet, Mercedes said, "I know where you've been sleeping, and girl, you're going to kill your back that way. Come home with me tonight. We have an extra bed since my cousin moved out."

The new girl nodded, and Mercedes smiled briefly before wheeling the cart back out to knock on the next door.

Home was a second-story apartment in a red-brick apartment block about an hour away by bus, including fifteen minutes waiting for a transfer in the misty drizzle. The new girl resented having to pick the bus fare out of her meager tips, but when they climbed the stairs after dark she could see from the steam on the kitchen window that a meal was waiting. Mercedes opened the door to the warm sounds of television commercials and a running faucet, and the larger of two small boys lying in front of the TV set looked over his shoulder and said, "Hi, Mom," then turned back as a cartoon started.

From the kitchen, a woman was already talking to Mercedes in Spanish, running through the events of an exhausting day, from the sound of it. Mercedes cut her off, also in Spanish, and gestured toward the new girl, who closed the door behind them and relaxed into the noisy, steamy apartment. The woman who turned from the sink looked about ten years older than Mercedes, but it was hard to tell under her heavy makeup.

"That's my sister Lucia. Sit down," Mercedes commanded, pointing, then she launched into a fresh round of Spanish directed at her sister, gesturing toward the single plate set on the kitchen table. The woman barely glanced at the new girl, not smiling, and shrugged. Wordlessly, she opened the kitchen cabinet, removed a plate, gathered up silverware from a drawer, and set them all on the low counter that separated kitchen from dining area. Then, grabbing the magazine that had been open in front of her on the counter, she walked out of the kitchen, past the children in the TV room, and into the hall.

"Is she okay?" the new girl whispered as Mercedes moved around the counter into the kitchen and started scooping some chicken and rice out of a pot on the stove onto the plate.

"She's fine, she's okay. She watches the kids until I get home, then she has to go to sleep to get up early to open at the department store." But by the time Mercedes had finished serving up her own plate and brought it to the table, another TV had started up in the back bedroom, Spanish voices clearly audible through the thin walls, clashing with the English-language cartoons. "Eat."

The new girl obeyed. The food was good, and she said so.

"It's been a while for home cooking, huh? Lucia's a good cook. She won't let me pick up McDonald's for everyone on the way home; she says the boys have to eat everything fresh." She shuddered over a forkful of chicken. "I couldn't do it with my hours at the motel, but she's going to try to get me hired at the store when she's been there a little while longer."

The new girl felt the warmth of the meal spreading through her. The chicken leg on her plate was so tender, the meat fell off the bone with the gentlest prod of her fork. She thought about what it would be like to have a girlfriend, someone to talk things over with while they waited in the kiosk. She imagined them in their uniforms, side by side on the bus, laughing about—what?

"It's my turn!" "No, *mine!*" The cartoon show's credits were rolling, and the boys were struggling for the remote. When one started wailing, Mercedes snapped her head over her shoulder, the smile dropping from her face like a mask.

"Boys!" she shouted. "It's bedtime! I'll be in your room to tuck you in in five minutes, so start brushing your teeth *now!*" She looked back at the new girl apologetically. "I'll go make sure you've got clean sheets and put the boys to bed. You have more food if you like, watch TV." She gestured vaguely, then got up and walked through the TV room, stopping a few times to pick up toys on the floor before vanishing around the corner.

As closet doors opened and closed somewhere in the apartment and the two boys squabbled over something—"Give it!"—the new girl eyed Mercedes's purse where it lay, unzipped, on the kitchen counter. One half of her brain was still riding the bus into work the next day, and the other half was adding up her tips, subtracting bus fare, calculating if the rest would cover brown hair dye. There was no need to steal money when all that stood between her and real earning potential was a little plastic rectangle saying *Mercedes Rodriguez, California, brown hair, blue eyes, twenty-four years old* lying in an unzipped bag three feet away. If the universe was handing out mercy, she'd take it.

9

Tom doesn't come home after eating breakfast with Jane. He doesn't come home for lunch either.

It occurs to me for the first time that Tom has not so much as mentioned the Julie Fund since our daughter's return. Surely he has thought about what we could or should do with the money —whether we should proceed with the scholarship in Julie's name or if, as Julie hinted, we could convert it into a kind of scholarship for her. Or maybe, now that Julie is twenty-one, it's her money, her decision. "Sole beneficiary." Then what about the trustees, the administrator? Tom has dealt with everyone, even our lawyer, for so long that I find myself completely at a loss as to where to begin.

Tom's desk is in the room where Julie lies sleeping. I gave her a Valium after she got out of the bathtub, and she swallowed it with her skin still steaming, slipped under the covers, bathrobe and all, and closed her swollen eyes immediately.

Now I walk down the hall and, after listening for a moment

to her gentle wheezing from just outside the door, nudge it open. She hasn't moved, not even to roll over; the covers are still where I placed them, her red hair sticking out in strange directions, the way short hair does when you go to bed with it wet. I can just see a faint pinkish shadow seeping out from under her head on the pillow.

I turn my back to her and sit down at Tom's desk, conscious of the magnified squeak of the office chair, the brittle sound of its wheels rolling over the plastic carpet protector. At one point I jerk around, positive I heard Julie stir, but she's still lying motionless, facing away from the desk.

Tom's desk is almost antiseptically organized, writing tools neatly ensconced in sectioned pencil holders, notepads and graph paper slotted away in stacking mesh trays. A tiny, dry-needled cactus perches on the windowsill behind the desk, just catching a sliver of light from a four-inch suspension of the wide-slat blinds. A studio portrait of the four of us sits in the corner of the desk, and in front of it, a shot of Julie—not the one we used for the missing-person picture that was all over the news, but one from the Grand Canyon, the last family vacation we ever took. It's a posed shot. From that trip, there are countless pictures of Jane straddling voids, her feet on two boulders, hands on hips, elbows akimbo. Julie, who had just gone through a growth spurt and seemed unsure how long her limbs were, kept slipping as we climbed the rocks, and stayed well away from the edge. In the photo, she's perched uncertainly on a rock, one foot up in front of her, elbow on knee, chin in hand.

After a moment I move the mouse and am relieved to see the monitor come to life with no password prompt. The desktop photo is a landscape, some generic tropical island at sunset, and the folders are arranged with painstaking neatness. I do a file search, typing in key words one after the other—*Julie, fund, trust, trustees, donation, reward*—thinking there must be a spreadsheet somewhere, a record of incoming donations and search-related expenses, or at the very least a file with the contact information of the trustees. Nothing comes up, and I find myself wondering whether Julie's done this same search recently. If so, she couldn't have had better luck than I'm having. I open the web browser and check the history—nothing. Which, considering she just told me she's been looking up her case on the Internet, makes it look an awful lot like she cleared the browser history herself.

Pushing away this thought, I start pulling out desk drawers but encounter only the expected debris of empty mechanical pencils, rubber bands, and paper clips. A side drawer holds stacks of blank tax forms that make my head spin just to look at them. I slide them all shut as quietly as possible and tug the handle of the file drawer. Locked.

Shit.

Who needs computer passwords if you keep the hard copies under lock and key? These must be client files—highly confidential. Suddenly I feel certain the information on the Julie Fund is in this drawer. I think I've seen a desk key on his key chain before, but keys always come in twos; there must be a spare somewhere. I open the shallow drawer again to make sure there are no diminutive keys jumbled in with the paper clips. In a fit of inspiration I lift up the plastic separator and peek under the molded plastic, where I find some dust, at least, but no key. I open the other shallow drawers so I can rifle through them, but there's nothing to rifle through. How can anyone be expected to find anything in all this not-mess?

This time the noise behind me is real, and I whip around, cringing at the creaking chair. Julie has turned her face toward me, but
her eyes are still closed, and after another murmur and a sigh, she
goes silent again. I wonder if she's faking it, if she opened her eyes
and saw me, closed them when I turned around. After a frozen
moment in which my limbs go numb anticipating her slightest
movement, I decide it doesn't matter. If she's seen me, it's already
too late, and I might as well get what I came for. And maybe she
hasn't. Choosing to believe the latter, I rack my brain one more
time for the key's hiding place.

I've never been a big snooper. You'd think after Julie's disappearance I would have watched Jane like a hawk, would have
flipped through her phone, once she got one, for her contacts and
text-message history, read her diary—not that Julie's diary, which
the police scoured, contained anything more interesting than
track practice and homework and *i*'s dotted with hearts. Still, I
used to think that by resisting the urge, I was honoring Jane's privacy. Now I realize the urge was never there; I just didn't want to
know. Jane's rebellion was healthy, proportionate—the constantly
re-dyed hair, the piercings. What more could I gain by prying? I
thought if I let her have her private world, if I let her slam the
door and listen to her music, one day she would come out and
thank me for giving her the space. Now that she's left the house,
the city, the state, I realize she *wanted* me to pry. I remember the
stack of notebooks she was carrying as she left the house this
morning. Those were journals; she actually left her old journals in
the house when she went to college. She left them for me to find.
And now that I'm just catching up to her need for me, it's too late.

And then I know where the key is, and that Tom has hidden it not just from the world at large, but specifically from me. He put it in the very last place I would look.

I reach for Julie's picture, turn it around, and find the key tucked under one of the metal clamps that holds in the photo. I pull it out. I open the drawer.

At the back, behind fifteen inches of client files, there's an unmarked folder. I pull it out. Then I rearrange the files to hide the missing one to the best of my ability, lock the drawer, replace the key, and extract myself from the room full of Julie's warm, sleepy breath as quickly and silently as possible, taking the folder with me.

I am expecting, perhaps, something thicker, a dusty file full of newspaper clippings, our correspondence with the parents' group, media, and law enforcement. Instead, I find a few forms clipped together, folded because they're larger than letter size: the bank documents for setting up the trust. I scan the top part, but it's all standard language, dense as a block of wood to me. There are appended documents, and when I unfold them I see the notarized signature at the bottom of the fund-administrator form. *Alma Josefina Ruiz*. I have no idea who that is, but she holds the purse strings to what I now see was an impressive $240,000 of collected donations in 2008. Who knows what's left now, but it might be enough to pay for GED classes, or even a few years of college if she gets into a state school.

I don't remember an Alma. But then I don't remember much of anything from that period. I drank a lot. I slept for days at a time. I took pills so I could sleep at night after having slept all through the day. Above all, I didn't want to know details. I wanted everything to blur, fade, go away forever. I wanted to be left alone.

Now, faced for the first time with everything I blocked out quantified starkly in dollars, I finally feel how alone I have succeeded in making myself.

I check the time and wonder when Tom will be getting home. He used to go to the support group for parents of missing children on Sunday evenings, but does he still, now that Julie is home? Is he allowed? What would it be like to be surrounded by the faces of those whose children are still and always missing after your own prayers have been answered?

Then I remember.

Ask Alma if anybody knows what hers looks like.

It was the billboards. The last night I ever went to the support group with Tom, they turned on us, on me, about the billboards.

"Your girl is everywhere," a woman—Connie, I think her name was—said that final evening. "I see her face every time I run out to the corner store. When was the last time you saw my girl Shawnna's face? Do you even know what she looks like?" She turned from side to side, staring down the people sitting near her. "That's right. I guess you know she's black, that's about it. Fourteen-year-old black girl, probably just ran away, right? Nobody gives a shit. Ask Alma if anybody knows what hers looks like."

In my memory, Alma has downcast eyes, dark lashes, hair in a tight, tucked-under French braid.

The group leader said something about the importance of each focusing on our own feelings, and Connie said, "Pissed off," and a mumble started up around the circle among the parents of kids who had been abducted in more ordinary ways: picked up from school by an ex-husband and whisked across state lines, like Alma's daughter, or talked into driving off in an older boyfriend's truck. Kids who were too poor or too brown, too old or too badly behaved to wind up on the news night after night for weeks and months after they were gone.

Julie's wide-eyed innocence, however, seemed made for TV. She was a character in a comic-book crime: one of America's pink-cheeked, golden-haired daughters, stalked by a psycho and stolen at knifepoint from under her very own roof. That round face with the flat upper lip that made her look childish in precisely the way adult women are supposed to try to look childish; her ice-blue eyes, the limp, pale flag of her hair. I used to look at the stubby eyelashes that were dark near the roots and that vanished toward the tips and think, *When this girl puts on makeup, we will all be doomed.* Of course, we didn't have to wait that long.

One by one, the group members' faces turned toward us with envy, even hatred. As if our worst nightmare had been orchestrated to steal the spotlight from theirs. As if we were lucky to have had our daughter stolen by a true psychopath.

I say *we*, but I'm the mother. They stared at me, and I felt myself turn to stone.

"I'm so glad we're talking about the anger we feel," the group leader said. "I'm so glad we're sharing these feelings."

She's just as dead as all of yours, I wanted to say. But instead I walked out and never came back, leaving Tom behind to give conciliatory speeches. I never asked how he got home at the end of the night.

Suddenly I feel sure it was Alma who gave him a ride.

Karen

's seventeenth birthday party consisted of three people: Karen and Melinda and Bob McGinty.

"Happy birthday," Melinda said, handing her a cardboard box. Melinda's iron-gray cap of hair was as smooth and prim as ever, but she wore earrings that bobbed against her turtleneck, and her large teeth were visible through a stretched-open smile. Even Bob looked pleased.

Karen opened the little box. In it lay a necklace with a horse charm.

The riding thing was how Karen survived public school in Red Bluff, California, a wasteland of baseball-playing thugs dating girls with faces like sour milk. Because she rode, she didn't have to take gym, and she had a social status independent of what she wore. That was fortunate, because dressed in the skirts and tights and sweaters the McGintys bought her—and some of it wasn't even bought but handed down from a niece who'd dropped out of high school fifteen years ago and was roughly her size—Karen looked awkward at best. Melinda and Bob didn't have a daughter of their own, although they'd tried, and their son hadn't been home since he was eighteen. Whatever it was he was off doing in New York, if he was still there, it was nothing he wanted to tell his parents about. They got a postcard every year or so, Melinda told her, adding, "So we know he's still alive," in a matter-of-fact way that suggested a lot of tears had already gone into that phrase.

Karen had heard all this, or some version of it, before. She'd stopped being surprised when foster parents told her the story of why they were fostering. It happened so often she almost always knew exactly for whom she was substituting: a child never born but longed for, begged for, and finally given up on; a dead child; a missing child; an older brother or sister who drove away on a motorcycle forty years ago and never came back. She learned to distrust the big families, where the real siblings presented a united front against her, tolerating her in front of the parents but ignoring her behind their backs. ("Don't worry about learning all our names, you won't be here long.") The parents might act like they had too much love and needed to keep giving it away, but there was, of course, the money. She didn't blame them, but she wouldn't thank them either.

Whatever role Karen was playing for her temporary parents, she was never interested in playing it well. She knew she was just killing time before aging out. Fostering with a family had risks, but it was usually safer than the streets. And when it got unsafe, when a father walked in on her changing and lingered a moment too long before backing out and shutting the door, when a cousin came into her room during the family barbecue—well, she had calibrated the precise moment past which she could no longer measure out her body's worth in string cheese and Snack Packs. At that point, she would run away, taking something small with her.

Nothing valuable; she didn't want to end up in juvie. She aimed for sentiment instead. Things that wouldn't be missed for some time but would spill tears when they were. Two years in foster care had left her with a small collection of these trophies, including a Precious Moments figurine with an onion head and teary eyes clutching a teddy bear whose ear had chipped off in her backpack; a souvenir thimble from Niagara Falls she had found in the drawer of a foster mom's bedside table; a finger painting, yellowed with age, *Deacon, 4 yr.,* in a preschool teacher's handwriting in the corner. She'd hesitated over the last one, remembering the sick little boy, but then she remembered what Deacon's older brother had done to her and the hard smack Deacon's mom had given her when she ratted him out. She kept it folded up in quarters so she wouldn't see the messy swipes of red and blue paint.

But the McGintys were different. They gave her plenty of space, because they themselves liked a lot of space. They were both retired, but Melinda volunteered at the library every morning, as if constant pillow-straightening and counter-wiping were not enough of an outlet for her precision. At first Karen thought she'd been brought in to babysit Bob during Melinda's library shifts. Each morning after Melinda drove off, Karen had waited for his perversion to emerge, but Bob only nursed his coffee for an hour or two before heading out to his woodshop to putter away the day. She'd go upstairs, close her door, and lie on her bed for hours at a time, staring up at the light fixture, gripped with a suffocating feeling she couldn't understand, like a hand wrapped around her throat. It had been a long time since she'd been bored.

Horse camp saved her from certain desperate acts of vandalism she was beginning to contemplate. Melinda signed her up for eight weeks at a ranch run by an old friend of hers just down the road. Karen assumed it was a favor between friends, because although two months of camp sounded expensive, Melinda didn't seem to care whether she went or not. "Bob'll take you if you want to go," she said. "Or you can walk half an hour down the FM 229, that'll get you there. Starts at ten in the morning every weekday." Karen was noncommittal, but when the time came, after Melinda left for the library and Bob folded his paper and wandered off to the woodshop, and she saw they really weren't going to push it, she decided a walk sounded better than another morning alone with the wallpaper. Besides, she had a kind of distant curiosity about horses. As a child, she'd had fantasies of a silvery-white steed invisible to everyone but her who galloped the horizon silently as a cloud, watching her from afar.

When she first entered the stables, the sweaty, rank, shiver-skinned reality of horses made her ashamed of the fairy-tale version she'd envisioned. They frightened her, all twitching muscles and rolling eyes and hooves that hit the earth with a shudder she could feel through her sneakers. But as a rule, Karen showed fear only when it helped minimize damage, and she could tell right away that cringing wouldn't get her anywhere with animals this powerful. Besides, the half a dozen other kids at the camp, many of whom were already accomplished riders, were years younger than her. The youngest was nine. When Karen petted the giant head of a chestnut mare on her first visit to the stables, she made sure the instructor, the nine-year-old, and anyone else watching saw that her hand didn't tremble.

She went back the next day, and the next, and over eight weeks, she got pretty good at being around horses—riding them, taking care of them, cleaning up after them. Not great, but comfortable. At the end of the summer, Melinda left the library early every day to watch her ride, and as much as being on the back of a strong, fast animal meant to Karen, watching Karen seemed to mean even more to Melinda.

It was the horse charm that made Karen understand how much, though. Looking down at the flimsy charm, she thought that nobody had given one like it to Melinda and that she must have wanted one, probably from someone in particular.

"We want to get a real one for you someday," Melinda said. "A horse, I mean. Our finances just aren't in order this year, but it'll happen sometime." The McGintys occasionally referred to a distant, more prosperous past in which they'd owned horses, but this was the first they'd ever mentioned buying one.

"Wow, thanks," Karen said.

"You've made good grades this year," Melinda continued. "We're proud of you." Bob nodded agreement. "Anyway, we'd like to talk about taking the next step. We want to adopt you, Karen."

My name isn't Karen was the first thought that came into her mind. "I love the necklace" is what she said. "Thank you so much." She meant it. The charm on the thin gold chain was cheap, one side flat and the other sculpted to look three-dimensional. But the horse was running.

"You don't have to decide right now," Melinda said. "We just wanted you to know that we consider you our daughter."

What Melinda wasn't saying but Karen heard in her words was the concern over her aging out. Karen had listened to the stories in the group home. She thought of the Petes with a shudder.

She weighed her memories of them against Melinda's long,

strong face, which was more than plain, almost ugly. Strong, bitter lines cut a path from the corners of her mouth to the underside of her chin — that son — but a smile softened her eyes to a watery gray. Karen's future with Melinda and Bob might involve horses, but it would also involve community college, a job in Red Bluff or Redding or even Sacramento. More: A baseball thug of her own, maybe a walk down a church aisle trimmed with ribbons and foldout bells made of tissue paper. And then, one day, this house with the clapboard siding and peaked roof would be hers, and she would sleep in the master suite that faced the wooded mountains and take her own children to the coast once a year. Snug as a fork in a drawer.

"This is the best birthday I've ever had," Karen said. It was close enough to the truth, even if it wasn't really her birthday, just a random date that happened to stick.

The next time she was out riding at the stables, she imagined leaning forward just a little more, urging the powerful creature to a trot, then a gallop, until it looked like the horse charm on her necklace. Leaping over the low wooden fence and cantering through pastures and woods and then up into the mountains. That was sheer fantasy, of course, another version of the silvery-white steed; she didn't know how to jump, would kill herself and maybe the horse too trying. Horses didn't do well in mountains, and neither would she. Anyway, how far could a girl get on a horse these days?

So she started thinking bus routes. It was time to head to Portland, where she'd heard there were more strip clubs per capita than in any other city in the U.S. That sounded like cash waiting to be made with no strings attached. When the time came, after Melinda left for the library and Bob folded his paper and wandered off to the woodshop and Karen set off down her usual path, she was surprised and relieved at how natural it felt to turn in the wrong direction on FM 229 and just walk away. She'd wrapped the necklace chain twice around her ankle, and the little gold charm clicked against her anklebone as she walked. Every eighth step or so, the charm slid into her shoe and got trapped against her skin for a second, then it popped out with a thwack, worked its way around her ankle, and slithered down again. The rhythm was nice, like the tiny horse was galloping away, and she was riding it out of town instead of a Greyhound bus.

10

"You think he's cheating?" Alex Mercado says, casual but interested, like someone discussing odds in a race he's not betting on.

"No. I don't know. I just—" A shadow passes the narrow, frosted window outside my office door, and I shift the phone to my other ear. There's always someone lurking around the department, even on the weekends.

"You want me to find out if he's cheating," he rephrases. "I'm happy to follow him, find out where he goes." *It'll cost you* runs the unspoken part of the sentence.

"Would you just look into something—someone—for me instead?" I say, lowering my voice. "Alma Josefina Ruiz."

"Basic background?" he says. "Or follow her?"

"Background," I say hurriedly. "She's a trustee for our donation fund. The fund administrator, actually."

"Ah," Alex says. "Maybe that's why the name sounds familiar. Shouldn't be hard to find out what's up with her." *And if she's seeing your husband.* "Oh, and do you want me to keep tailing Julie? I found out where she's going." Before I can ask, he says, still in that maddeningly offhand voice, "She goes to church."

"What? What church?"

"The Gate."

I'm speechless. The Gate is the megachurch whose billboard I pass at the 610 flyover on my way to work every day. They meet in the goddamn Astrodome.

"She doesn't go in," he says. "She just sits in her car. Your husband's car," he corrects himself. "In the parking lot."

"What is she doing?"

"I don't know. It's a freaking compound, there's a lot going on in there. Three Bible study groups around that time, a singles bowling league, and something called the Circle of Healing." He sounds amused. "You never went to that church?"

"We never went to church at all," I say. "I mean, Julie went with a friend once in a while after a sleepover. Trying it out, the way kids do." I think of the televangelist's enlarged grin on the billboard. *Faith every day, not everyday faith.* "I just can't imagine Julie wanting to go someplace like *that.*"

He's silent for a moment. "Did you watch the video, Anna?"

"Yes, I watched it. Gretchen Farber. That band in—Portland, was it?"

"And?"

"And—yes, it looks like her. Maybe. But the image is so fuzzy, it's not like you can say for sure." It feels like honesty, because I watched it only once, in the middle of the night, with the sound off. And because I can hardly be sure of anything these days.

"Cell-phone video," he concedes, but I get the uneasy feeling he's humoring me. "Not a great image."

"Exactly," I say. "And Portland—"

"—is not Mexico," he finishes.

There's a pause, so I go on the offensive. "May I ask why you were looking in Portland?"

"I wasn't," he says. "I've been checking police reports filed all over around the time Julie arrived, anything involving a woman her age, hoping something might turn up. There's a missing-persons report out on this Gretchen Farber—not in Portland, actually, but in Seattle. It's from a couple days after Julie showed up—"

"After she came home."

"You have to wait three days to file a missing-persons report for an adult, especially if it's the husband or boyfriend filing—in case it's what they call a lover's quarrel. This was filed by a boyfriend, Calvin something. Anyway, I got lucky"—*Lucky*, I think—"because there's a video of her. Don't worry, I'm looking into it, calling the bars, trying to nail the ID." He pauses, and I can hear papers shuffling. "There's one other possibility I'm exploring."

"You mean for identifying the impostor?" I ask, attempting to sound sarcastic, but Alex doesn't skip a beat.

"Charlotte Willard," he says. "Same age as Julie, ran away from her home in Louisiana shortly after Julie—uh, disappeared. Maybe it's nothing, but there's a Charlotte from seven years ago—going by a different last name, of course—picked up in San Francisco, spends a while in foster care, and then sort of falls off the map. Switched up her name again or something."

"So?"

"So, I'm not sure," he admits. "But I think Charlotte may be Gretchen. And Gretchen may be—well, Julie."

"And why would this Charlotte or Gretchen or whoever she is be posing as my daughter?" I hear my voice climbing to a higher pitch and try to wrangle it back down, unsuccessfully. "What could she possibly want?"

I push the Julie Fund out of my mind, though Alex surely hasn't forgotten why I called him in the first place.

"Honestly, Anna, I don't know yet. I'll let you know when I find something else."

His tact annoys me. "Say what you're thinking. You think it's the money, don't you? The money in the fund?"

"I won't know what to think until you get me that DNA sample."

I hang up without saying goodbye and open the browser on my desktop.

The Gate's website features an elaborate series of Flash animations, which I click through impatiently until I find the Circle of Healing. When I click on the link, an animated drop of water falls into the middle of the words, pushing them out into concentric circles that ripple over the whole screen. When the screen goes smooth again, this description appears:

> *We invite to the Circle of Healing all who feel broken.*
> *When we ask forgiveness in the Circle of Healing,*
> *God will show us that we have already been healed.*

At the bottom of the screen, a series of faces fade in and out, each with a testimonial: an elderly woman blinded by cataracts until the Circle of Healing taught her she could already see. An African American teenager saved from dropping out of school by the Circle of Healing. A man, once homeless, discovered the path to financial security through the Circle of Healing. *God's plan is for abundance,* the quote says. *The Lord makes His Kingdom great!*

I scribble the meeting times on a Post-it note and go back to the search screen, where another listing is a link to a recent magazine profile of Reverend Chuck Maxwell, the man whose face looms over our local urban landscape on billboards at every bottleneck. The article is called "'It Ain't Luck, Chuck': How Rev. Chuck Maxwell Landed the Biggest Pulpit in Texas":

> *Chuck Maxwell is handsomer in person than on the billboards for his Houston megachurch, The Gate. The 42-year-old pastor with the grizzled beard and piercing stare is 6 foot 2 and unexpectedly graceful. It's easy to see how this man has built a spiritual—and financial—empire.*

Oh, it's going to be one of *those* profiles.

> *Maxwell has never been ordained in any denomination, nor does he hold degrees in religion or philosophy; indeed, he never finished college. Yet every week he stands in what was once the Houston Astrodome and delivers a sermon to 30,000 parishioners and up to 10 million remote viewers via his television and Internet ministries.*

I skip down a few paragraphs.

> *After dropping out of Texas Christian University, he snagged a production job for Houston's fire-and-brimstone televangelist Jim Wilton. It was there that Maxwell says he began to have strong ideas for a Christian message he felt uniquely suited to deliver.*
>
> *"I wouldn't say I had a falling-out with the Baptist Church,"*

he says. "But the message was so negative: 'You're messing up! Get right with God!'" He laughs. "But God doesn't want you to focus on your sins of the past! God says, make it new!"

My English-professor eye snags on *make it new*, Ezra Pound's modernist slogan, and I enjoy a brief moment of imagining the elitist, anti-Semitic old creep rolling in his grave. I keep skimming, and Maxwell keeps preaching endless reinvention, spreading the word that nothing matters but the present moment. Could that be what Julie's after? The profile goes on for three more pages, covering Maxwell's massive donations to a nonprofit for missing children—that, of course, catches my eye—but I can't stomach reading to the end. The thought of Julie needing Maxwell's message—*Erase the past, live in the now!*—is too repellent to dwell on. Jane and Tom and I are, after all, Julie's past. Or we're supposed to be.

Which brings me to my final call.

I get out the piece of paper Jane gave me, still wadded up in my pocket, and stare at it. The area code looks familiar, but I can't quite place it until I look it up: Seattle.

Jane must be playing some kind of trick on me. This is the phone number of a friend of hers, her roommate, somebody she's put up to this. I feel a hot rush of anger, followed by a guilty twinge. I've neglected Jane—willfully ignored her, at times—over the past eight years. Every time I looked at her, all I could see was her failure to scream in the closet that night, the three hours she spent huddled among her shoes with tears and snot streaming down her face while Julie—I know it wasn't Jane's fault, but I couldn't help it. Casting doubts on Julie's identity would be a particularly cruel way to get back at me, but effective. My hand is shaking.

I dial the number and wait. It rings half a dozen times, as if someone on the other end is staring at the caller ID, deciding whether to pick up. Then someone does.

"Stop this," Julie says.

I'm shocked into silence.

"Well, say something, Cal," she says, her voice weary. "I finally picked up one of your mystery numbers, so say something. I know it's you. Calling from every stop on your grand tour of my life, aren't you?" She pauses. "Well, you found me. You're here. So what is it you want to say?"

I hold my breath.

"What dirty little secret have you found out about me now? I guarantee, no matter what it is, there's something worse about me you still don't know."

I know nothing, absolutely nothing.

On the other end of the connection, Julie says, "Fuck you, Cal. I left. It's over. *Go home.*" The call ends.

Charlotte

sat in a dingy room with the social worker and a bearded man who kept trying to get her to tell him the name of her pimp. Officer Pete used that word too, but she didn't know what it meant, just that there was a thrill of secrets around it, like a curse word. It made her think of pimples, but she wasn't telling the bearded man that.

"I don't have one of those," she said, unable to make herself repeat the word.

"Come on, what did he tell you?" said the bearded man. "He told you you were special, he'd treat you right?"

The only person she could think of who fit that description was John David. Was he a pimp? *Her* pimp? She wasn't sure. There was no way this bearded man could know about John David, was there? But a deep black well hovered just under that thought, waiting for her to slip and fall in. She shook her head.

"He convinced you to start trading it for money, right? Only he gets all the money."

Now she understood, and a wave of heat exploded just under her jaw. "I've only done that a couple times," she mumbled.

"Okay, just once or twice," he said in a too-nice voice. "Just to help him out. So you want to protect him, because he protects you, right? You think he's your friend? Maybe your boyfriend?"

"I don't have a boyfriend," she said, the heat spreading up from her jawline until even her eyeballs felt hot. She pushed all her hate out through her eyes and straight into his bushy brown beard. At least Officer Pete believed her. She drew a breath to say so but realized she didn't know Officer Pete's real name.

"He bought you things at first?" the beard continued to prompt her. "Maybe he got your nails done."

She pulled her hands off the table self-consciously. There were lines of black beneath the ragged nails, and one had a red, puffy bump of skin around the corner where it was torn. She noticed the social worker, a brown-skinned woman with a pair of glasses on a chain around her neck, shake her head and roll her eyes quickly, then look away.

But the bearded guy went on for another five or ten minutes before finally standing up. He flipped a card onto the table in front of her, pressing one finger down on its corner as he said, "If you remember anything, call me at this number. Just remember, he's a predator. You're the victim here." As he lifted his hand away, his sweaty finger tugged the corner of the card just enough to knock it out of its perfect alignment with the fake wood grain on the table. She watched the card settle into its skewed position in front of her, memorizing the angle to keep from reading the name. When she looked up, the man was gone, and the social worker had taken his seat across the table from her with an expression of clear relief.

"I'm Wanda, Charlotte."

She almost jumped. Although it was the name she'd put on the paperwork, the first one that popped into her head, nobody had called her that yet—the cops who'd shuffled her from room to room had said "you" or "young lady" or, when they were talking about her like she wasn't there, "the juvenile." Hearing the name said out loud for the first time, she realized how weak and stupid she had been to use it just because it made her feel brave to claim it as her own. Now it sounded like an accusation.

"Charlotte," Wanda went on, as if determined to damn her as often as possible, "I was told you'd like to be in foster care. We call it out-of-home care these days. Do you have a safe home?"

She tried to think of home, but instead she saw a pair of blank, staring, upside-down eyes. Their un-wet opacity.

"No."

"You don't have a home?" Wanda prodded. "Or you feel it's not safe for you there?"

It sounded like a trick question. This Wanda wasn't like Officer Pete, mouthing off after a long day, or the asshole with the beard, drilling down in hopes of finding something in her he could use. No home, or not safe? She stared at the corners of Wanda's mouth, watching for a flicker to tell her which one the social worker wanted to hear, but Wanda only waited, her face relaxed and expressionless.

"I'm. It's." Where to begin? "Not safe."

It wasn't exactly a lie.

Wanda just nodded, an expression not so much of approval but of completion, a box ticked off. "And Charlotte, are you hoping to be in out-of-home care for just a short time or for a longer while?"

Multiple choice again. She'd been good at tests, once. "I want an emergency placement," she said, remembering what Officer Pete told her to say.

"I'd like that for you too, Charlotte," the social worker said. "Unfortunately we have a shortage of options just at the moment. Child Protective Services will handle all that, I'm just making the referral. But I have to tell you something. If you're entering out-of-home care right now, you're very likely going to have to stay in a group home for a time while they look for a placement for you."

She nodded. Group.

"It'll only be temporary, but I just want to prepare you for that. Are you sure there's not a friend or family member you could stay with? Somewhere you'll be safe? Think."

She thought, hard this time. All the places she could go, she'd need to be a kid, and she wasn't a kid anymore. Kids didn't go to dirty apartments and have babies scraped out of them. Kids didn't do with Petes what she'd done with Petes. Kids didn't do to other kids what she'd done to the girl in the basement.

She didn't know what she was.

"I'll go to group," she said.

As the two of them left the police station, she said, "What about my things?" But even before Wanda opened her mouth to say the words, Charlotte knew the stolen knife was gone forever.

It didn't matter, because in group, only the biggest kids got to have knives. They hid them in their mattresses or taped them to the bottoms of drawers. Nobody stole them and nobody told on the kids. One of the scrawny little boys tried making his own out of a plastic butter knife that he snapped in half. He showed it around, bragging, until one of the big kids took it away in the night and did something to him that didn't show.

Because of obvious rules like that, group was easier than she'd thought it would be. In her mind she called the biggest kids Enforcers. She herself tried to be an Invisible, obviously the safest course of action.

Her roommate Beth was an Eager. Eagers played along with whatever the counselors asked, volunteering in group sessions and earning gold stars and sparkly toothbrushes and puffy stickers for good behavior. The stars and puffy stickers were worse than pointless; too permanent, they left a hard, sticky gum behind that ruined clothes and had to be scrubbed off skin with a scouring pad. The undersides of the chairs and the walls behind the beds were lousy with them.

Toothbrushes were different. She'd lived without one before, and the flimsy plastic stick they handed her when she first arrived was better than nothing, but its thin row of stiff, hard bristles hurt her gums. One day she picked up Beth's toothbrush and flipped it over, looking into the pink translucent depths of the sparkly plastic, letting her eyes slide along the buried bubbles and shimmering threads that caught the light as she turned it from side to side.

"Hey, put that down. That's mine," said Beth from the doorway.

"It's nice," said Charlotte, but she didn't put the toothbrush down. She waited to see what Beth would do. Beth, who was only eleven, wriggled uncomfortably. "It's pretty," Charlotte added encouragingly.

"Thanks," said Beth. After a brief interior struggle, her wide eyes almost filling with tears, she said, "You can have it." Her teeth dragging on every syllable.

Charlotte put it down with a thwack. "That's gross. I don't want your used toothbrush."

But later on, she took it anyway.

11

Monday afternoon, I get in the car and head to the Gate.

Ironic, isn't it? I've been telling Tom for two weeks I'm going to work, and Julie's been telling us she's going to therapy, and now we're both lying to go the same place. I turn into the parking lot, where new construction shields the former Astrodome from the neighboring NRG Stadium, and take note of the aerial walkway between the two buildings. The Gate must get a healthy amount of foot traffic during playoff season. As if on cue, the digital marquee flashes—WITH GOD, ALL THINGS ARE POSSIBLE—and I give an anxious snort of laughter.

There are a hundred or so vehicles clustered around the entrance. It's not Julie's therapy day, so I know she doesn't have a car, but I still feel nervous that I might see her, or she might, at this moment, be seeing me. The parking terrain is vast and includes a five-level garage that looks empty from here. I park and approach the modern, streamlined, steeple-and-stone façade that has been added to the gargantuan inverted bowl in an unsuccessful attempt to bring it down to human scale. I open one giant glass door and enter a lobby as airy and clean as an airport VIP lounge. Screens hang from the ceiling at regular intervals, their resting faces the church's glowing-gate logo. The sea-green carpet is dotted with pristine rugs of white shag across which clean-lined chairs face one another in decorous intimacy. Very soft music is being piped in over invisible speakers, and off in the corner of the vast lobby, a vacuum cleaner drones. Monday must be a slow day.

There's a mounted map of the church just to the right of the entrance, and a brief consultation points me in the direction of a corridor with the word FAITH hanging over it in brushed steel. The room number I'm looking for is 19F, and I find a moment to wonder whether there's a LOVE wing where all the room numbers have *L*s in them. The vacuum cleaner shuts off, and, looking back, I see my tracks, a line of slightly darker sea-green footprints trailing across the sea-green carpet. *That must be where God carried me,* I think. I've always had trouble taking religion seriously, but this place seems like a massive joke.

The heavy wooden door to 19F is closed and windowless, and after only a moment of hesitation, I push the door open on one end of a room the size of a high-school gymnasium. A hundred or so people stand hand in hand in a flattened-out oval that runs the length of the room, eyes closed, heads bowed, some rocking back and forth rhythmically, others stock-still. I enter and close the door softly behind me, and the low murmuring of the circle enfolds me. I had imagined chairs or somewhere to sit and observe, but there is no room for anything in the windowless hall except the humming, breathing circle. Without opening their eyes or looking at me, the two supplicants nearest the door release each other's hands and take a half step outward, opening the circle and extending their arms. My stomach turns over. This feels much more real than I was expecting and at the same time embarrassingly fake. When I step forward and grasp the hands on either side of me—one the dry, rough, thick-jointed hand of an old man, the other the horrifyingly moist and malleable hand of a teenage boy—I am officially an impostor.

At first I can't tell where the murmuring is coming from; amplified around me on all sides and in all keys, it doesn't appear to originate from any one place. I keep my eyes open and run them over as many members of the circle as I can see, but if there's a starting point for the praying, it must be somewhere close to the other end of the oval, the part hidden by its longer side. Looking around, all I see is an endless train of sweatshirted senior citizens, pimpled teenagers, and ponytailed women in yoga pants, all echoing one another's words. I close my eyes, and after a moment one of the voices seems to separate itself from the muddled sea of noise it's been swimming in and rise a few inches above. It's an ordinary man's voice, the vowels pinched by that indefinable Houston accent. Nevertheless, I can hear the words, crystal clear, as if they were being spoken directly into my ear.

"Found." The word drops like a stone into the pool of murmurs. "What was lost has been found. Furthermore, it was never lost."

"Furthermore, it was never lost," echoes the rest of the circle.

"Do you look to your Heavenly Father, who offers you armfuls of blessings, and ask for a single favor? If you are handed a plate of food at a wedding, do you beg the giver for a bite? You have what you need right in front of you. Do the lilies of the field cast their faces down in supplication? Do the sparrows moan to the heavens in despair? No. The lilies raise their faces to the Lord in awe and delight. The sparrows lift their voices in songs of praise. They decorate God's creation with their thanks. Does a grateful daughter clothe herself in rags? No—she shows the world her father loves her. She is thankful for his love. What was lost has been found. It was never lost. What was lost has been found. It was never lost. What was lost has been found. It was never lost."

"What was lost has been found. It was never lost." Some of them continue to chant the phrase while others move on with him, repeating his words just a few seconds after he says them, as clumsily as wet sand on a beach casting itself in the image of the waves that roll over it.

"What you need is already in your life," the speaker goes on. "Christ was wounded forever that we might be whole."

Some of the chanters change their mantra at this. One begins weeping loudly.

"Our Lord has a hole in His side so that we can be whole inside."

At this abjectly dumb wordplay I stifle a snicker, but as the phrase ripples through the circle, taken up by the chorus of voices, the suppressed hiccup undergoes some kind of emotional alchemy in my stomach. Unbelievably, I feel my eyes start to prickle.

"We are whole in every aspect of our lives. Do you want a new job? You're already doing it. A spouse? You're already married, but neither of you know it yet. Relief from a debt? It has been paid, now and forever. A release from pain? There is no pain except in your mind."

A second weeper has begun, this one gasping for air in between sobs. Every sob that rings out is immediately encircled and washed away in the mumbling tide, so that the next one feels entirely new, as if it's from a different planet.

"Rejoice! What was lost has been found. It was never lost. It was you who were lost. The son who was dead is now living again; he who was lost is found. But he was never truly dead; he was never really lost."

I can't take much more of this. I snap my eyes open. Nobody notices. Then I spot someone across the circle from me. An elderly woman sitting in a wheelchair, wearing a Mickey Mouse sweatshirt.

I yank my hands away and grab blindly for the door, my sweaty fingers slipping on the handle as I heave it open and run, run, back across the sea-green carpet, where my tracks have already been vacuumed away.

Back in my office, I dial the number and the phone rings and rings, but Alex Mercado isn't picking up, so I'll have to find what I'm looking for on my own. I type the damning words into the search engine and wait for the most recent news story to come up: BOMB SHELTER REMAINS BELONG TO 13-YEAR-OLD GIRL, EXPERTS SAY.

The lead photo shows a one-story brick bungalow in River Oaks, an old central neighborhood shaded by massive trees and, these days, condos crowded onto too-small plots. The house in the photo was being leveled to make way for one more condo when bulldozers uncovered extra pipelines going to a bomb shelter buried in ten feet of concrete in the backyard. Another photo shows twisted pipes leading to a broken concrete shell. There are no pictures of what they found inside. I keep digging: The house was seized in 2008 from the owner, nursing-home resident Nadine Reynolds, for delinquent property-tax payments. Sold at auction to an out-of-town investor who rented it for years without crossing the threshold, it changed hands several times before being picked up in 2015 by the most recent developer, who decided it would make more money as condos.

But it's the photo that's important, not the house. I wind up on the Texas DPS website, where there's a statewide database of missing persons, over three hundred listings. So many missing; so many unidentified bodies, each one corresponding to a lost daughter or husband or wife or son, like a massive jigsaw puzzle with pieces scattered all over the globe.

I click through the most recent Harris County listings and see the thumbnails of male faces with eyes closed, oddly dignified and brutally sad. Then a head-shaped outline with a question mark. The death date is indeterminate, 2008 or 2009, the approximate time all of our lives fell apart. I hold my breath and click, and the photo that has been haunting me pops up, the horrifying details cropped in order to focus on a single rotted scrap of faded black cloth shaped like two circles connected by a partially eroded isthmus of faded black.

I can see why I didn't recognize it at first. After all, it's been eaten by the air in the bomb shelter for eight years. No one could have recognized it right away, not even someone who's been carrying around the memory of her daughter's nightshirt for eight years. A nightshirt now reduced to a pair of Mickey Mouse ears.

I just want the body, I once said in the support group, before I left forever. *I just want something to bury.* The chorus of police voices and therapist voices and media voices chanting in tandem —*The first three hours, the first three days*—made it hard to conceive of a world in which my daughter was living. Now I feel a strange numbness settle over me at the thought that she hasn't been. That she isn't. I didn't recognize it right away, because I didn't want to. I didn't want Mercado to be right about Julie being dead. I didn't want him to be right about *anything* that had to do with my daughter. I wanted to be the one who knew her better than anyone.

My cell phone is ringing; it's Alex, calling me back. I hit the green icon to pick up, ready to make a full confession. But I never get a chance.

"I have some bad news," Alex says.

Petes

is what she called them, even the ones who bought the pills and weed she'd stolen from the shopping cart under the bridge without even asking her to suck their dicks or let them shove them inside her. She'd learned to spit in her hand and wrap it around fast, so there was a chance they'd forget about putting it inside her if she moved quick enough. And if they remembered, it'd go a little easier, be over a little faster.

By the time she got to San Francisco, she'd lost track of the men who got her there, but at least she remembered their names. Their names were Pete. Two Petes in the bus station. A Pete in the bathroom of a Diamond Shamrock gas station. One Pete on the bus she'd tried to fight off with the knife, but then she'd let it go and took his wallet instead. He sat next to her the whole way to Sacramento with his dirty fingers interlaced with hers, like they were girlfriend and boyfriend. She turned fourteen between Petes, but she wasn't sure when exactly the day passed, and anyway, to

Petes she was sixteen, to police, eighteen. She had the birth year for eighteen memorized, and when asked to move along—*How old are you, young lady, aren't you supposed to be home at this hour? Oh, really, what's your birthday?*—she gave random dates from that year, once accidentally saying that day's date without realizing it. That policeman said, "Happy birthday," and made a face.

The last Pete turned out to be a cop. And when she got into his car and he asked for her date of birth, she'd rattled one off and he just looked at her and shook his head. "You sure you're eighteen?" he said. "You know you could be charged as an adult."

He hit something and a siren went on, and she looked and saw that the doors didn't have locks on the inside, and her door didn't even have a handle.

"January eleventh, 1989," she said immediately. It wasn't the right day or the right year, but it put her two years closer to her real age.

"That's more like it. We're going to get you a social worker and get a case opened up on you before you get into a situation you can't get out of."

I've been in one, she thought. *I got out.*

"I know you think you're tough and all," he said, giving her a quick sidelong glance. "But you were about to get picked up by somebody who would have hurt you pretty bad. Juárez owns this block. That was one of his boys in the beater, just before I pulled up."

The rust-blotched Honda had slowed and the driver had rolled down its window, but then he rolled it up and sped away before she could step off the curb.

"They took off when they saw me. They know I'm a plain-clothes cop," he said. "It's a good thing, too, because you were about to get pounded to within an inch of your life. Then you'd get dumped somewhere conveniently near Juárez's place—that's not his real name, by the way, he just wants everyone to think he was a big shot in Mexico—and he'd talk you into a kind of a deal, like you'd crash at his place and work for him, and he'd make sure nobody hassled you out on the street, make sure nobody ever came after you again. And a week later you'd see the one who raped and beat you sitting in your living room eating a Pop-Tart on your sofa and you'd figure it out, but it would be too late."

She sat silently during this lecture. Officer Pete, as she had begun to think of him, had a weariness to his voice and a tic of flicking his nose. He did it regularly, a little more toward the end of the speech, so quickly his other hand didn't even whiten on the steering wheel.

He cleared his throat. "So, anyway, you're welcome," he muttered. "Now we're going to meet the nice social-worker lady who's going to open a case file on you and get you in a foster home."

She started upright. "I don't need to be in a home. I'm eighteen."

"So you said the first time. What's your birthday again?" He laughed. "I bet you can't remember either one of them."

"I don't need to be in a home."

"I don't want you on the streets getting knifed by some pimp. You haven't been on your own very long, have you?"

She considered the question. Was John David on her own? She didn't know, but she shook her head anyway.

"I thought so. You've been in town for less than a week?"

Two days.

"You don't love this work you're doing, do you? It's not your passion?"

She shook her head again.

"Okay. So you need a place to stay for free. At the very least, you'll go to a group home for a while."

A group home. She'd heard of them. If she didn't know any details, it was only because kids on the street who said "I just ran away from group" weren't saying it to share their life stories. They were saying it to scare the shit out of you.

He saw the expression on her face. "Relax, I'm not driving you straight there," he said. "You'll talk to Wanda, and Wanda will figure out what to do with you. If you're so scared of group, tell her you want emergency placement and then you want to be adopted by a nice family that doesn't beat you or whatever yours did." He flicked his nose again and stole a glance at her that he probably thought was surreptitious. "I'm sorry about whatever it was. I guess it was pretty bad. Still, this is a hell of a dangerous way to survive. You dead set against going home?"

She thought about home for a long moment. It seemed less real than what she had done, not just with the Petes to survive, but the other time. She remembered a wicked little blade and scrambling out of a hole on hands and knees slippery with blood. She thought of who was waiting for her at the hole's mouth. Whose blood was drying on the bunker floor.

"It wasn't—" she said, and tried again: "I just needed to get—"

"To San Francisco. I know." He sighed deeply, and she hated him with every fiber of her being, the stupid Pete. "You didn't invent it," he said.

She knew she didn't. Petes did. Janiece did. John David did.

12

Tom is finishing off some reheated food at the kitchen table when I get home. There's no sign of Julie.

"Where's the money," I say. The words are thick and wavy, as if seen through a streaky window.

He puts his fork down. "Anna," he says, already desperate enough that I know I'm right.

"Where is the money in the Julie Fund," I clarify, "and are you fucking Alma?"

"No."

"Liar." I can't believe it even occurs to me to feel anger at this. I have been lying, Julie has been lying. Jane, too, about school if nothing else. Tom, though—I honestly didn't know there was a part of me left that still needed him to be truthful, to be the good one, but there was. I wanted to have all the bad feelings to myself, cope with Julie's death—*Yes,* I tell myself, *her death*—in the worst, most self-destructive way possible. And he let me think I was do-ing just that. This is the ultimate betrayal, then. Not that he was the liar, the cheater, this whole time but that he let me think *I* was.

"Anna, listen," he says. "You were drinking so much. And you wouldn't talk to me, you wouldn't listen. I was so alone. You wouldn't even come to the support group with me."

I want to yell that I stopped going to the group because it was killing me. The hope, yes, but also the sight of other people's pain, the thought of other people's daughters. Only my pain mattered.

"Do not put this on me," I start.

"You left, and I needed someone. I didn't love Julie any less than you did. I didn't miss her any less than you did."

"You're the one who managed the fund," I say. "You're the one who kept up the message board, distributed the flyers. You ar-ranged the damn billboards. You talked to the trustees. And you put *Alma* in charge of the money."

"Yes," he says.

"Where's the money, Tom?"

"I can't talk to you when you're like this."

"Like what? You stole Julie's money and gave it to your whore!"

"Anna!"

"Deny that you gave it to *Alma Ruiz,*" I say, spitting out the name.

He puts his head in his hands. "I gave it to Alma. Yes. Some lowlifes working for her ex-husband came forward with a ransom request—maybe the ex's girlfriend ditched him and he figured out raising a kid alone isn't such a cakewalk, I don't know. I made her the admin so she could sign off on my emptying the account, and I gave it to her for ransom money, and she got her daughter back."

"Now deny that you slept with her."

There is a long pause.

"Deny it. Go ahead. I want to hear you."

"Once," he says, miserable. "After that—we went our separate ways."

"I guess you'd served your purpose."

He stands up, suddenly angry. "You don't get to say that."

"I think I get to say whatever I want right now," I say, but he's talking over me.

"You think you're telling me something I don't know? Yeah, maybe it was about the money, and maybe I was so damn lonely and messed up—anyway, we had it and she didn't. I don't blame her, I would have done the same in a heartbeat to get Julie back. If I thought fifty thousand dollars was all it took, I'd have slept with anyone for it. I'd have *killed* for it." He's trembling. "You would have too."

I can't think. I can't let myself. "What if we had needed it for a ransom for Julie?"

"But we didn't." He swallows, looks down, then back up at me. "You want me to admit it? I thought she was dead, Anna. It was easier to believe that than to hope." This breaks him. He bows his head, starts to shudder, dry-eyed, crying without tears. It is gruesome. "Can you forgive me?"

Right here is where I'm supposed to go to him, put my arms around his neck and let him hug my waist, and start crying as I confess that I, too, believed the worst. And follow that with the horrible truth: that I was right, and therefore he was right too.

Right to fuck Alma, right to save Alma's kid instead of holding out hope for our own. That by the time he was giving the money away, Julie was dead. Dead, dead, dead.

But I can't even think about doing any of that because I hate him for not believing in Julie's return. All these years, I doubted it only because I thought he believed. The thought of us side by side, each locked in our private mausoleums, mourning Julie alone, year after year, is depressing and enraging. All these years I've been jealous of his faith. If I'd known he was doubting, I could have been the one to hold out hope. It could have been *me* going to those meetings, *me* keeping the search alive for as long as the money held out. It could have been me.

"Anna, please," he says, looking up.

I walk out of the kitchen without saying a word. I've got to get to the meeting I set up with Alex after he told me about the Julie Fund, but first I need to find something in my nightstand. The IHOP on I-10 is too close to the house, but I want this over with fast, before I change my mind.

The manila envelope has grown fatter, as if it has been eating steadily since the last time I saw it. It no longer closes but gapes open on the sticky table between us, the contents partially obscured by the dog-eared flap. I wonder what Mercado has collected in that envelope about Tom and me, about Alma Ruiz, about Gretchen Farber. My life, in layer upon layer of sedimentary lies, beneath which, at the very bottom, I can see a glossy corner of the truth: the photograph. I hold the flap to the table with one thumb and pry the picture out.

I hold it in my hands and force myself not to look away. The original is so much bigger than the thumbnail, and so much more horrible. Bones bleached a dirty yellow by the flash, skull slumped to one side, a crescent of reflected light cradled in each blank eye pit. Scraps of black clinging to the rib cage in that shape I now recognize as an awful parody of a child's cartoon.

I just want the body.

I try to paint my daughter's face over the skull's awful blankness. I build up the soft cheeks, fill in the eye pits, give her blue eyes and white-blond hair that spills over the ground. But it is too much, and instead I find myself thinking of Julie, of not-Julie, of the woman living in my house who says she is my daughter—for money, for kicks, for some other reason too awful to imagine. Her face intrudes even on this moment. The photograph goes blurry but I keep staring, the tears rolling down my face.

"I'm so sorry, Anna," Alex says softly, and he puts his hand on my forearm, where the muscles that keep my fingers pressed around the photo are jumping. He leaves it there for a long moment, then pulls back.

I set her down on the table as gently as I would lay a baby down in a crib.

"You're sure, now," says Alex, voice still low but with the piercing, restless quality already coming back. "Why?"

I reach into my purse, pull out the photograph, put it on the table, and turn both photos toward Alex.

He immediately sucks in his breath. "The nightshirt," he says. "I don't know why I didn't—"

"I had to see them together to be sure." The photo is from Christmas morning nine months before it happened. She's sitting up on her knees in front of the last Christmas tree we ever had, holding her new diary in one hand and the too-large box we'd purposely wrapped it in to throw her off the trail in the other, smiling with the goofy, groggy happiness of a child still young enough to care about Christmas.

"Why don't the police have this?" Alex mutters, still staring.

"They asked for recent pictures," I explain. "I just didn't think to—I mean, look at her. She's still a little girl." But it was only nine months between when the picture was taken and when Julie disappeared. How could she have changed so much in nine months? It's the smile, of course. This is the last picture of Julie smiling the way kids do, with her mouth all the way open, showing her teeth. Shortly after that, she became a close-lipped teenager. And then she was gone.

"No, no," he says. "I mean, there's not even one photo of her in that nightshirt anywhere in the case files, just a description. I assumed you just didn't have any. That's exactly the kind of carelessness that would never have happened if this had been treated—" He breaks off, shakes his head, looks at the two photos again, and sighs. "Well, this puts that theory to bed anyway."

"What theory?"

"That Julie ran away."

I stare at him.

"Oh, come on, Anna. You had to know that was a possibility. It just didn't look like a kidnapping." He shakes his head. "Why do you think they investigated you and Tom so closely?"

"But Jane saw—"

"Eyewitness testimony from a ten-year-old? At that angle, from a dark closet, in a dark house? Not particularly reliable," he says. "Honestly, Anna, there was always more than a little reason to believe she'd made it all up or was convinced to lie. Or, if she did see something, didn't understand what she was seeing."

"But—" *They gave her a lollipop for sitting so long with the police sketch artist,* I want to say, but the words sound stupid even in my head. "The investigation—"

"Sure, big, high-profile case, leave no stone unturned. With no other leads, they were ready to take her story seriously, in public at least. Behind closed doors, though—believe me, I was there, I know where it was headed. I saw all the signs."

"No," I say. It seems important to keep saying this, because what he is implying is actually worse than my worst nightmare. It's something I have never even repressed. I never had to, because I simply never thought of it. Although now, with the word *runaway* instead of *abduction* ringing in my ears, I suddenly wonder why not.

As if reading my mind, he pries back the index finger of his left hand with the index finger of his right and starts on his list of evidence. "Minimal signs of forced entry. Almost staged, like someone just jiggled a lock pick around for a while, then opened the door with a key. The alarm wasn't even on."

"We sometimes—"

"I know, you didn't set it every night, okay," he says. "Could be. Or could be she disarmed it herself." He moves on to the middle finger. "No weapon."

"The knife—"

"*Your* knife, which he takes from the kitchen after he breaks in. He comes to this house in the middle of the night completely unarmed. And he walks straight up the stairs; he knows exactly which room—"

"We went over all this with the police. They said he must have staked out the house."

"I'm not saying he didn't," Alex reminds me. "I'm saying what the police were saying. I was there, remember? I've seen the file."

I sink, deflated, back into my booth.

"They didn't believe there was any man. And even if there was —she almost had to have known him, Anna."

I struggle to keep from raising my voice, and it comes out strangled. "Look, I don't care if she knew him beforehand or not. She was thirteen. That's child abduction."

"Absolutely. Still a crime. But a very different kind of investigation. Runaways are a lot harder to find, because they don't want to be found." He waits for a second as if weighing whether to speak, then goes ahead. "I don't know how to put this. If she'd been in my neighborhood, there would have been no question that she was a runaway."

"But Julie was only thirteen—"

"So was Stephanie Vargas. She climbed into a car with a friend of the family in 2005. My little sister went to high school with her brother. We didn't lift a damn finger for the Vargas family. She and her brother were staying with an uncle while Mom visited relatives in Mexico." He sighs. "Stephanie was a straight-A student. She played the clarinet. She practiced every day." He looks straight into my eyes. "Her body was found less than a mile from her house. Dumped in a drainage ditch."

I shut my mouth. His face looks older, years older, and I can see the shadow of punches thrown. It fills me with rage. "So you knew," I say. "You knew about this, you knew they weren't really looking for Julie because they didn't really look for this other girl, and instead of coming forward, instead of fighting for all those girls"—*For Julie, Julie, Julie*—"you just fucking quit?"

"I didn't quit. I was kicked off."

"That's not what you told me before."

"I lied."

You and everybody else, I think. "So why didn't you come to us back then?" I ask, relentless. "If you're such a white knight, where were you eight years ago? When it mattered?"

"I can't say for sure, but if I had to guess, I'd say blackout drunk in a public restroom somewhere," he says. "Or in a parking lot, or behind a dumpster. It takes effort and determination to get kicked off the force just for being a drunk. Really fills up your social calendar." He sighs. "Look, to be honest, even after I sobered up, I wasn't too sure of myself." He leans forward. "But I've tried to find her. Please believe me, Anna, I've tried."

"Why do you even care?"

He shrugs uncomfortably. "Some cases you never forget. They just nag at you. You're sure you screwed the pooch, but there's no proof."

We both stare at the photos on the table.

"Until now. We don't need a DNA sample, not with this. I can take it to the police. You lay low; you don't even need to be involved. They'll compare the forensic report on the remains with Julie's records. And we'll find out what we already know." He looks me in the eye. "Just say the word."

But I can't say anything.

"Do I have your permission?"

I look away. I nod.

"I know it's too late, Anna. I know I can never undo what I did, or didn't do, while I was drinking. But this is all I've got." He pauses. "It's all I can do to make amends."

"I don't want your amends."

I want my baby.

Baby

woke up without opening her eyes. Her insides hurt, like her stomach was a fist squeezing itself as hard as it could. Or like falling asleep with a rubber band in wet hair and trying to pull it out in the morning. Like something that wouldn't let go grabbing at something that wasn't there anymore. She doubled up to push the walls of her insides tighter together to fill the hole, but her body moved sluggishly, and when she tried to wrap her arms around her knees, her wrists felt pinned to the ground by powerful magnets. She stayed like that, curled on her side, knees to chin, arms dead.

Her body was slow, but her mind was waking up fast. The absence that hurt her stomach sang in her ears like an alarm bell, ringing louder and louder, shivering up and down her spine. She had won. Esther was bleeding out of her onto a fat strip of towel wedged thick between her legs. Esther was gone at last and, with her, the last of John David.

She tried to conjure up his image, the way she had seen him

once, wearing a wobbling halo of light. But when she saw a halo of light now, it was the glowing globe in the kitchen where she lay hard-backed on the table with her legs spread wide, and the darkness at the center of the light wasn't John David but a man in scrubs with a surgical mask and gloves who gave her a sweet pill to melt her to the table until she sank right through it. Then her spirit went up, up, toward the light fixture, where the outlines of winged insects with burned-out guts lay in a dusty pile. With her last bit of will she flew up into that globe light and let her tissue get burned right out of her. And now she was an outline only she could fill in.

When she woke up again she was in so much more pain that she could hardly stand it. The bed hurt her bones. Where was she?

Because it was dark outside, it took a moment to realize she wasn't on a bed at all. She lay on a slanted, corrugated slab of concrete under a bridge, the smell of gasoline and something sour filling her nostrils. Janiece sat a few feet away, her head and shoulders emerging from a mass of blankets. She stirred, and Janiece turned toward her.

"Hey, Baby, you feeling better?" Janiece asked. She leaned forward and adjusted some of the blankets without leaving her own nest. "You been making some noise there."

She opened her mouth to say *It hurts,* but there was only a gasp of air where her voice should be, just as if the fist in her belly were squeezing her lungs too.

Janiece nodded. "Yeah, you got the cramps," she said. "They're nasty. I had the cramps real bad after mine."

At the thought of Janiece with a baby in her belly, she blinked.

"I got nothing to give you for it, Baby," Janiece continued. "Aw, don't look at me like that. They don't send you home with nothing over at Smith's place. They give you one big double dose to knock you on your ass, but after that it's 'Naw, you gonna sell it' or 'You gonna snort it.' Baby, they don't give you nothing at Doc Smith's. They don't trust you for shit." She was talking more to herself now, but loud, as if she had an audience under the bridge, where the pigeons were wedged up under the shit-streaked concrete like a row of stuffed animals on a shelf.

She opened her mouth to speak again, but her breath kept snagging.

"What is it, Baby?"

"Stop calling me Baby."

Janiece just looked at her, unimpressed. "Well, you ain't Wig Girl anymore. What's your name?"

She thought for a minute. She stayed silent.

"That's right, Baby," Janiece said. "You can be Baby for a little while, it won't kill you." She leaned over again, put out her hand. The fingers touched Baby's hair and Baby couldn't help it, she relaxed. The fingers were warm and heavy against her scalp, and the rough dry skin caught her hair and gave it little pulls, and her own skin tingled around the pulled hairs.

Baby lay on her side all night, but she didn't sleep. Her stomach ached so much she couldn't imagine feeling anything else. "You just need something to eat," Janiece said. "Hang on, we'll get something when Pete comes by."

Baby didn't ask who Pete was; she just nodded.

They waited and waited for Pete. Cars swooshed by at random intervals, sometimes several at a time, sometimes thirty seconds with none and then only one every ten seconds for a while. Baby counted them but she couldn't see what color they were, or what kind. Janiece stared car-ward, immobile as the pigeons.

When Pete finally came, though, Baby knew she, too, had been sitting like a pigeon all this time, because Pete brought so much motion to the concrete ramp that Baby felt self-conscious, even while fresh rounds of cramps made her insides rattle like the wheels of the shopping cart that Pete pushed in front of him. When he got close, he pulled some scraps of blanket from around his wrist and tied them around the shopping cart's wheels so it wouldn't roll down the concrete slope.

"Took you long enough," said Janiece. "I thought we were gonna rot over here. Look, Pete, I gotta get her taken care of so I can go get something to eat. I'm starving. I've been taking care of this baby all day and all night."

"What do you need, J?" Pete asked without looking at Baby even for a second.

"What do you have to take the edge off?" she said. "Opes?"

"You wish," Pete said. "I can get you some later but you have to hook me up, understand?"

"Tylenol?"

"No way. Sorry."

"What the hell are you good for, Pete? Why have we been sitting here all night waiting for your sorry ass?"

"Go down to camp if you want Tylenol."

"Not with this one," she said, looking at Baby again. "She can't fend yet."

"Or the clinic."

"We're not going to any more clinics for a while," Janiece said in a low, gravelly tone.

"Fine," he said. "What I've got's a little weed, that's all I've got for now."

"I knew you weren't useless." She smiled. "Come on, Baby, I

got something for you. It's going to help, trust me." Baby willed her limbs to move, but the bumpy concrete was harder to navigate than she thought. "Come on, do you want it or don't you? It's going to fix those cramps up for you. And then I can go get us something to eat."

Baby pushed herself halfway upright and saw Pete looking at her for the first time. A warm, rank scent filled the air, something like the insides of shoes but also like the steam off a cup of tea, not entirely unpleasant.

"Here, honey," Janiece said, pushing the joint in her face.

Baby had seen a joint before when a boy brought one to school, though some other boys said it was oregano. It was certainly not something she ever would have associated with the smell that hit her in the face when Janiece handed her the twist of brittle paper, warm from the burning breath that had already passed through it.

"You gotta be kidding me," Janiece said, seeing her confusion. "Like this, Baby, see?" She kissed the wrinkled tip of the joint with her cracked and puckered lips, sucked, held the lungful of smoke, and exploded it out with a cough. "You really are a baby." She passed the joint, and Baby took it, tentatively kissed the moist tip, and sucked in. The smoke surprised her, a square feeling in her chest, something with corners and hard edges. She tried to hold it but her lungs convulsed, punching the smoke back out into the air. She started coughing uncontrollably.

"That's fine," Janiece said. "Take another. Don't worry about me, Baby, you finish that yourself. It's all for you. I was just showing you."

"Sure," said Pete. "I don't want any. Never saw you turn down a joint, though, J."

"I was just showing Baby how," she said. Meanwhile, Baby was coughing again, but a thick syrup had dripped down over her so she hardly even felt like she was coughing. Then came a deliciousness in her stomach that was like the easing of the fist, or maybe, when she noticed it, the fist was still there, clenched as tight as ever, but she didn't care anymore because all the muscles had started turning into elastic one by one, or something gummier that could stretch forever, like Silly Putty. Her skin shivered under scores of hair follicles that seemed to have turned into little antennae, and her whole body dissolved into points of light. Or bubbles, like the ones in a soft drink. She felt so happy, so safe. Even the under-freeway had turned into a vault, and she was something precious tucked away inside, hidden where no one could find her.

"You feeling a little better, Baby?" said Janiece, and now she could nod. Her mouth opened up as if on its own, and "Yes, thank you," came out as if from a pull-string dolly.

"So polite! That's good. That's real good. You keep puffing on that. But you're gonna get hungry next. I gotta go get some food from the camp. Here's Pete, he's going to look after you while I'm gone."

Baby shook her head from side to side at the sight of Janiece rising to her feet. Suddenly Janiece looked very skillful standing on her two feet, since the whole world was tilted and she was balancing perfectly on the side of it. Baby twisted her neck to make the world go straight again, but it settled back into a slant and she remembered that it really was slanted, and that struck her as funny, so funny that she started laughing and laughing. Her stomach hurt from laughter, not from cramps, unless they were the same thing. She had forgotten what the cramped feeling was about. There was nothing inside her. She was Nothing.

By now Janiece was gone, and suddenly Baby understood what

was happening with crystal clarity. It was too late for her to move, of course, she was pigeoned against the concrete like a doll on a shelf with huge, glassy eyes that wouldn't stay closed, even when Pete began fumbling at her clothes under her sleeping bag, and the smells of him became overwhelming. *Okay,* she told herself, because the panic was starting to rise in her, thick and warm, and she knew beyond a shadow of a doubt that screaming for Janiece or anyone would do absolutely nothing, because this was just another path she had chosen to walk down, remember? From now on she was choosing everything that filled her, and right now it was Nothing, right now it was Pete, right now it was a thing she had to do to earn the warm syrup of smoke coating her insides with glitter paint.

This slow, syrupy world gave her all the time she needed to understand what to do next. It was like she was in a bubble with the man named Pete and the sleeping bag and the pigeons and the cars, whose headlights never illuminated the place behind the pillar for more than a quarter of a second, but in those flashes she saw that Pete had fists and that there was a knife concealed in his pockets, and why wouldn't there be? It wouldn't be the first wicked blade she had stolen.

Baby lay still, waiting for it to be over. Nothing watched for an angle.

13

I watch her all week long, waiting for something to happen.

Now I am thankful for her short red hair, which both reveals and defamiliarizes her face. I retrace its contours, not with a mother's intimate knowledge but with a stranger's curiosity. I try not to superimpose the real Julie over the false Julie, compare line to line, but rather to learn every curve and dimple anew. Her chin is fine and pointed, but her jaw is sharper and squarer than it looks at first glance, her forehead higher and shadowed with the very first creases that no amount of blank-facing will completely smooth away. I try to determine the degree of the slight angle between the bridge and the tip of her nose, trace the flanges of her nostrils.

I do not look at her eyes if I can avoid it. Too dangerous. She'll feel me looking, and I'll feel something that may or may not be real.

Even so, I'm making her uneasy. She drops a glass in the sink

Wednesday morning and it shatters; Tom has to take her by the shoulders and move her aside so he can clean it up. She runs to her room and closes the door, dramatically but as quietly as if she's performing a role in a silent film. She can get up and down the stairs with hardly a creak or thump. I wonder if she is pacing in her bedroom; if so, we hear nothing of it downstairs.

Tom and I don't talk about it. We haven't spoken since Monday, and he sleeps in Jane's empty room, where he has moved his computer desk. I assume he works in there during the day. Perhaps Julie comes and goes while Tom stares at his screen and tries not to notice.

As for me, I go to work too. Once I'm in my office, door locked against the department secretary, I'm oblivious to faculty and students passing in the halls; nothing can hurt me. I put my cell phone on my desk and lay my head down next to it, waiting for Alex to call, waiting for news about the DNA test. Sometimes I grow impatient and imagine calling the police myself, telling them my doubts about the woman in my house. Things would move much more quickly after that. But I threw Overbey's number away and finding it again would take more willpower than I have at my disposal.

Besides, this way, like Alex said, I don't have to be involved. She'll never know it was me. That's the beauty of ID'ing a corpse rather than a living girl.

And what will happen when they get the results? I imagine the police bursting into the house, ready to cuff her and drag her away. She's sitting on the sofa under the afghan, watching a movie; she turns around at the noise. I try to inoculate myself against the expression on her face as they come for her. Shock? Rage? But I never see it. Instead, I keep seeing her expression illuminated by the ultrasound screen: bottomless grief, hopeless despair.

And what if I'm wrong?

But these are the habits of denial. When I feel myself starting to indulge them, I force myself to think of the photo.

It's a short trip from there to thoughts of Tom's gun. When did Tom take the classes, when did he get a license to own a handgun? Just another thing he was doing on his own, though I know it doesn't take long. I know, because I once planned to buy one. I told myself that's why I went to the firing range: I was practicing to get my license, firing rounds into a piece of paper shaped like a man for entirely pragmatic reasons. If something like that ever happened again, I told myself, I wanted to be ready.

It was a lie. I wanted to pretend, in every possible scenario, that I was killing him. Every time the gun discharged and I felt the jolt go through me, I felt exhilaration at the thought that maybe I had missed the heart, hit a shoulder or a knee or the groin, so I could have the chance to do it again and again. I wanted to kill him forever.

One day when I drove to the firing range, I realized it wasn't really Julie's abductor I wanted to kill. It was someone else, the person who was really to blame for Julie's death—and even if she wasn't to blame, she was the only person I could hold accountable. A firing range is the easiest place in the world to kill yourself; you don't have to own a firearm to shoot one. It was raining hard, one of those summer downpours where the air feels inside out, like a monsoon, and I almost wrecked the car getting there. I was too drunk to write my name on the sign-in sheet that day, and they turned me away.

I never went back. That was the beginning of the end of the drinking, and when I sobered up, I decided not to buy a gun.

But there are laws of inevitability at work in our lives. While I was crying drunkenly in my car, shuddering away from the brink, Tom, somewhere across the city, was making a different decision. And now the gun is in our house, like it was always meant to be.

Now that I've lost her again, I can always use it.

Friday night after dinner, Tom goes up to Jane's room and shuts the door while I sit on the sofa and idly browse the cable channels. Something has to give; something has to break. I believe it will happen tonight.

Halfway into a rerun of *Roseanne,* Julie confirms it by striding quickly past the sofa on her way out. I hear the garage door open, catch a glimpse through the kitchen window of Tom's car backing out. Leaving the television on, I wait a few seconds and follow her in my car.

At night, the freeway is less clogged, and the rosary beads flash past instead of scrolling slowly by. The faded awnings and new construction and apartment buildings look flat and dull at night, irrelevant. I can barely distinguish one from the other. Up ahead, the Range Rover weaves expertly around slower cars, in and out of lanes—*Julie's a good driver for someone who's only just learned,* I think to myself with some sarcasm. Though there are plenty of cars on the road, I can always see her. The SUV sticks out over the other cars, highly visible even to me in my squat little Prius. I know where she's going before she puts on the turn signal.

At night, the Gate is a bald hill wreathed in glowing glass. The surface parking lot is full—there's something going on, one of the nighttime services that are among the church's most heavily attended offerings. I turn into the garage, where suited attendants direct a line of creeping cars farther and farther up, and a steady stream of people flows back down a central staircase from the roof. I go where I'm directed, ascending past thousands of cars to the top level of the garage.

Every time I pass the staircase, I glance at the line of people, and just as I'm turning the corner to the top level, driving toward the open spots in the distance, I finally catch a glimpse of Julie heading downward with the rest of the crowd. She's wearing a long skirt and cardigan I bought her just a few weeks ago, when things were so different.

I park and walk down the staircase with the rest of the stragglers: a lean older couple wearing matching denim shirts and shining belt buckles, the woman carrying a leather purse dangling fat silver charms; a black woman about my age, in jeans and a ruffled blouse, herding two children in front of her; an elderly woman with a cane; a towering Latino man with a potbelly and a bullet-shaped head who pushes past everyone impatiently. All of us emerge together onto the surface lot, then stream down a walkway to the lobby, which is teeming with people. The hanging monitors and clerestory lighting feel different at night, surrounded by the faintest hint of a stadium echo that no amount of plush carpet and soft, shaggy area rugs can dampen. It makes the air feel a little fizzy, so that it's obvious this structure was originally built for excitement.

The escalators that cleave the entryway in half are covered with people, but I don't see Julie anywhere. I hurry past the information desk and step onto the escalator to avoid the enthusiastic greeters, only to be delivered straight into the hands of a thin woman with large, bright-awake eyes behind oversize glasses at the top of the escalator. "Program?"

I take the glossy trifold, still scanning the crowded horizon for Julie, and she spots my hesitation.

"Is this your first time visitin'?" she asks with a heavy Houston accent, flattening the vowels, chewing and pinching off the consonants.

"Um, yes." I nod, and she puts her hand on my forearm.

"Well, listen, honey, here's what you're going to do. You're going right back down this escalator and—you see that desk on your right? Well, now, usually Sheena is up here at the top of the stairs with me, but you can see her down there—"

I start to panic. What if Julie sees me, stopped here at the top of the escalator? "Can I just seat myself?"

"Of course, honey," she says but then calls after me as I'm moving away: "It's just since you're new, we'd rather you got one of the *really good* seats."

For my money, a good seat is one where you can see the lay of the land without attracting attention. I walk around the stadium's curve on the second floor, following the flow of people past a room with a sign saying COMMUNION, more video screens, and an unmanned, recessed information booth that used to be a concession stand or bar when this was a stadium. Then I step into the sanctuary itself.

It is cavernously huge. Cluster lights illuminate dust motes a hundred feet away against the bluish-black vault of what used to be the Astrodome, only the intricate starburst pattern of rectangular skylights on the ceiling hinting at its former identity. Gone is the Astroturf, replaced by acres of beige carpet; the folding seats lining the walls have been tastefully reupholstered in navy. Jumbotron screens flank the stage, and a TV camera on a crane swoops over the red-carpeted dais as if it's limbering up for the show. I find a seat halfway down the top section, close to the aisle, and sit down.

After a few minutes, the lights dim and the stadium, still steadily filling with people, erupts into applause. Audience members stand in waves, shouting, "Jesus lives!" and "Praise Him!" over the band, which has started up a dramatic, throbbing hum. Seven singers emerge from the depths of the altar, dressed in television-friendly stage outfits and holding wireless mics. All at once, the music bursts out, a heavy beat thrumming through the whole stadium, as loud as any rock concert, basketball game, or monster-truck rally. The laser light show begins, brilliant beams of green and blue sweeping the stadium. One moves across my face for a split second and I feel a shot of adrenaline, the chemical response to being bathed, suddenly and forcefully, in a powerful light. My heart feels as if it's actually leaping up, like in the Wordsworth poem; I've always wondered what that would be like.

The music thuds explosively onward. It's a soaring pop anthem, the song you hear near the end of a film about teenagers in love. The Jumbotrons cut between the singers' faces, the band sweatily playing their instruments, and a montage of images: fast-motion sunsets and sunrises, flowers opening in a tenth of a second, young people driving a jeep across dunes, a beautiful blond girl lying on her back beside a campfire, a black baby stumbling forward on chubby legs while a white woman kneels with her hands out, a sailboat speeding across a giant lake in time with the clouds.

After a few minutes of this, the singers part and recede around a lone figure who walks to the front of the stage. The people begin pumping their fists, the cries of "Praise Him!" louder and louder.

"I'm here for you," he says simply. "And so is the Lord."

I recognize the voice from the Circle of Healing, but this is my first glimpse of Chuck Maxwell in person. He looks like a country-pop singer at the Houston Livestock Show and Rodeo or the long-lost father on a soap opera. The Jumbotron gives me a close-up of the kindest, crinkliest pair of blue eyes I have ever seen.

"I'm here to tell you, the Lord has great things in store for you, His children," Maxwell says to screaming and applause. "And you're here for one reason: to listen, to know, and to praise His Holy Name. Because nothing happens by chance in this great universe the Lord has made. He's bigger than your problems. And when He calls your name, they'll be *gone!*"

"A-*men!*" a voice just behind me yells out.

Maxwell pauses and lets them scream for a while, a smile crinkling his beard around his neck. "Listen," he says. Another dramatic pause. The music is swelling and people are shifting from side to side, shaking their heads back and forth. "Tell it, Chuck!" a voice rings out.

"I will tell it! I will!" he yells. "Why are you here today, people? Let me just ask you that, why are you here?" He puts the microphone out and cups his other hand behind his ear as the audience yells in one voice: "It ain't luck, Chuck!"

He puts the mic back by his beard and says, "That's right, y'all. It ain't luck. Nothing is luck in this universe the Lord has made for us. He loves each and every one of us, we are all His very special favorites, and He will bring us something that is beyond our imagining very soon. And whatever it is He has in store for us, y'all"—he pauses again—"it's gonna be *worth* it!"

The screaming and clapping erupts once more, and the singers melt forward to begin a song, obscuring him from view temporarily. The man sitting to my left taps my shoulder and hands over a blue plastic bucket filled with envelopes and cash, a crisp hundred-dollar bill sitting at the top of the pile. I pass the bucket to the usher at the end of the aisle, who smiles beatifically at me although I haven't put anything in.

"Y'all, His blessings are gonna rain down upon us," says Maxwell confidingly as the music subsides. "I know you're worried. I know you've got the day job or the sick kid or the people coming after you about the bills. I know you've got the son-in-law who hasn't come to Jesus yet. You turn on the news, and you think this world is getting darker, turning its face from God. I'm here to tell you some of the best news of all: *Don't worry about it!* Let the Lord look after your neighbor and your kid and your landlord and your boss. What you're waiting for is coming, and the only reason it hasn't come yet is your faith ain't *strong* enough yet!"

The music starts up again, but this time slower, more hymnlike. "Now, this next song, I and my team of prayer leaders will descend down off this stage, and anyone who wants to can come on up here and pray with us. Just go on up to the head of your section, and a prayer leader will listen to you and pray with you, pray you get the wisdom to see what the Lord is already giving you. And the rest of you can take your seats and just listen to these inspired singers tell you about God's love."

As the crowd rises as one and surges toward the dais, I begin to understand what the "*really good* seats" are good for. Lines form, filling the stadium floor and trailing up the aisles, while Maxwell and a handful of other elders begin quietly conferring with the first few who make it to the stage. I sweep my eyes back and forth, searching for a redhead in the crowd, but the stadium floor is rapidly becoming an undifferentiated mass of people milling forward for their personalized prayers.

Just as I'm deciding this is an impossible task, there she is, on the prayer-cam, the features I've been studying so minutely blown up and hanging overhead on a Jumbotron screen. I watch, transfixed, as Maxwell appears next to her, his face tilted down toward hers, his eyebrows bent into a serious, compassionate expression, one hand resting on her shoulder. The redhead turns her face up toward his, stands on tiptoe until she's almost his height, and draws so close it looks like she's about to kiss him. She puts her lips to his ear and whispers something. Maxwell's expression changes dramatically. His eyes go suddenly wide, his eyebrows shoot upward, and his mouth opens in a gasp, like he's been kneed in the groin.

The camera cuts to someone else.

I drag my gaze from the screen down to the stadium floor, desperate to find her before the moment is over. There she is, one hand steadying herself on Maxwell's padded jacket shoulder so she can stay on tiptoe, the other pointing a finger at his chest. He jerks backward as she sinks down to her heels and turns to walk away. Two men in suits who have been standing nearby emerge from the crowd and start moving toward her, but Maxwell gets there first. He lunges, grabs her forearm, and leans in close, his whole body tensed toward her, enfolding her in a terrible intimacy. He gives her arm a single shake, and she tears out of his grasp and pushes off to the side, losing the two bodyguards, and my gaze, in the crowd.

When I look back at Maxwell, he's already talking to the next woman in line, their foreheads so close they're almost touching, and yet even I can tell his mind isn't with the woman he's absolving. It's with Julie, and Julie is gone.

I start up out of my seat to follow her but then stop myself and sink back down again. She's on the ground floor, and I'm upstairs; by the time I get out of the Gate, she'll be halfway to Tom's car, and I'm parked farther away than she is. Anyway, I have no idea what I've just seen and thus no idea what I'd say if I caught up to her now. Only one thing is clear: Judging from Maxwell's alarmed expression and the ferocious intimacy of his body language on the stadium floor, they know each other. What did she whisper in his ear? A threat? What could Julie possibly have on Maxwell?

Not Julie, I remind myself.

As the service comes to a close, the music swells and thunders, the screens flash and go black again, the slices of red dawn outline the Gate logo, and, in the grand finale, it opens. When the praise band finally decrescendos, the people around me look happily exhausted by the barrage of positivity. I stumble out, feeling emptied. Out in the night air, I check my phone; there's a new voicemail from twenty minutes ago. The signal must be spotty inside the concrete stadium, because I never felt it buzz. Then I see the number and hurriedly put the phone to my ear to listen to the message.

"Hi, Cal. It's Gretchen."

It's the same voice that cried, "Mom, Dad," when she hugged us in the emergency room, the same voice that whispered, "You must have really wanted to find me," before breaking into tears. And now this voice confesses out loud that she, the woman living in my house, is not my daughter. After everything I know, it shouldn't surprise me. But this is more damning than a fuzzy You-Tube video, more damning even than a crime scene photo. Only now do I realize I've been holding on to some last, slender thread of hope. These words—*It's Gretchen*—are the sound of it snapping.

The message continues. "I need your help, Cal. I'm scared." She starts crying. "If you're still at this number, you're in Houston. And if you found me here, maybe you already know everything about me. Maybe you know the worst." She sobs thickly. "If you come for me after finding out the worst, I'll know you still love me. I'm going to the Water Wall to confront the man who did this to me. He'll be there at midnight. Please come. I don't want to go alone."

On the voicemail, there's the sound of a horn honking, followed by a clatter, as if she's dropped the phone. Then: "Cal, I don't know if this makes any difference, but for a few weeks, I was —we were—I think it was a girl."

The voicemail beeps. "Press seven to repeat this message. Press eight to delete this message. Press nine to save—"

I press 9. When I confront her, I want to have her own voice in my pocket as proof. By the time I reach my car, it's 11:35, and I know I have to find her now, tonight, before I lose my nerve, and demand to know what she's doing here, why she's tormenting my family.

Now that I know Julie is only Gretchen after all, a blurry face on a YouTube video, a second-rate performer, an impostor, a fake, I have no choice. It's been Gretchen this whole time. And soon it will be midnight.

She

didn't feel the blow but she felt the black. It was like water she was sinking into, or that was sinking into her. There was a redness at the top of it, and the closer she got to the red the more it hurt. Whereas the black was as soft and lustrous blue-black as clouds of birds taking flight. The black was as soft and lustrous green-black as the ocean floor. The black was as soft as the black velvet pillow that swallows the diamond ring. The black was as black as her sleeping self.

She swam toward the red, she fought red-ward even though the black was trying to swallow her like a diamond, it was wrapping eyeless tendrils around her ankles and dragging her gently down, it was surrounding her with silent caws and carrying her into a blue-black sky. But every time she rested into its softness, she heard Charlotte screaming. Then there was a blow and the screaming stopped.

Then another noise, a mewling, that didn't sound like Charlotte or like anyone. Was it her? Her tongue was dead in her mouth, a dead bird with blue-black wings. The noise went on, a gurgling and then another thud that she felt inside her eyelids.

If she concentrated every red particle of energy to her fingertips, she could just feel the ground. It was slick and hot and red; she could feel the red stinging her fingertips. Or maybe it wasn't a feeling but a smell, a pointed smell that was both clean and dirty at the same time. It was the smell of losing a tooth, which was also a taste, warm electrified metallic.

She tried to pull her fingers back but the birds had all been clubbed out of the air one by one and she must be made of them from head to toe. So her dead-bird fingers rested in the electric red pool that smelled like teeth.

There were words being said, a litany, a prayer. They were being said in a voice she knew well, John David's voice, but they were angry. Maybe they were God's words, and it was God who was angry.

"You little shit. Goddamn little shit" were the words said over and over again.

The bird in her mouth twitched and she knew it was alive after all. It wanted to scream. She clamped down hard.

"What am I going to do. What am I going do. What am I going to do."

Thumping, retreating, ascending, and fading. He ascended into heaven. He had rolled the stone away and now He was climbing the basement stairs into the sky.

She opened her eyes.

Charlotte lay crumpled before her, upside down, four feet away, staring at her through eyes filled with blood.

She stared into Charlotte's upside-down eyes. They seemed full of wisdom.

Charlotte was trying to tell her something. Charlotte was the brave one, Charlotte was the smart one. She had even stolen the wicked little blade from John David's trash can to saw through the duct tape.

No, that was Julie who had stolen the blade.

Charlotte wasn't looking into her eyes after all. She was looking at Julie's right hand, curled an inch from her face. She was staring at something Julie could feel lying under the back of her hand, digging into one knuckle with a sharp corner. A wicked little corner.

When she moved her hand, the blade scraped the floor underneath and then there it was, a cold slice of air a few inches from her face, doubled and blurred but unmistakable. Her left hand slid toward it, fingertips dragging electric trails through the red liquid that was even now less hot than it had been, even now just barely warmer than the air itself. Her bloody fingers closed around one side of the blade.

Feet appeared on the stairs and, next to them, the head of an ax.

For just a moment, she squinted her eyes shut again. Just to remember what life was like when she didn't know that Charlotte was dead, and she was next.

An unexpected noise of retching came from the corner. She opened her eyes and John David was on his knees, facing away from her and Charlotte. He was not praying. A puddle of vomit snaked away past John David's knees toward the place where the blood was, where she was.

Before the puddle reached her, she was up on her feet. She hardly knew how she got there; her head was like a cinder block, but she stacked it on top of her body and stacked her body on top of her legs and then she was standing, towering over the broken doll that was Charlotte and the hunched figure of John David groaning in the corner. He spat, groaned again, and gasped for breath. A wave of dizziness swept over her suddenly, the red coming back to cloud her vision with blue-black dots swimming around the edges, threatening to rise up again like smoke. She put a bare foot out to steady herself, and the noise made the emptied-out John David whirl around on his knees, one hand still on the ax handle, one foot already making contact with the floor to push himself to standing. But as he pulled the other foot up, the heel of his boot came down in the snaky trail of vomit and his boot shot out from under him like a Russian dancer's, and he landed hard on the hand still holding the ax, so hard that his full weight crushed his fingers between the ax handle and the floor and he yelped in pain.

She stood, holding the razor blade out in front of her, but as he scrambled for purchase on the floor that was slippery with so much blood and vomit, she gave a cry and ran up the narrow stairs, not quite on all fours because she was still clutching the razor in her left hand but almost, using her arms like in dreams of running on all fours, some kind of throwback, maybe, to a time when hands were useful for something more than holding a feebly small razor blade that, although wicked, was nothing in comparison to the vast, smiling cruelty of an ax. Her knees, her everything, was slippery with blood.

"Esther! Esther!" The voice was behind her, beneath her, but how far? "Esther, come back! I won't hurt you!"

She was at the top of the stairs, and he was at the bottom. She looked at him there, so tiny, and saw the beginnings of a bald spot coming out at the very top of his head. She had never been taller than him before.

"Esther!" he cried again, but his hand was still on the ax, choked up now near the head. His voice grew wheedling. "I never meant to hurt you, Esther. Charlotte was the bad one. I only knocked you out so you wouldn't have to see."

"My name's not Esther," she shouted, but it came out in a whisper.

"No," he agreed.

She was shocked.

"It's Ruth. For you have seen much."

She stood stock-still.

"Ruth," he said, "you have passed the test. You have made a blood sacrifice."

His tone had lost its frantic edge and grown soothing, honeyed. "You did the right thing, Ruth. She tried to run away, and you stopped her. Now we can be a happy family again, just you and me."

"I—"

"You called for help. She overpowered you, and you called for help. And I came."

Although her head was swimming she knew that was not what had happened at all.

She shook her head to clear the cobwebs. "My name is Julie." That was the only thing that made sense, but it made his hands tighten around the ax handle. She turned and ran just as he sprang up the stairs after her.

His legs were longer than hers, but she darted around the corner just as he reached out to grab her ankle, the ax handle clattering clumsily against the stairs. She got around to the other side of the kitchen table as he appeared at the top of the stairs, but then realized she had pinned herself against the wall. He held the ax with both hands, shifting its weight from one to the other as if he enjoyed the feel of it in his palms. "Don't make me kill you, Esther," he said.

"I thought my name was Ruth now," she said, this time forcing the words to come out loud and strong.

"Whoever you are!" he yelled. "Don't make me kill you, because I will if I have to, but God does not want you dead."

"God is shit," Julie said.

"God is love, and *you* are shit," he returned. "Never forget that." He slammed the ax blade into the middle of the table, and the Formica cracked down the center with the blade stuck in it. She grabbed the table from her side and shoved as hard as she could, just hard enough to make John David fall on his ass, the ax still in the table, and she almost laughed at how funny this was, but now John David was scrambling along the floor after her, grabbing for her ankles with his bare hands, knocking aside the chair she threw back at him until finally she was at the door.

She managed to get one foot onto the concrete step before a hand grabbed the pitiful bedsheet that was still tangled around her like a robe. She tried to slam the screen door behind her, but it bounced on his arm. She leaned back as hard as she could, hurling her entire weight against the door. His hand jolted loose for an instant, but then the fingers gripped her upper arm and squeezed hard.

"I've got you," he said, panting, and his hot breath warmed her cheek through the screen door. "I've got you." He leaned hard on his side of the door, and she could feel his weight through the mesh, curiously soft and intimate against her own, and what a time to remember his bulk on her, what a time to remember those nightmare communions, what a time to suddenly feel more his than ever, in this moment of almost-freedom, of failed freedom.

"What happened here is your fault," he breathed through the mesh. "You aren't Ruth. You aren't Esther. You're *nothing*."

But in her bloody hands, something wicked still remained.

She slashed blindly with the blade at his fingers, and when they opened, she ran.

Nothing nothing nothing
Nothing nothing nothing nothing
Nothing
She ran to the rhythm of what she was.

There was something, though, curled right up in her core, and every pounding, naked footfall sent shock waves through her legs to say hello to it.

Goodbye, she told it.

I don't care, she told it.

You're nothing, she told it. But she knew she was wrong.

She remembered a distant promise of help—peaches in syrup, canned corn—and ran hopelessly toward it. Every ounce of effort went into not tripping on the uneven sidewalks or getting smacked in the face with low-hanging branches or tangling herself up in her sheet, which was trailing. She could not take the time to look back and see if he was ten steps behind, twenty, or none; one fall, and his hands could close around her throat, bloody hands she'd slashed open herself with the wicked little blade, the same blade she'd used to commit the sin that could never be erased. Oh, Charlotte. Poor, poor Charlotte.

She ran through the old Houston neighborhood of hunched brick houses concealing God knows how many pulped skulls and ruined little girls, houses with who knew how many buried secrets in the backyard, zigzagging crazily around corners. The quaint old fairy-tale curves of the houses with their thick climbing vines nauseated her, and she ran past them in search of the larger streets that would signify civilization, and possibly help. But the streets were eerily bare—was it too early, even, for morning walks?

She emerged from the stifling neighborhood onto a corner with a stoplight and paused to catch her breath. A small park lay on her right next to a long, rectangular building with a covered walkway running its whole length. She recognized the sculpture on the lawn, a canal of rusty metal sunk into the grass in a random, nonsensical pattern like a dropped ribbon, and vaguely remembered visiting this museum on a long-ago field trip.

Looking around, she realized that it wasn't morning after all; though the light was at half strength and she felt that she'd lived through a long night, the colors weren't right for sunrise. The sky was a dingy, opaque white that made her feel as if she were still indoors, just in a bigger room. The trees loomed large, so dense and saturated with green, the color seemed to bleed off the edges of the leaves. That and the fact that the trees were absolutely motionless in the dead air made them look like fake trees on a stage set, or in a dream. She ran into the empty street and, craning her neck to the right, saw a freeway.

Then she saw it, towering above her, taller than the trees, taller than the lampposts. *Missing:* A girl, blond, beautiful, and pink-cheeked.

It wasn't her. Nothing like. She looked at the billboard and then down at herself, barefoot, filthy after months in the dark with him and the things he'd done to her. And now she had the something that wasn't nothing curled up in her gut to remind her of those things. To remind her, too, of what she'd done to Charlotte. The girl on the billboard knew nothing about that. She was perfect.

The next moment, as if someone had ripped a Band-Aid off the sky, a wall of rain fell down. In a few seconds it made a river that flowed past her bare feet and hid the billboard almost completely.

She started running again.

By the time she got to the food pantry, the rain had slackened to a drizzle like laundry being squeezed out, and the sun was poking out from behind wet-flannel clouds, making the last drops sparkle in midair. The ground was already starting to steam, but she shivered in front of the thin plywood stall. It was padlocked shut.

"If you need anything," the woman with the peaches had said. She needed lots of things. Her stomach swam with the sickness that could attack her at any time of day, especially when she hadn't eaten. The only thing that kept her from vomiting was the thought of being found on her knees on the concrete, alone, in front of the pantry stall. She circled around behind it.

A figure leaned against the back of the pantry stall, sheltered behind it on the concrete slab, smoking a cigarette. The woman heard her and swiveled her head slowly in her direction, as if she anticipated being bored by the sight. She took her in from head to toe with a long look, exhaled, and waited with the cigarette held between two fingers down by her knees. She seemed like she was used to waiting.

Suddenly the woman snapped to attention and took another,

quicker drag off her cigarette. Then she leveled it out in front of her, pointing. "Wig Girl!" she said. "I know you. You're that wig girl. Where's your wig at?"

The girl opened her mouth to say something, but just then the cigarette smoke from the woman's outstretched hand caught the breeze and drifted toward her. The rush of nausea it induced sent her to her knees in the mud, and she puked into the long, wet grass behind the wooden stall, but there was nothing to puke, just acid that burned her throat. Afterward she couldn't see anything but green and yellow flecks for a while, and then there was a moment of blackness before she felt a warm hand on the back of her neck.

"Wig Girl, you don't look so good," the woman said as she helped her to a sitting position on the concrete. The flecks cleared, and she saw the woman's face more clearly. The weave was gone, and the woman's short black hair shot back away from her face in stiff little flames. "My name's Janiece. And your name's about to be Mama, if I'm any judge."

The girl breathed in and out, taking long gulps of the now smoke-free air. "I ran away," she said, and then paused. She couldn't think of the words for what had happened. She'd lied. She'd killed. She'd tried to be good. She'd failed.

"Yeah, I got that," Janiece said. "You got people you can go to?"

She shook her head.

"You need some clothes? A place to stay?"

She nodded.

"You need to get rid of that?" Janiece pointed.

For a moment she was confused.

"Whose baby you having, honey?" the woman asked a little more softly.

The retching came from so deep within her this time that she thought she would be torn to pieces. Except that wasn't even a possibility. To have pieces, you have to be *something*.

Janiece watched her as she came up wiping her mouth with the back of her hand. "Okay, then, never mind about that. You need some food in you either way."

She looked mutely toward the food pantry behind them.

"Oh, hell no," said Janiece. "Rhonda's a nice lady, but one look at that four-months-gone belly and she ain't letting you out of her sight. They got a room for you."

"A—room?"

"Look at that, it talks! Yeah, they got a special room with a special movie. They're *Catholics,* understand? You don't want to mess with Catholics in your condition, shit."

"She said—if I needed—"

"If what you need is a lecture on keeping your legs closed. And I ain't saying you don't."

"I need—" Every word felt pulled from a bottomless well. Sometimes the bucket hit water, and sometimes it went down and down and dangled in space.

"I know what you need, and I can tell you right now, you can't get it—not without a bunch of papers signed by your folks back home. Hell, it's probably someone there did it to you in the first place."

Home.

You're nothing.

"Come on. You're coming with me." Janiece helped her up and sighed. "Whoever did that to you, I hope he rots in hell, because getting it out is going to be a whole lot of trouble. Money too." A sideways glance. "But we'll talk about that part later."

She thought about hell. She thought about heaven. She thought about what was inside her, the life, the heartbeat. Then she thought about John David, his weight on top of her again and again. She hadn't crawled out of the hole after all. It was inside her. Its name was Esther.

14

In 2002, a rock climber named Ryan Hartley scaled the Transco Tower using a small pick. When he reached the thirtieth floor —almost halfway up—he jumped.

On his broken body they found a note protesting the war in Iraq. Presumably he chose the Transco Tower because it was a symbol of Houston's oil boom: sixty-four stories of silver-black glass thrusting heavenward, alone in the middle of a retail and residential area, the tallest skyscraper ever built outside of a central business district. Pure energy shooting out of the center of the earth, as if a geyser of oil could be caught, purified, and transformed into a prism of light. As if anything could be that pure.

Opposite the tower, across a rectangle of grass, stands the Water Wall fountain, a horseshoe-shaped artificial waterfall exactly sixty-four feet tall, each foot representing one floor of the Transco Tower. Once, we took the girls there after Christmas shopping at the Galleria. Jane, three at the time, pulled away from my hand

and ran up to the edge of the water, and Tom took off running to catch up with her. Adventurous Jane stopped right at the bottom of the steps and looked straight up at the curved wall. Then, dizzied by the rushing water, she took a step forward. Her legs buckled under her. She sat down and let out a wail.

Julie, five, lay on the concrete, her head tipped back to see the giant arc of rushing water from a safe distance. While Tom gathered Jane up in his arms, I lay down next to Julie so that I could see what she saw. I remember her warm head nestled into my temple, her wispy hair blowing against my cheek. Together we listened to the sounds of Tom comforting Jane, barely audible over the noise from the waterfall. The water slammed down the wall so fast that it hardly looked like it was moving at all.

When Julie spoke, her words went right into my ear. "Mommy," she said. "Is the sky falling down?"

I made a mental note to repeat it to Tom later that night, after the girls went to bed, and said in a loud voice that the water noise turned into a whisper, "Don't worry, honey, it can't get us here."

I felt rather than saw her brave little smile.

Seen from a distance, silhouetted against the lit-up Water Wall and framed by a stone archway, they could be a couple taking engagement photos: Gretchen and Maxwell, their hands clasped together, Gretchen leaning backward in a graceful bow shape against his weight. Then he jerks her forward like a dancer and clasps his arms around her, and they become one dark figure, waltzing back and forth in front of the illuminated wall of water. But as I hurry toward them over wet grass that gets muddier closer to the fountain, I see her elbows angling out as she tries to push him away, his arms pinning them back down again. They are both fighting to get at her purse, which looks as if it has been wrapped around her neck in the struggle. I break into a run.

I always forget how loud the Water Wall is up close, a pounding roar that changes pitch and intensity with my every step, fading one moment into the background in the manner of white noise, then throbbing with renewed intensity. A mist fills the round concrete plaza in front of the curved wall of the fountain, making the ground treacherously slippery, and at night the light is a yellowish, jaundiced glow emanating from the underwater fountain lights. Just as I cross under the archway onto the plaza, the conjoined silhouettes tilt alarmingly and skid on their fulcrum. Gretchen stumbles backward over something lying on the ground and then she's down, her head bouncing at the impact, Maxwell collapsing on top of her. He continues to flail for a moment like some deep-sea creature washed up on the shore, then pulls back, separating their bodies. A sliver of light outlines his beard and briefly illuminates a panicked snarl of animal rage on his face before he leans into the darkness, reaching for the purse that is now lying halfway under Gretchen's limp body on the wet concrete.

The man who did this to me. That's what she called Maxwell on the recording. I don't know what he did or who she is, but seeing his hand reach toward her motionless form, I know I have to stop what he's going to do next.

I propel myself forward as hard as I can, and then my shoes are sliding on the wet concrete, just as Gretchen's did a moment before, and my feet slip out from under me. I manage to get my hand out in front of me and drop to one shin, but my teeth close on a millimeter of tongue when I hit the ground, and a flower of heat spreads through my mouth. Maxwell sees me and springs to his feet, still straddling Gretchen's limp body. When he opens his mouth and speaks, his deep voice carries over the rushing of the water behind him, just as it carried over the sea of voices at the Circle of Healing.

"I know what this looks like," he says, panting. "But you don't know what this girl is capable of. She's dangerously disturbed. She lies. She's a killer."

"I don't believe you," I say, but I can't hear my own words, and I know that the lying part is true.

"She's been stalking me, making threats. She tried to blackmail me. She wants my money." He gestures toward a duffle bag lying slumped on the wet ground a few feet away. "She forced me to come here, threatened me. And then she attacked me." I look down at the unmoving body on the concrete. "I swear, I was defending myself! She's got a gun in her purse!"

But it's a mistake, because now I will never let him get that purse in his hands. "If all she wants is your money, why would she attack you?"

He licks his lips. "Like I said, she's disturbed. I'm successful, I help people." His voice rises petulantly, his beard bulging over his Adam's apple. "Girls like that can't stand a—"

"Girls like what?"

He looks at me with a faint air of surprise. "Whores."

I suck in my breath through clenched teeth. "You don't talk about my daughter that way," I say. And even though it isn't her, it suddenly is.

He lunges for the purse but I get to him first and push him into the trough at the base of the fountain with so much explosive force that the next thing I know I'm kneeling in six inches of water on top of his chest. Behind me, his legs flail and jerk in the water, kicking toward my back, my head, but I am mostly in the air and he is mostly underwater, which makes me heavier, temporarily. My knees are on his shoulders, and I can feel his hand grabbing for my hair, and *Good luck, motherfucker,* I think; I cut it short when Julie was born, I gave it to motherhood, along with dangly earrings and peace of mind and the ability to *not! give! a! fuck! about! anyone! And! dreams! of! my! own! And! a! heart! in! my! body!* With my fingers snarled in his tangled hair, I slam his head on the bottom of the fountain as hard as I can, like punching through the bathroom door when I thought Julie was hurt on the other side, but the water puts up too much resistance and what I get instead of a smack is a splash and a host of crazy shadows leaping up and careening away to the rhythm of my rage.

Behind me a voice cuts through the thundering water. "John David." There's a click I recognize from my fantasies. In the split second that my grip relaxes, he is scrabbling backward, kicking me away, until he's up against the water-covered slope. And then I see a look on Maxwell's face that says he wishes he hadn't kicked me away so quickly, and when I turn, I know why.

Gretchen is standing, holding the gun.

The pounding of the falling water is like a blank piece of paper, and the gun is the point of a pencil hovering a millimeter above it, sketching the three of us invisibly on the air before committing us to the page.

Our bodies hold the corners of a triangle open: The man with his hands up in front of him, back pressed against the slope, water pouring over his shoulders and pummeling his neck so that his head shakes with the effort of steadiness. Me on one knee in the water, frozen in the act of rising. Gretchen, standing with the gun.

"Esther," says Maxwell. "Please."

She ignores him, addresses me instead. "He's right, you know. I've had sex for money, more times than I can count. That makes me a whore. I've done a lot worse things too. Lied and stolen from the people who loved me. Used them. Left them."

"Julie," I say, forgetting.

She snaps toward me, and the gun flickers my way. When I flinch, the gun moves to Maxwell again. "Don't call me that. I'm done with Julie."

Something breaks off inside. It feels like a piece of my lungs, or like the water in the fountain is boiling and the skin is falling off my foot from the ankle down. That is all an exaggeration. What I should say is that it feels like all the parts of my body are going their separate ways. It feels like I am being abandoned by everything that has ever felt like a part of me. Maybe once you've been left by the most important person in your life, you can never be unleft again. Maybe you're destined to be abandoned even by your own guts, maybe your foot walks off with your thighbone, why not, stranger things have happened.

Like, for example, right at this instant, Gretchen, or Esther, or whoever she is, is pointing the gun at Maxwell and saying words that make no sense.

"I went back to our old place, John David. It took me forever to figure out where it was. I couldn't remember what the house looked like from the outside, but it doesn't matter, because it's not there anymore. Just an empty lot, except for the police tape, and a cross, and a bunch of flowers and teddy bears." She pauses. "I guess after you convinced me I killed Charlotte, you just bricked up the bunker and started over. God knows I've tried to do the same." Her face is already too wet from the spray in the air for me to see tears, but I can hear her gasping. "But other people care about that dead girl in there. You should see all the candles. Nobody knows who she is, but they don't just smooth it over and move on." She takes a step forward. "Neither do I. I didn't kill anyone. I'm not thirteen anymore, and you can't tell me it's my fault." She takes another step forward and levels the gun. "I won't let you."

"Help me, Anna, please help me," Maxwell says, a couple of yards to my left.

As unobtrusively as possible, I steady my foot on the bottom of the fountain.

"Stay back!" she yells.

"Okay," I say. It feels like there's a wall between us, seething with metric tons of water that I have to push through. "Gretchen."

That gets her attention. Her head jerks toward me.

"I know who you are. And I know about Cal." I'm rising slowly to my feet. "I know it was his. Maybe you love him."

She says, "Don't."

"I just want you to think about what you're doing. Think before you pull the trigger."

"I've had plenty of time to think."

"Me too," I say. I'm standing now, still in the water. I begin to slowly inch one foot forward. "I don't think you're a killer."

"I'm nothing."

But she's not nothing to me. For the past month, I've fed and clothed this girl. I've held her sobbing body on the bathroom floor. I've sat in waiting rooms praying for her to be okay, and I don't pray. I can't take my eyes off her now or the gun will go off. One foot is almost to the lip of the fountain. Every step I take toward her, her face looks younger and younger. I am fighting the wall, dragging my feet through her resistance as if it's a river running fast. "You're my daughter."

I am close enough to put a hand across her wrists. They are stone, untrembling.

"Julie."

She shakes her head at me. "Anna," she whispers with frightened eyes.

"Mom." I gently wrap my fingers around the muzzle of the gun, expecting any moment to feel a searing, scalding heat.

"I'm not who you think I am," she says, and I'm barely close enough to hear it.

"Whoever you are, I love you," I say. And then I have the gun in my hands, and I'm feeling for the safety, slowly and carefully, as I keep my eyes glued to hers. "And whatever he did, it's not worth ruining your life over."

"He kidnapped Julie." Her eyes are wide and blue. "Mom. It's him."

The words slow everything down, expanding the waterfall's roar around an eye of silence. At my feet, the duffle bag has burst open, and shiny stacks of paper are sliding out, dampening and unfolding in the mist. As the breeze flip-flops one of them over the concrete, I see that it's a church bulletin.

Somewhere inside the eye of silence, Maxwell is screaming: "She's a liar, Anna!"

But something she said a moment ago is ringing in my ears. The bunker. The police tape. *Our old place.*

"I see you know my name," I say to him, and pull the trigger.

Esther

was a virgin, an orphan girl living with her uncle Mordecai. But Esther was made for great things.

One day the King of Light called her to his palace, for he needed a new wife, and she was the most beautiful virgin in all the land. Esther was scared. She was only a girl, and she did not want to shame herself in the King of Light's palace in her dirty clothes. But she recognized the voice of God in the King of Light's call, and she knew that when the Lord calls, He must be obeyed. So she went to the king. He saw her and loved her immediately, but he refused to touch her. "Your garments are dirty," he said. "You must not defile my bed."

What happened then?

Esther wept for shame.

Esther wept for shame. But the King of Light said, "Don't cry, my child. Have faith in the Lord, and one day you will be cleaner and more beautiful than you have ever imagined." And what did she think?

She thought he must be mistaken.

Because?

Because she was unworthy.

But?

She did not question the King of Light.

Why?

Because he spoke with the Lord's voice.

"What must I do?" Esther asked.

"You must live in the palace with my concubines for a year," he said.

Esther heard the Lord's voice in the commands of the king, and she knew that the Lord must be obeyed. So she bowed her head and went to live with the concubines.

The concubines bathed and perfumed her and braided her hair. For a year they did not clothe her, so that she would learn humility. They taught her ways of pleasing the King of Light. They beat her when she spoke, but never left a scar. She never thought of running away, for she was willing to endure all for love of the King of Light, who was chosen of the Lord.

How did she feel?

She felt so alone. She felt like she was dead.

But?

But she knew that her clay was being shaped for the spirit.

So?

So she endured.

Other maidens were sent to the house of the concubines, and she saw them weep and complain, and some of them fled. But in the whole year, Esther never wept a single tear, and though other maidens were sent to the King of Light's bed, Esther knew they had not pleased him, for they returned to the house of concubines afterward and became the king's slaves.

One day, a year after she had first seen the King of Light, he called her to his bed. He was so pleased with her that he chose her to be his queen, the Queen of Light. And from that day forward she has been God's chosen.

What does she do?
She follows the Lord's commandments.
How?
She listens to her king.
Who is her king?
The King of Light.
Who is she?
The Queen of Light.
Is she happy?
This was the part she got wrong at first. Too many times. She had a round, red spot on the inside of her upper arm from the first time, purple and faded. The new ones were on the insides of her thighs.

But not today.
Is she happy?
No.
Why isn't she happy?
The Lord does not want her to be happy.
What does He want?
He wants her to be good.
And?
He wants her to be clean.
And?
He wants her to be beautiful.
She is, Esther. She is.
And then she closed her eyes. The part that always came next didn't hurt at all anymore.

During the day, he preached, and she, his first disciple, held the basket. She wore a sheet wrapped around her, all the way up and over her head at first, like a hood, until he spied a wig in a trash can out in an alleyway behind a building. From then on she wore the wig. It was a black, curly wig with a plasticky halo of frizz at the crown, and half of it was longer than the other, like something you would get at a Halloween store in a plastic bag. The underneath part of it was stiff and scratchy from being crumpled in one position for too long. It poked into her head. It smelled like garbage.

John David said it was to cover her hair, which had grown almost down to her waist and darkened from white-blond to gold. Her hair, he said, was a powerful blessing. God had wreathed her in light. She covered it when they were outdoors so that others wouldn't make her unclean by looking at it.

With the wig, she no longer had to wrap the sheet over her head. She got her peripheral vision back, and this meant she had to relearn to ignore the way people looked at them. She kept her face down most of the time anyway. She barely heard the words that John David yelled at passersby, although she could see their feet as they hurried past them. In his hands, a cardboard sign; at her feet, a basket. If she stared down at the feet hard enough, if she willed them to, sometimes a pair would stop in front of her and throw money into the basket. When this happened, John David never faltered in his harangue, but she could feel how pleased he was with her.

On the best days, they sang.

He would take the money out of the house, away from her, and come home late, smelling sweet and sour, and collapse into his bed without visiting her in the little room. This was the thing she liked most in the world: when he was pleased with her and fell asleep without touching her.

She wanted to be alone with herself, sometimes. She wanted to meditate on her sins. They were legion.

Once they went to the soup kitchen, but the soup kitchen was filled with men who looked, to her, like wild beasts in their dank overcoats and stained sweatshirts. Most of the men left her alone, but a few didn't. A man she sat next to at the long cafeteria table grinned and put his hand between her thighs. She froze. John David was gone for only a moment, and when he came back and saw the leering, stubbly face, he knew what was happening. The man knew too, and he jerked his hand away like it had been burned and picked up his tray and skittered off.

Esther was filled with shame. Later she was punished.

The food pantry, by contrast, was frequented by women with shopping carts and squalling babies who lined up outside until it opened. The food pantry was just a shed in the parking lot of a church, and it wasn't heated, and the people who ran the food pantry were as cold as the cans of peas and corn they passed over the counter. Some days it was all soggy green beans, and when they opened the cans at home and ate the beans, John David made her drink the olive-green salty water with its floating bits of bean skin afterward, because her wrists looked alarming poking out of her robes. Other times they got refried beans, her favorite, and small cans of peaches and pears in syrup. She saved the curled-up aluminum lids, tabs still attached, under her bunk, where they were—not hidden, exactly, but hers. She had no secrets from John David, and he could see everything anyway. He knew the lids were there but benevolently let her have a dark place to hide. While the bed creaked beneath them, she meditated on the accumulation of silver curves, imagined herself ice-skating along their dramatic slopes, hopping from one to the other, or even sailing in them like little boats, and then the boats turned to flower petals bobbing in a pond, and then for one horrible moment they were metal again, scratching and screeching against one another. And then all was silent and he was gone.

One morning, John David didn't come downstairs for her.

Esther waited anxiously in bed. She was not allowed to leave the bed until he bade her to every morning. She was afraid that if she got out of bed now, he would come back and beat her. Or, worse, that he would never come back at all. It might be a test.

Perhaps there was some reason he wouldn't let her out of bed. Perhaps the floor would kill her.

She thought about the lids under the bed. They would not let the floor kill her.

She listened. She waited.

Later, when she had woken and slept innumerable times, her stomach began growling too loudly for her to ignore. It was like a vacuum inside her. She got up, put her feet down without thinking, realized that the floor had not electrocuted her, thanked the lids, and went upstairs. There was only one can of creamed corn on the counter. She opened it and ate it. The sweet starchiness went straight into her bloodstream; for an instant, her brain felt oxygenated and fizzy.

"Where are you?" she dared to ask out loud, partly because she knew he wasn't there and wouldn't answer. She reached for the feeling of his omnipotence, but it shrank back, and she felt that he was not only gone, but also no longer looking at her. The thought made her cold, and she shivered.

On the third day, Esther went to the food pantry alone. It was the bravest thing she'd ever done, but she knew the way. She kept her head down as much as possible and wore a scarf tied around her wig—*A babushka*, she thought, the word surfacing from another plane of existence, as words sometimes did these days. She stood in line.

The women standing in line stared at her. One elderly woman with a babushka like hers leaned forward over a grocery cart she had pushed across the bumpy parking lot. A very tall woman with a short, tight skirt and a long blond wig snuck glances. A junkie, a twitchy woman of indeterminate age with long, greasy brown hair, stared openly for a moment, then looked abruptly away.

A woman with a weave turned away from the counter and walked down the line, humming and swinging a plastic grocery bag clanking with cans. A box of animal crackers rattled on the top of the pile. Esther could feel her approach, could feel everyone else feeling her approach. She needed food.

"Sugar, where your friend at today?" the woman asked.

Esther kept her head down.

"I said, where your friend at?" the woman repeated. "He is your friend, isn't he?"

The others pretended to mind their own business, but the twitchy woman in front of her, angry red marks glaring through the open cuffs of her oversize shirt, was the only one who seemed truly unconcerned with the conversation. Esther could feel the tension mounting. Another woman came shuffling away from the counter, cradling her cans in a windbreaker with its sleeves tied together. There was only one woman ahead of her in line now. She held her breath.

"Sugar, I'm talking to you. Who's that man used to come here with you?"

She had to say something. "He's my dad," she whispered, keeping her head down.

"Mm-hmm. Where'd he run off to?" the woman asked immediately, as if this question were on the tip of her tongue.

Another word floated up through Esther's brain and came out of her mouth in a whisper: "Laundromat." She pointed to her right, as if indicating something around the corner, just a few blocks away at most.

"Huh." The woman looked her up and down, taking in her dirty white sheet and sneakers, which were separating from their soles at the toes, and lingering on the wig. "Your mama know where you at?" the woman demanded.

Esther didn't hesitate. "She's dead," she said, eyes on the ground.

"Uhh-huh." The woman appraised her skeptically.

"Leave her alone, Janiece," said the tall blond with the teetering heels in a low, guttural voice. "It's some custody shit."

The woman named Janiece snapped back. "Mothers gotta be with their daughters. Especially when the father is *unfit*." She drew out the last word with a big pause between the syllables and looked pointedly at the blond woman's heels and ropy, exposed legs.

"Fuck you, J," said the blond, then sighed. "Besides, for all you know, her mama could be worse. I know mine was."

The argument continued, but by this time the junkie was

shuffling away from the front of the line, her baggy jeans and the pocket of her flannel shirt weighed down with cans, and Esther stepped up hurriedly. All the cans of franks were gone, but there was a can of chickpeas and another of refried beans, so she pointed to them wordlessly. The pantry worker was an older woman who was there often. With an expressionless face, she pushed an extra can of peaches across the counter. "Here," she said, "I've been saving these for you. If you ever need anything, let me know."

Esther couldn't bring herself to nod in case he was watching from somewhere close by, testing her. But she made eye contact with the woman for just a moment and tried to thank her for the peaches with a half smile. The woman named Janiece was gone when she turned back, and the tall blond woman had folded her arms and was muttering to herself. The junkie was weaving back and forth down the sidewalk. Suddenly she put her hands up toward heaven and crowed toward the sky.

Esther hurried home, tennis shoes tripping over the tangled sheet. She wondered if John David would know she'd gone out of the house, and if so, what her punishment would be. If this had been a test, she had failed. Esther thought about Abraham in the Bible tying up his son, Isaac, the raised knife flashing in the early-morning sun, like John David told her. God, too, had sacrificed His Son, Jesus. Always sons, never daughters. Were daughters too important? Or was it the opposite?

She walked into the kitchen, ate, went down the stairs at the back of the pantry, and lay down in her bed to await further instructions.

From her bed she heard the back door creak open, and two pairs of feet started moving through the kitchen upstairs. She almost didn't recognize John David's voice at first; it was pitched higher and reminded her of someone she had known a long time ago, a man with a guitar. He was talking with a second voice, and though she couldn't hear the words, the tone was friendly.

The second voice belonged to a girl with heavy footsteps. A chair screeched across the floor, accompanied by a squeal of pain and a burst of laughter. Whoever she was, she was clumsy.

"Esther!" he yelled into the pantry. "Esther, come up here!"

She glanced at the wig, the sheet draped over the foot of the bed. As if he could see her, he yelled, "We're not going outside, don't worry about your shoes and stuff. Just come up and meet someone."

Meet someone. She walked warily up the stairs in her night-shirt. A young girl, maybe a little younger than Esther, stood in the kitchen next to John David. She was short, with dyed-black hair pulled into scraggly pigtails. She wore a black T-shirt and a short black skirt that poofed out above her knees, exposing smudged white legs over faded rainbow socks.

"Esther, this is Charlotte," John David said.

She saw with a shock that he had shaved his beard. A memory fizzed through her brain of a guitar with an embroidered strap, a room with posters on the walls. His skin that had been hidden under the beard looked pinkish and bumpy, like chicken skin; his mouth looked small and thin-lipped; there was a tiny cut above his Adam's apple.

Charlotte rhymes with *harlot*. Esther kept her eyes on the floor, but she was aware that Charlotte was staring at her and became suddenly self-conscious about her appearance: ratty nightshirt over jeans he'd stolen from a dumpster, dirty, naked feet sticking out from the frayed cuffs. She wondered if the nightshirt smelled bad. It had never been washed.

"Charlotte, Esther's my niece. She's been crashing here for a little while." There was that voice again, the new-old John David who reminded her of when she was someone else, a long time ago. He turned and addressed himself to Esther in that kind, friendly voice and it made her want to cover her ears and sing until she couldn't hear it anymore. But she knew better. "Esther, can Charlotte use your computer to check her e-mail? She's a long way from home, and I know she would really appreciate it."

Esther didn't have a computer. She knew what was required of her, though. She nodded without looking up.

"Great. I'll just take her down and get her set up in your room. Do you mind hanging out up here for a few minutes?"

Esther nodded acquiescence and stepped away from the door. As they passed her, Charlotte said, "Thanks." Esther looked up at her quickly, caught a glimpse of brown eyes with a shimmer of green or gold in their depths. She put a hand out to grab Charlotte's arm.

But Charlotte had seen the narrow door in the back of the pantry by then. "Whoa, is this like a secret passage or something?" she said.

"Bomb shelter," John David said, hovering behind her shoulder.

"No way!"

"This house belonged to my grandparents," he said. "My grandfather was a fighter pilot in the Pacific. He was scouted for NASA in '61. They could have moved out to a big house in Clear Lake. But my grandmother believed the Cold War would end in a nuclear holocaust. She believed Jesus would scourge the earth." His voice sounded far away. "She convinced him to build an underground bunker here."

"That is trippy," Charlotte said appreciatively.

It was trippy. Esther had never heard any of it. Thinking about John David's grandparents made him seem suddenly very ordinary.

"You can't have a basement at sea level, but with about ten tons of concrete, you can have a fallout shelter."

The words tumbled through her head, a history lesson, casually delivered, as if the man speaking weren't outside of history, weren't divine. As if he were just a man living in a house.

"Your niece is so lucky. This is the coolest bedroom ever." Charlotte's voice receded down the staircase with her footsteps. As the two of them vanished into blackness, Esther understood for the first time what was going to happen.

She understood for the first time that it had happened to her.

She curled up on the sofa and put her hands over her ears, but she still heard it. No words, just Charlotte's voice getting higher and shriller, and then a thump and another thump, something dropped on the concrete basement floor with a clatter, muffled yells, the sound of shoes sliding against the floor as if scrambling for purchase. A short silence. Something heavy being dragged. And then a sort of stuttering bark she recognized, after a moment, as the sound of duct tape being ripped off a roll.

John David appeared at the top of the stairs, looking weary, and dropped a bundle of clothes on the pantry floor. He filled a plastic bucket with water at the kitchen sink and handed it to Esther. "Bathe her," he said.

The concubines bathed and perfumed her and braided her hair.

The sponge was a new blue kitchen sponge, soft on one side and scratchy on the other. The bucket was unexpectedly heavy and swung a little as she took it, splashing a bit of water over the edge onto his shoes.

He walked to the sofa to lie down. The exercise had exhausted him, drained him of the emotional electricity that usually seemed to vibrate off him in waves. Lying with his eyes closed, he looked smaller. She took a step toward him, but he drew his elbow up over his eyes and turned toward the sofa back. In a moment he was snoring.

She wondered what he was doing up here all those times while she trembled in her room downstairs. Napping on the sofa? Fixing himself a sandwich? These thoughts filled her with dread. She turned away and walked to the pantry door. She stepped over the pile of clothes, pulled this way and that like a cast-aside doll. The black T-shirt lay on top, inside out and twisted double, so that the picture on the front was only a blocky outline puckering the fabric, the letters on the back backward and illegible. She started down the stairs.

Before she could see Charlotte, she smelled her; she'd peed herself. Then her eyes adjusted, and gradually a glimmer of whiteness grew and spread into the shape of a torso. Charlotte lay naked on the floor. Her hands were duct-taped behind her back, her shins duct-taped solidly together in a silver column, so that in the dim light it looked as if her legs had been cut off below the knees, her white feet lying nearby like a pair of sneakers. A piece of duct tape was pressed over the bottom half of her small round face, a little bump showing where the lip ring was. Her eyes were closed.

The concubines bathed and perfumed her and braided her hair.

Esther knelt down, her knees making cold contact with the concrete. She put the bucket and the sponge on the floor beside her and waited.

This was too much. She would go back upstairs, tell John David she couldn't do it.

Esther inched toward the body on her knees, trying not to look, feeling hot tears coming to her eyes. She put out a hand, moving closer and closer to where angry pink circles blotched the soft white belly in clusters of four, like fingertips, over her ribs, then pulling back. She took up the sponge and dipped it in the water, which had started out lukewarm but was nearly cool by now. Careful to keep the rough side of the sponge facing away from Charlotte, she very gently applied one wet, soft corner to the bruises that stained the white expanse of stomach, as if the water could wash them away.

The girl's eyes flew open.

Esther started backward with a shriek.

Charlotte, unable to scream, moaned into the tape and raised her head only to shake it wildly back and forth, strands of her too-black hair coming out of her pigtails and floating in front of eyes that were all white. She rolled onto one shoulder and jackknifed her bound legs back and forth until she managed to kick Esther hard on the side of her knee.

Esther gasped and put a hand to her leg. But the impact of the kick overbalanced Charlotte and she fell back and hit her head on the concrete. Then she lay still.

Esther picked up the sponge, which had landed close to her feet in the scuffle. "I'm just going to give you a bath," she reassured Charlotte. "It won't hurt."

The concubines bathed and perfumed her and braided her hair.

"I have to bathe you," she said. "You have to be made clean."

The girl began moving her legs again, but slowly this time, as if tired out by her initial fury, bracing her feet against the floor to push herself around, leaving her head limp. Still flat on the ground, she rotated clockwise by inches, like a fat white goldfish in a koi pond. Every minute or two, she would stop and lie still for a moment. Then she would start again. When she was facing away from Esther, she stopped and lay completely still.

Esther got up and walked around to Charlotte's other side so she could see her face, wondering if Charlotte would begin inching around to escape her again. But Charlotte appeared to be looking at something.

Esther got down on her knees and put her head close to where Charlotte's head was and looked. And she saw them. The lids, curled up on the floor like they were hiding under the bed.

No, like trash.

They smelled like trash. The whole room did. It reeked with a faint sickly-sweetness that Esther had never noticed before. She'd been sleeping on a bed of garbage. Her stomach turned. She looked around at the tiny, windowless room. Not a basement. You can't have basements at sea level. A prison. A torture chamber. The bed covered with its tattered blanket. Her whole world, so small.

When she looked back at Charlotte again, she knew that Charlotte didn't belong here. She'd never submit to this atmosphere. She would disrupt everything, had disrupted everything already. She had twisted the room inside out, changed it somehow, like the inside-out T-shirt. Esther could almost read a message coming through the thin fabric of her reality, but the letters were backward and didn't make sense. She had to straighten everything out.

She had to get rid of Charlotte, and she knew how. It would be a sin, but then, John David had told her often enough she was a sinner.

Esther crept up the stairs. John David lay on the sofa, unmoving, and she was struck by how peaceful he looked. With his newly shaven face and without his towering height above her, he looked more like a boy than a man. There, as she'd remembered, was the tiny red bump on his Adam's apple where he'd cut himself shaving.

He'd *cut* himself.

There was a razor in the house.

The most logical place to look was the bathroom attached to John David's bedroom, but she had never gone in there. All of the bedrooms were off-limits, so that even stepping into the dark, doglegged hallway gave her a shiver of discomfort. She had seen only the kitchen and the bunker, though she was allowed to use the half-bathroom up here instead of the tiny metal toilet in the bunker, which required buckets of water to operate. When she peered into the bedrooms at the end of the hall, she understood for the first time that it was an ordinary house, even comfortable. The beds were covered with bedspreads and sheets. There were lamps, teal carpets, and wallpaper—one room covered in flowers, one pebbled with gold. On the nightstand in the unused bedroom stood a bronze deer and a box of tissues with a knit cozy over it and a dust ruffle sewed to the bottom. The upper reaches of the single white tissue were coated with dust, and a few severed threads of cobweb floated in the still air.

John David's bedroom looked much the same. She had pictured him on a pallet of some kind, but he slept on a king-size bed under a painting of a landscape, somewhere dry with mountains, as different from Houston as she could imagine.

The bathroom cabinets still held grandparent clutter: Nearly empty bottles with varying degrees of stickiness settled around their bottom edges. Small, beaked vials of eardrops and eyedrops. Silver cards bubbled with fading pills. Plastic pill cases marked with the days of the week. Nothing useful.

As she turned to go, she spotted one more thing: a trash can behind the door. She could just see, under a wad of tissues and curled-up dental floss, a wicked glint.

She looked down at Charlotte, whose eyes wobbled with tears, her penciled eyebrows tilting upward at the middle, chin dimpled beneath the duct tape. Esther put a finger to her lips. "Shhh," she warned.

Then she ripped off the duct tape.

They stared at each other. Charlotte's eyes were so big that for a moment, the rest of her face disappeared, and Esther felt like she was looking into a mirror, staring into her own eyes, and the rest of her became disconnected. Esther took a bundle of used Kleenex out of her pocket and began unwrapping it cautiously until she felt the razor blade in her hands: a small, wicked thing. A sin.

She showed Charlotte the blade and said, "Hold still." The duct tape around Charlotte's wrists was accordioned into thick, sweat-stiffened pleats. Sawing at the tape, she felt all the girl's resistance—to John David, to the hole they were in, even to her. The tension was hot in Charlotte's wrists. Charlotte had fought John David. She would fight anyone, and she'd never stop fighting.

Julie, that worthless whore, had lain down without a struggle.

The names popping into Esther's head were tumbling over one another, confusing her. Every tug of the blade through the duct tape freed her a little more—freed whom, though? Charlotte? Esther? Or the other girl? She kept cutting, hearing the soft protesting squeak of the tape against the absurdly small blade as she worked it patiently back and forth, the heavy tape grabbing and twisting at the tiny blade so that she had to stop and unstick it from time to time with a small smacking noise. After an eternity, the last fibers on one side of the thick sleeve of duct tape gave. Charlotte wrenched away from her, twisting her arms apart so that the skin stretched white and red until one of them pried itself free. Her arms were surprisingly strong for being so short and thin, but Esther knew they must be sore from being taped behind her back.

Charlotte was the bravest, strongest girl she had ever seen. Tears came to Esther's eyes, and she started wriggling out of her nightshirt, keeping it right-side out as she shrugged it off over her head.

"Here," she said.

Charlotte took the warm shirt right away and slipped into it without so much as glancing at Esther. Then she held out her hand for the razor and started hacking at the tape on her shins. Esther grabbed the sheet off the foot of the bed and wrapped it around her torso and shoulders, tucked it under her arms. She'd worn a sheet many times before.

"Give me a hand, would you? Get this off," Charlotte said, and Esther started peeling the damp swaths of slashed tape away from her calves while Charlotte kept working on the tape with the razor. "Okay," she said. "I'm getting the fuck out of here. You're going to help me, or I'll cut you with this." She held up the razor blade. "Got it?"

Esther nodded with a smile. She knew Charlotte wouldn't really hurt her.

"What's your name?" Charlotte asked.

"Esther."

"Is that your real name?"

Esther thought about that, but Charlotte was already back to working on her knees. "That guy is a sick fuck," Charlotte said. "Come on, tell me your real name."

"My name is Esther."

"Like hell it is," Charlotte said, and with a snap, she jerked the blade through the last strand of duct tape. As she clawed the tape away from her legs and stood up, the blade dropped to the floor. The barest nudge from Charlotte's foot sent it skittering away as lightly as a leaf. It stopped and spun in place on an uneven bit of concrete for a moment before coming to rest. "Come on. Look, you helped me. You have guts. We're going to get out of here. Now, what's your name?"

Julie started to speak, but Charlotte wasn't looking at her anymore. She was looking at something right behind her and opening her mouth.

15

The visitation room at the Harris County Jail is a hellish, echoing cacophony; there are no handsets to use to communicate through the Plexiglas windows, and the speakers embedded in them barely work, so dozens of visitors, many with children in tow, are reduced to screaming through the glass. After Tom's first visit, I tell him not to come back, and please, for the love of God, not to let Julie come either.

Instead, I call Jane. Once a day, in the morning, I dial her cell phone using an insanely expensive third-party account and listen to her talk until my fifteen minutes is up and the call auto-terminates. She sounds remarkably normal—tells me about her summer makeup classes, complains about finishing her papers, contemplates joining a kickball league. It's like my transgression has opened a floodgate in her, and Jane is bubbling over with the details she'd wanted me to work so hard for before. They are details of a life that turns out to be gloriously mundane, only superficially rebellious, on the level of hair dye. Having to define herself in relation to someone who wasn't there and who was therefore always perfect was existentially confusing for Jane. Now, with an actual person to compare herself to, she doesn't seem to need the big gestures anymore. From what I can tell, she is flourishing.

It's a little exhausting to listen to, but she repays my years of neglect by not asking me any questions about myself, not even a *How are you?*, which I appreciate. She doesn't ask about Julie either, but Tom says she and Julie e-mail regularly.

("Of course I knew it was her," Jane said when I finally got up the courage to ask, speaking in a tone that suggested I was not a bad mother, just stupid. When I reminded her she was the one who told me Julie was lying about the cell phone, she said, "I don't see what difference that makes. I lie all the time, but it's still me.")

A tiny, lonely part of me is angry that Jane hasn't offered to come home, but long days of contemplation have convinced me that she's waiting for me to ask, and until I stop being afraid she'll say no, we're at an impasse.

In the meantime, I can't say I don't enjoy living vicariously through Jane, a little bit. How exciting to believe in your own ability to defy the world's expectations of you even as you fulfill them, one cliché after another. I have spent my own life looking to my left and right and finding only the well-worn tracks of my own thoughts and behavior hemming me in. Maybe it's a side effect of studying the Romantics, those fetishists of originality who unwittingly invented two centuries' worth of platitudes; maybe that's why I can't seem to respond normally to those who love me and whom I love. But I try, with Jane. I listen, I imagine the thwack of a wet kickball against a shoe on the quad, and at the end of every phone call, I feel the dingy, fluorescent-lit jail cell settle a little heavier on my shoulders.

There were witnesses—a teenage couple trudging up the lawn to make out by the glowing waterfall that night. The young man has a criminal record that will keep him off the stand, but the young woman will testify that, although she couldn't see Julie and me from where she was, the victim was clearly visible in the fountain lights, holding up his hands and pleading for his life. She heard a shot and saw him sink into the water, but she didn't make the 911 call.

I did that.

As luck would have it, the judge assigned to our high-profile case is a former district attorney, notorious for following her cases up the chain of appeals, attaching herself to the prosecution, and even submitting testimony condemning defendants she's already ruled against. She's also vocal about her relationship with Christ, and, if I had to guess, I'd say Chuck Maxwell donated to her campaign. The thought of a godless academic rotting away in the county jail, a facility well known for abuses, perhaps getting softened up for a plea bargain at the hands of her cellmates, must appeal to Judge Crofford as much as it does to the prosecution, who file motion after motion to delay my bond hearing, using every excuse from the live-stream footage of Julie whispering in Maxwell's ear to the inflamed public sentiment over this appalling attack on a pillar of the community.

It's true that jail is dirty, overcrowded, humiliating, and excruciatingly boring—you can't get phone calls, incoming letters are limited in length and heavily censored, and the official process for getting a single book approved and ordered from the publisher can take months. I'd pay a lot of money for something to read to take my mind off my dismal surroundings. But if Crofford expects the inmates to harass me, she's wrong. The women leave me alone. Word must have spread pretty quickly among them that I shot the man who kidnapped and raped my daughter.

That's the rumor they've heard anyway. Proving that's what happened is much harder, of course, and my self-defense claim rests on it. At the police station I begged them to check his DNA against the bunker-house crime scene in River Oaks, and I used my one phone call to leave a message for Alex Mercado. I have to admit that although I can see the resemblance in the shape of Maxwell's low brows and hooded blue eyes, the bearded, square-jawed billboard minister doesn't otherwise bear much resemblance to ten-year-old Jane's police-artist sketch of a skinny, ponytailed guy in a hoodie.

And then there's what Maxwell is saying: that Julie and I were blackmailing him together.

Yes, Maxwell is very much alive. Not for lack of my trying. My shot hit him low on the shoulder, and he went down on his back into the shallow water before I saw the bullet wouldn't kill him. That's for the best, because if I had seen right away, I would no doubt have kept on shooting until there were no bullets left. I'm glad I didn't, and it's not because I feel Maxwell's death would have been such a great loss to the world; it's not even that I prefer to see him humiliated and exposed and put away for life rather than dead. It's just that if he'd died as a result of my shooting him, prosecutors might be pushing for a capital murder charge right now—in Texas, even an accidental death that occurs during the commission of a felony can be punished with the death penalty, and blackmail is a felony. When I pulled the trigger, the preservation of my own life was not high on my priority list.

But everything's different now, because I have my daughter back.

I wish I could say it happened in a flash, that standing there at the Water Wall with a gun pointed at Chuck Maxwell, I could suddenly see thirteen-year-old Julie in twenty-one-year-old Julie's face, like a Magic Eye poster you've been staring at for weeks that suddenly leaps into focus. But that wouldn't be right, because I always saw her there, from the very beginning, from the moment she appeared on our doorstep. I knew; I just didn't *believe*. Her lies and evasions made doubting easier, gave me something concrete to focus on. My new version of Julie was like the optical illusion of the candlestick-shaped negative space between two profiles. Imagine two faces—Julie then and Julie now—staring at each other in profile across a gash of grief. All this time I've been seeing only the ugly shape of what's between them. The negative space of trauma.

I haven't talked to Julie since I was arrested, so I still don't know what's in that black hole, but I'm ready to accept what's on either side of it. Julie, before; Julie, after.

In the pretrial hearing, the prosecutors ask to have the trial date pushed back. At first I think it's more intimidation—keep me stewing longer—but then I hear the words "River Oaks murder victim," and I know Alex Mercado must have gotten my phone message. The lead attorney on my case asks again for bail while the police investigate a link between Maxwell, Julie, and Charlotte Willard, a thirteen-year-old girl who disappeared from her home just across the Louisiana border in Beauregard Parish about six months after Julie did. It's Charlotte Willard whose DNA they eventually matched to the remains in the bomb shelter, and it was Maxwell's grandmother who originally owned the house; I imagine Alex has left me messages to that effect on my phone, but I'll have to wait to check them. I remember what Julie called the house: *our old place*. Alex was wrong about Julie being dead, but he wasn't wrong about everything. He just had the girls mixed up—who'd escaped and who was dead. It could have gone either way, really. I think of the awful photograph again, and the horror that befell this girl who is not my daughter suffocates me. I cry for her mother and wish once more my shot had killed him.

The judge denies bail again, but my attorney looks hopeful. In the hallway, she tells me of an anonymous blog post whose writer claims to have been sexually molested by Maxwell at the Gate, her mother allegedly ejected from church membership for bringing a complaint. A former member of Springshire Methodist, this one named, alleges that Maxwell was fired from a briefly held leadership position in the youth group nine years ago after abusing her daughter. Both women were immediately served with cease-and-desist orders from the Gate's attorneys.

But by this time, other people's daughters have started coming forward.

As an inmate at Harris County Jail, I can't receive phone calls, uncensored letters, or unapproved books, but I have unlimited access to legal documents related to my upcoming trial. At our next meeting, my attorney hands me a fat folder. "A transcript from the deposition," she says. "I think you should read this, Anna."

Any distraction is welcome, and I tell her so.

She sighs. "What's in there—I want to warn you, it's not an easy read."

Thumbing through what look to be hundreds of pages in Q-and-A format, I see one name after another highlighted in yellow. I feel a surge of horror. "Are these all Maxwell's victims?"

"No," she says. "Just one."

Julie

still feels like someone else.

She's me. I'm her. I don't mean to say I don't know that.

Maybe I'm just embarrassed. Julie seems like such an idiot to me now. She used to have an imaginary friend when she was very young. It was a horse from a book, I don't even remember which one. A white horse with a silver mane. When she rode the bus in elementary school, she used to look out the window and imagine the horse galloping alongside the bus. She'd make little motions under her backpack like she was feeding him sugar. It was more than a fantasy; she could almost see him.

I could almost see him. It was me. I have to tell Julie's story as if it were my own. For her sake, I'm going to try.

I must have been about five when I asked my mom who God was. It's one of Julie's earliest memories. *My* earliest memories.

She laughed and said, "Just some guy." When I asked where he lived, she said, "Probably San Diego." Then she told me to go ask Dad.

I did, but I don't remember what he said. I liked the idea of God living in San Diego. That's where Grandma and Grandpa retired to—which I guess was the joke, how much better it was than Houston. At the time, I knew there was a joke somewhere in her answer, but I didn't understand where. I knew she was laughing, but I thought she was laughing at me.

Anyway, that summer—or maybe this happened before, I'm not really sure—we actually went to San Diego to visit Grandma and Grandpa. They had these special buckets shaped like sand castles, so if you packed them with wet sand and turned them over, they looked like towers, with tooth-shaped ridges around the top and dents on the sides for windows. I remember I got sand stuck in my eye trying to look in through the pretend windows, and it hurt really bad. Dad helped me rinse the grit out, and after I was done crying, he said, "It's more fun anyway to just imagine what's inside." So I did. By the time Jane put her fist in one of the towers and the whole castle crumbled to the beach, I didn't mind. I had already built a new one in my mind, and it was better, because nobody could destroy it.

I'm not saying that these things had anything to do with what happened later on. I'm just bringing them up to say Julie had a history of belief. She wanted to believe there was an inside to the castle, even though she'd packed it full of wet sand herself. She wanted to believe God was a beautiful man who lived with her beautiful grandparents on a beautiful beach, and maybe someday they could all live together inside that beautiful imaginary castle.

On the same trip, Dad told me glass was made out of melted sand. How was God any harder to believe than that?

I keep trying to find the *before*. But once something like that happens to you, there is no *before* anymore. It takes the before away. And if there's no before, then there's no order I can tell it in that makes any sense, and no reason to choose one particular place over any other.

I'd start with the shame, but everything gets there eventually. So, no hurry, I guess.

I met Charlie in Sunday school the summer after the seventh grade, when I went to church with Candyce.

I don't know if my parents would even remember Candyce. She always wore these big bows in her hair that her mom made with a hot-glue gun to match her outfits. Julie was a little jealous of them. I was jealous, I mean. I can't imagine caring about that, but Julie did. Candyce's mom bought her pretty clothes and made pretty bows to go with them. My mom just sort of looked at me when I wore pretty clothes, her lips pressed together. She's very serious; she's a professor.

Anyway, I went to Sunday school for the first time with Candyce, and there he was—not Chuck Maxwell from the article I found all those years later, not even John David yet, just Charlie, a skinny guy with a guitar leading the class in a half hour of songs. I liked school fine, but this was different. There was one kid at school who was, I don't know what you're supposed to call it, but in seventh grade they said "retarded" and threw French fries at him in the cafeteria. His name was Jason. In Sunday school Jason sat with the cool kids in the front row, and nobody bothered him, not even the boys. He looked so happy, singing along and doing the arm motions that went with the songs. It was almost like he had friends. Charlie made everyone feel that way.

The rest of church was confusing to me. The hallways were hung with felt banners showing scenes from the Bible: women putting babies in baskets and floating them down the river, women carrying water jugs on their heads, women washing Jesus's feet with their hair. But the sermons were always about traffic or primetime television or an article in *Newsweek,* which didn't seem to have anything to do with the banners and the hymns and the Bible readings. Candyce and I would tune out and write each other notes on the church bulletins using the golf pencils in the backs of the pews, make little cartoons with speech bubbles. Her parents didn't care as long as we stayed quiet.

After the service, Candyce and I would link arms and walk down to the Sunday school room, which had sofas and a big-screen TV and posters on the wall that looked like graffiti but with Bible verses. There was no sermon in Sunday school, just goofy songs, and then what Charlie called "real talk," where we sat on the floor in a circle.

Sometimes it would start with a Bible verse, but pretty soon kids would begin talking about their problems. A lot of the problems were about girls: what they wore, who they danced with, whether they were godly and how godly were they and how much did it matter. One week they spent the whole time debating if it was okay for a girl to lie and say she liked her friend's outfit if she actually hated it. I remember one guy in the eighth grade wanted to ask a Jewish girl out, and they talked for an hour about whether or not Jews were going to hell and, if they were, whether it was their responsibility to share Jesus's message with them. Some kids were concerned about the silver James Avery crosses that were popular, whether girls should be wearing them if they were wearing them only for looks.

I watched from the sidelines. In our house, my mom was all-knowing, and my dad could answer any question in a way I understood. But it turned out there were questions I didn't even know needed asking, a whole world happening in another dimension, and my parents didn't seem to know anything about it. It turned out there were battles being fought all around me, that every word and action had a deeper meaning, and even the jewelry that a person wore could be related to something called salvation.

Charlie didn't egg them on; he just sat on the floor and listened, nodding when the arguments got more heated. Then, toward the end of the hour, he'd finally start talking, and everybody would shut up. He'd explain that God was watching us, and that He loved us more than we could possibly love ourselves, and that all we had to do was try to be worthy of that love. Jesus, he said, had become a man so He could understand what it was like. He understood how hard it was not to sin, and He paid the ultimate price so we wouldn't have to. Class dismissed.

In other words, Charlie didn't give us any answers at all.

Candyce was happy to supply the answers that Charlie wouldn't. "No offense," she said one day while we were walking down the hall after service, "but the Bible says your parents are going to hell."

That was the day I cried in Sunday school. I was so embarrassed I couldn't even speak when Charlie asked if I wanted to stay afterward and talk. But I nodded: *Yes.*

• • •

There's no before anymore. Everything in my memory is colored by what happened, like one of those old photographs where the tints are all weird. His offer to drive me home after Candyce rolled her eyes and said her parents were waiting in the breezeway, so could I please hurry up? His smile when he said Candyce and I shouldn't tell our parents or anyone else he was driving me home, because there was a lot of insurance paperwork he'd have to fill out first. His assurance, when Candyce left the room, that he was willing to risk it—because I was special.

I mean, he didn't come out and say that, but he implied it. I was special. Me, Julie, unchurched child of unchurched parents. Not even Easter-and-Christmas parents but never-ever parents.

When Charlie and I sat together in his office with the door cracked open, and I asked how God could damn my parents and Jane to hell, he told me that only God could judge, and anyone who said anyone else was going to hell was trying to do God's job. And that wasn't right.

"But not believing in God isn't right either," I said. "The Bible says you have to believe in Jesus."

"The Bible also says it's easier for a camel to get through the eye of a needle than for a rich man to go to heaven," he said with a smirk. I wasn't sure whether we were rich or not, but I knew for certain Candyce was; I'd slept over at her house enough times.

Then he said the important thing wasn't whether anyone else was damned but whether you yourself were saved. He said I was very brave to come to church on my own. He said I had the soul of a seeker.

My whole life, ever since I could remember, I'd always hated the thought that no one could ever know what anyone else was feeling or thinking. The fact that no one could ever be inside my head with me seemed like the loneliest thing in the world. I wanted so bad for there to be something that could make those boundaries just disappear. Something so big it was like air, a magic flowing across the planet, connecting everyone and everything.

When Charlie spoke to me, I saw the boundaries disappearing. Now I see a careful distance narrowing.

Charlie drove me home from church three times. Each time he dropped me off in the parking lot at the CVS at Kirkwood, and I'd buy something cheap—candy or a magazine—so that when I walked the four blocks home, I'd have an explanation for why Candyce's parents had dropped me off there. I had the answer all worked out, but my mom never asked. It was spring, and she was usually doing something in the yard when I got home with my plastic CVS bag. I guess she never thought about how uncomfortable it was to walk four blocks in church flats.

In the parking lot of the CVS, my conversations with Charlie went deeper than the ones we had in his little cubby in the church office, where the church secretary kept barging in to use the copier. In the CVS parking lot, Charlie told me that he wasn't sure he even believed in hell. He told me everybody wants a rule book, that people want an instruction manual to life. They want to be told exactly what to do. But Jesus came to destroy all that. Jesus came to erase the laws that were written on the stone tablets and write them on our hearts instead. He told me Jesus wants us to *feel* what's right, inside, when we pray to Him. "God sent Jesus as a man," he said. "To teach us how to be men."

His hand rested on the back of my seat, and I could smell that he used some kind of prickly aftershave and see that he had blue eyes and that his blond eyelashes were longer than I'd thought.

"Never forget this," he told me, and I haven't. "People will always let you down. Candyce will let you down. Your parents will let you down. *I* will let you down. Only God will always be there for you."

I nodded, staring into his eyes. His thumb was touching my shoulder, just a little. He took his hand off the seat back, letting out his breath.

I'd been holding mine too.

Back in my bedroom, I changed out of church clothes, but instead of going downstairs, I crept into bed and pulled the covers over my head.

God sent Jesus as a man to teach us how to be men.

Who had God sent to teach me how to be a woman? Was it Charlie?

When I went back to Sunday school the next week, he was gone.

One of the church elders, a woman in her fifties, ran the Sunday school class. She told us that for personal reasons, Charlie had had to resign. It was unlikely he'd be able to return to the position, she said. They were already beginning the search for a new youth pastor, and in the meantime, fellowship would be suspended and Sunday school would be taught by members of the Christian Education committee.

"Can we say goodbye?" someone asked.

"I'll get a card," Candyce said. "We can all sign it."

"That would be very nice," the elder said. "Now, get out your Bibles and turn to First Corinthians, chapter thirteen."

Even I knew that verse. It was printed on the church bulletins and embroidered on some of the tapestries in the halls. But this time, the words seemed to be pointed straight at me: *If I have a faith that can move mountains, but have not love, I am nothing.*

Charlie had said he would let me down. And he was right.

With Charlie gone, church got very boring, and I stopped sleeping over at Candyce's house. At school, I went out for the track team and made it. I was not a good speed runner, but I could run distances, and I could propel myself into the air and sail over the hurdles with my legs in front of me. Looking around at the girls I'd be training with over the summer, all of us standing on the dusty track, our skinny legs sticking out of nylon shorts, I knew I didn't need Candyce or church or Charlie anymore. In eighth grade, I would have friends, real girlfriends who would show me how to brush my hair, put on makeup, and talk to boys. The girls on the track team had sleepovers and away meets; they painted racing stripes and Nike swooshes on one another's faces, finished each other's sentences. They were a tribe. When I was in eighth grade, my life would finally begin.

A few months later, I got the chat invitation.

His name was John David. There was no picture, just an outline of a head with a question mark inside it. According to his Facebook page, he was sixteen, and he had zero friends on his profile.

I tried to think of all the people I knew who went to high school. My friend Angela had an older brother named John; I'd had a crush on him once. Or maybe John David was somebody I knew from school who was just lying about his age, or some mean girls playing a trick on me. Maybe I was going to get reeled in with some phony "secret admirer" plot, and then they would take screenshots and post them for the whole school to see. Something like that had happened to a girl I barely knew, Rebecca. There were other things that had happened to Rebecca too. I unfriended her on Facebook so I didn't have to see them.

I refreshed the screen, half expecting to see the profile's friends shoot up to the hundreds, so that I'd know he was fake, a bot, an empty outline. Nothing happened, except the question mark took a little longer to load the second time. He couldn't contact me until I had accepted his offer, so I clicked on the question mark and a chat box popped up.

Hi. Who are you? I typed. I always spelled out words and added punctuation and capitals, even in chats with friends. I was reading *The Diary of Anne Frank* and couldn't stand how ugly most of my and my friends' writing looked in comparison with those sentences from a girl our age.

The chat box was blank for a few minutes. Then it started blinking as the person on the other end typed. The other person was not into spelling things correctly or capitalizing.

i don't want to give my real name

Do I know you? I wrote back.

There was a long delay while he typed, long enough to make me think he was typing from a phone.

we had amazing conversations together

I started to type another question, and then the chat box blinked again:

soul of a seeker

A wave of heat went up my body, starting from my toes and rushing up to my face until it was burning.

I typed, *Charlie?* but stopped myself from pressing the Enter key just in time and deleted it.

julie? u there?

I let out my breath slowly and typed: *I think I know who you are. You gave me a ride home a few times.* That sounded like I could be talking to a sixteen-year-old. I wondered how old he really was.

yes

Where are you now? You left without saying goodbye.

i had my reasons. u dont know my side of things

Side? I frowned and typed again: *Where are you now?*

i can't see you right now or tell u where i am. i have reasons. u were always smarter than the others. wanted to get back in touch.

It's nice to hear from you, I said, because I didn't know what else to say.

There was another pause.

god is with u all the time. i can see HIM all around u like a halo

My scalp prickled and I could feel his eyes on me suddenly, almost like I'd felt them on our last car ride home together. I wondered how far away he was.

Why did you leave? You left without saying goodbye.

i promise ill tell u the whole story soon but please for now just talk to me. i'm lonely

I tried to picture him in front of a computer screen or hunched over a phone somewhere, but I couldn't. I typed out the words *I miss you,* but then I backed the cursor up over them until they were gone and typed *Everyone misses you* instead.

He responded, *i miss u too,* just as if he could hear the real sentence in my head. *Something really important has happened to me since we talked. i'm going to tell u everything. god has a plan for me and for u too*

This time he didn't have to tell me not to tell my parents. He knew I wouldn't, and I knew he knew, and although the word *God* sent the old thrill spiking through me, it was Charlie's faith in me and the greatness of his need that caught the lightning-flash and amplified it, expanded it, made my entire body warm.

Go on, I wrote.

I saw the face of god, julie. he wants something from me. From you too.

From me? I could only retype the words.

from all of us, he wrote, after a long time.

The Plan felt like a special project we were working on together, or a game. Whenever I was chatting with Charlie—or John David, as I began to think of him—I existed in another dimension. In the beginning, I guarded the screen—my desktop monitor was visible from the doorway, and I jumped every time the floorboards creaked in the hall outside. But then I began to feel comfortable existing in both worlds at once: the ordinary world, which consisted of me eating dinner and finishing my homework and going to track meets after school, and the world of the Plan.

In the ordinary world, I was Julie, maker of As, runner of hurdle races. My grades stayed high, and I didn't drop my after-school activities. That was part of the Plan: No dramatic behavior changes. I worked hard to keep my weight from dropping too, but the pounds seemed to be falling off no matter how much of my dad's lasagna I ate. My mom blamed track and gave me extra helpings at every meal, but I knew it was the Plan working in me, preparing me for something John David called "privations to come."

In the ordinary world, I was ordinary Julie, but in the Plan, I was radiant. He told me that my loveliness was like a bruise in the exact center of a blinding light, like a sunspot. The fire of God shone around me. Even though we never met in person, never video-chatted—too dangerous, he said—I knew he could see me. He said he saw me when he closed his eyes and prayed; he said he saw me standing in front of the sun with it shining all around me. And there were things he seemed to know about me that he could not possibly have gotten from the Internet. He knew, for instance, when I started shaving my legs. I had to, for track; even though my leg hair was barely there, just a glimmer in the sunlight, really, the other girls would have thought I was strange if I didn't shave. He didn't like the thought of me taking a blade to my legs. He told me that afterward, I wouldn't need to do things like that. Things to appease the world.

I didn't know if he was close enough to be literally watching me or whether he was finding out some other way. I didn't want to know. Instead, I started pretending he could see me all the time so I could wear his gaze like a secret under my clothes, against my skin. It made Ordinary Julie a more exciting role, somehow. I performed my ordinariness for him: putting on lip gloss in the bathroom, giggling with other girls, reading *To Kill a Mockingbird* with my feet propped up on the ottoman, helping Mom with the dishes after supper, brushing my hair, writing in my diary—all for him. I even made up some diary entries that were totally ordinary, just listing what I did during the day, things Ordinary Julie did. I pretended to have a crush on this guy at school, Aaron. I felt sure Charlie knew how well I was performing my role, and I began to slip in little hints and references that only he would understand. I drew sheep on my binder and imagined him laughing at the joke. At the pep rally I got a sun painted on my cheek so he'd see it and understand the message. No matter how much I looked like a teenage girl to the others, he was out there somewhere, and as long as he was watching, I was divine.

The only time the two worlds touched each other was under the covers at night. Then I would try to whisper "Jesus," and "John David" would come out instead. Once I dreamed I was falling, flying apart, breaking into a million pieces, becoming the darkness at the center of the light. I clenched my teeth and waited for it to be over. When I opened my eyes, there were red stars.

That's when I realized I'd been in love with Charlie. A wave of shame rushed over me. It was stupid, the whole thing; a crush too embarrassing even to think about on someone who could never think of me that way, because I was a stupid little kid.

Or at least, that's how it had been—then. But I wasn't a kid anymore. The image of Charlie, faded now, seemed smaller than it had before. It had been months since I'd even seen his face. I did not have a schoolgirl crush any longer, because I wasn't a schoolgirl; that was Ordinary Julie. I was divine.

In our chats, the outline of a head and shoulders in the profile window reminded me of a blue shadow cast on the sidewalk by someone you can't see. The shadow was John David, and the everyday, ordinary Charlie who cast the shadow was no more important than the ordinary, everyday Julie. The embarrassing feelings were all for Charlie. John David was different. He was part of the light, surrounded by light. Not a shadow, but a real person standing directly in front of the sun, a person whose shape you can barely make out when you squint, hidden in blinding brightness. Tears came to my eyes, and there was a warmth in my chest, burning in my heart. I closed my eyes and saw the form of John David shining, haloed, a bruise in the center of brightness. He had already changed me. Walking toward him on the road made by his shining, I melted into him, and our darkness became pure light.

• • •

The Plan was an anti-plan, really. It was going to be a total surrender to God. That was all I knew. John David promised we would surrender ourselves to the source of the light together and sink into the sea of His love, and we'd never have to make a plan of any kind ever again.

One night I typed out the verse about the lilies of the field. He corrected me.

we won't be lilies, he wrote. *we'll be nothing. we'll be nothing at all.*

On the last night before the Plan, Jane looked at me while we were brushing our teeth and said, "I know something about you."

I was silent. I was counting to a hundred, like I always did when brushing. I could feel Jane's eyes on me in the bathroom mirror but pretended I was alone so my face wouldn't move.

"You think nobody notices," Jane said, trying again. Foamy toothpaste dribbled out of her mouth and she spat it into the sink. "You think you're so cool."

I did not think I was cool. My parents thought I was cool. My friends thought I was cool, and some of them were even cool themselves. But I wasn't. I only looked that way because of my friends, who were always calling me on the weekends to go to the mall, where somebody's older sibling would drop us off so we could try on halter tops at Wet Seal and smell all the perfumes at Sephora. There were slumber parties at Kristian's house with the whole team, and late-night chats with Lauren or Maya, some of which had begun to revolve around Aaron. I wondered if this was what Jane thought she knew. The made-up crush on Aaron had begun to take on such a life of its own that sometimes, in a moment of confusion, I thought it was real.

I refocused on the mirror and noticed that Jane was still staring, but this time her face was flushed and there were tears wobbling in her eyes. "How come you don't like me anymore?"

I reached a hundred just as the subject changed. It was not a coincidence, I knew by now. Nothing was. I leaned over and carefully spat into the sink, then straightened up and rubbed my mouth with the towel. "Why do you think I don't like you?" I asked.

"You could have just said 'I do like you.'" Jane sniffed.

"I do like you!"

"No, you don't," Jane went on. By this time the tears were squeezing out of the corners of her eyes and tracking down her reddened cheeks. Jane cried all the time now. Mom said she was hitting puberty earlier than I had, and at least it was all going to be over sooner that way. In her old-man pajamas, as I called them, the button-down flannel top and drawstring bottoms hanging off her, Jane looked bigger than me, even if she wasn't quite as tall yet. She didn't have boobs either, but there was something about her that looked like the beginning of something. Mom said she might even be taller than me soon.

I won't know, I thought with a pang.

"You're my sister," I explained, "I don't like you, I love you." I had meant it to sound funny, but as I said it, I knew that it was true. We had played and fought and done everything together throughout our childhood, Jane throwing toys when I turned my back and ignored her, me running to Mom when Jane wouldn't obey the rules of a board game or when she quit because she wasn't winning. Tears started tickling my eyes and I wondered, automatically and dispassionately, if I should let them fall, if doing so would benefit the Plan.

"How come you never want to hang out with me, then? You're

always hanging out with your new friends, and I have to stay home and watch TV by myself. You haven't even watched *Beauty and the Beast* with me once all summer."

"That movie is kind of dumb, Jane," I said. "It's a kids' movie."

"It's not dumb! I like the songs." Jane's favorite song was the one in the tavern. Whenever no one was paying attention to her, she'd start singing it, and if you didn't stop and do some of the voices with her, she would continue singing it, louder and louder. Jane was never afraid to be annoying, never afraid to take up space.

"I'm not a little kid anymore, Jane. I don't like princesses and cartoons and stuff."

"I miss you," Jane said.

Now the first tear came out, all of a sudden, after I'd thought the danger was over. *I'm right here,* I started to say, but the words stuck in my throat. "I'll watch it with you this weekend," I said instead, "I promise," and the lie somehow made me stronger, straightened me up.

Ordinary Julie would be there Saturday morning to keep her promise, I told myself. Ordinary Julie would stay behind to see what happened with Jane, watch over her, help her with her homework, tell her not to wear something that would make the kids tease her at school.

"Really?" Jane said.

"Yeah, sure." I looked back at the mirror. "What was the thing you were saying? What do you know about me?"

Jane's tears were gone now. She didn't smile, but she managed to look as if she wanted to. "I know you don't really like track," she said. "I know you're only pretending to like it so you can fit in."

I paused. I had never really thought about whether I liked track or not. It seemed so obvious that if you *could* play a sport, you should, whether or not you enjoyed it, because with a swarm of friends around you, any lie could become the truth. Suddenly I pitied Jane with her awkward face, every emotion going straight from her insides to her outside.

Jane would never be good at sports, I thought. She wouldn't be popular in eighth grade like I was.

"Good night," I said, and I wrapped my arms around her for a moment, long enough to remind us both how much fun we used to have together. When I was ready to pull away, I counted to three first. Ordinary Julie wasn't enough for Jane. She always wanted a little more.

That night I woke up to a rough hand over my mouth. I tried to gasp but couldn't, and, still half asleep, for a moment I thought I was drowning.

When I opened my eyes, there was a bearded man leaning over me. He nodded, and after a moment of paralysis, I nodded back, and he slowly, slowly removed his hand—keeping it near enough to clasp over my mouth again should I scream.

It was Charlie, but also not. His dark blond hair was straggly and long, long enough for a ponytail. His beard was darker than his hair, and a mustache covered his mouth with shadows. He smelled sweet and sour at the same time, like the smell that came out of the recycling bin when I emptied it after school.

That was my first impression of John David, and I immediately wanted to scream.

But I was Plan Julie, and so I repeated over and over in my head: *It's not really kidnapping. It's not real. I'm running away to meet my destiny. This is what I was born for. I am being chosen. He is choosing me.*

I smiled at John David, trying to show him I remembered, I knew. If he smiled back, I couldn't see it under his beard. His hand trembled as he pulled the blankets off me and reached out to help me out of bed, but when I put out my hand, he wrapped his around my wrist instead and pulled me to my feet slowly but forcefully.

We moved deliberately, playing the mirror game, flowing together across the floor, me anticipating his movements so that he wouldn't feel even a hint of resistance. I was so desperate to please him. My eyes did not leave his for a moment, as if we were dancing, his hand wrapped around my wrist, and the rest was all electrical current moving my feet silently across the floor. Then I saw what was in his other hand.

Although the word *knife* had been part of the Plan, I had never actually associated it with the knives hanging in the kitchen; I had never looked at any one of them and thought *Knife* and pictured it in his hand. It drifted up slowly, almost lazily, until it was level with my chest, and I thought, *He doesn't want to scare me* and tried even harder not to be scared. He circled around behind me and clamped his hand down on my shoulder. I felt the tip of the knife press into my back, not hard enough to cut, but hard enough so its cold metal tip separated the fibers of my nightshirt.

Now there was the relief of knowing exactly what to do, because there wasn't a choice.

I thought I'd given up control when we'd started discussing the Plan, but I hadn't—it had all been a game. But now, with him standing invisibly behind me, an unseen presence marching me forward with the pressure of a hand on my shoulder and the sharpness of a knife just to the right of my spine, I knew that the time to decide against the Plan had passed. Thoughts floated through my mind that did not sit comfortably next to one another; for instance, I did not know where he was taking me, and where was Jane? *Oh, safe in bed,* Jane was safe in bed. She'd stay there forever, tucked into a life that would never change.

Then Jane's face suddenly appeared.

I caught sight of her as we approached the open door to her room—we usually slept with the doors open. I could barely see her hiding in her cracked-open closet, down low by the floor, looking at me with eyes that were not closed and warm with sleep but wide and red-rimmed with terror. John David and I stood on the landing. Jane's face peered out at me from behind the closet door, desperately asking me what to do next.

I motioned with my eyes toward John David and willed Jane to sink back into the closet's darkness before he saw her. If she screamed once, it would all be over. He would get her too. And no matter where he was taking me, no matter what he was going to do to me, I would not let him do it to Jane.

Just before John David marched me down the stairs, there was a noise from the attic. I felt the knife's point lessen its tension for just a moment, the hand on my shoulder twist ever so slightly, and knew John David was looking away. As quickly as I could, I raised my hand and put a finger to my lips, *Shhh,* pushing the soft imaginary breath across the room to freeze Jane in place, *shhh,* and goodbye, *shhh,* and goodbye.

And that is how I lost my family, my home, my life, and my self —everything, everything—in one night.

16

One afternoon when I was pregnant with Jane, and Tom was off in an accounting class and we still lived in the little house near my university, Julie sat on the wood floor of the living room in a patch of sunlight. Her baby feet stuck out in front of her, and her wisps of hair were lit up white by the sun. She was concentrating on moving a blue crayon over a newspaper in front of her. When she accidentally squeezed the crayon too hard and it skittered away, she didn't cry, and she didn't get another crayon, even though there were dozens lying all around her. She screwed her face up, made her fingers into clumsy pincers, scooted herself toward the rolling blue crayon, and recovered it. Then she resumed coloring until the whole cycle started over again.

I watched her for maybe half an hour before it hit me: *She likes the color blue.*

It was the first time I understood that there was a whole world in there I would never see, a world so distant from me, and so distinct, that to say that Julie was made from me, that she was my daughter and I was her mother, seemed meaningless. I think I loved her more profoundly in that moment than I have ever loved anyone.

But that's memory for you. At first, I wanted the world for Julie, like all mothers do. Then, for a long time, I only wanted a body to bury.

Now, I just wish I could go back in time and hand her the goddamn blue crayon.

Reading through the transcript, devouring it, in fact, I learn the shape of her trauma, I study the names of all the girls she had to be to survive: Charlotte, Karen, Mercy, Starr, Violet, Gretchen. In her testimony, they struggle, they fight, they fail, but above all, they survive. Even as I choke back tears thinking of all she's been through, I hold each one dear, each of these girls, because each is a layer of my daughter, the one waiting at home with Tom.

But the girl whose story hurts me most is Julie. She's the one I thought I knew but didn't. Worse still, she's the one who knew *me*. Her words give me a picture of myself I don't recognize. I try to remember each moment she describes of her unfolding adolescence, to remember and possibly justify the role I played in it, but that feeling of otherness is monumental. I recognize the outlines of the situations, Jane and Tom and me reduced to characters in her story, but it's like seeing them, seeing us all, on an alien planet through an alien atmosphere.

I try to remember Julie asking me about God, but I can't. Who was I, what was I doing that I can't remember? I was finishing up a postdoc, then interviewing for jobs. *I knew she was laughing, but I thought she was laughing at me.*

My mom just sort of looked at me when I wore pretty clothes, her lips pressed together. I don't need a mirror to know what that expression looks like. I saw it on my mother's face over and over again. I didn't know it was on mine.

I had the answer all worked out, but my mom never asked.

I'd believed the girls were benefiting from my example, if not my undivided attention.

I guess she never thought about how uncomfortable it was to walk four blocks in church flats.

I read somewhere that Puritans would sometimes explain the death of a particularly beloved child as the parents' punishment for having loved the child too much. They blamed not the awful winters or the malarial swamps or the lack of good food or clean water, but a jealous God.

I never loved Julie more than Jane, I can say that with confidence. At the same time, there was always something about her. She seemed so complete in herself, so serene. Somewhere deep down, I thought Julie was perfect. Now I wonder: Was I so afraid of finding out she wasn't perfect that I almost killed her?

When they unlock the cell door, they don't tell me where they are taking me. It's strange how little anyone tells prisoners outside of directing them to put their hands out to be cuffed and pointing them down hallways. I guess nobody wants to be responsible for sharing privileged information.

I assume I am being taken to see my lawyer, because that's what has happened every other time I've been brought down this particular corridor. But this time, we take a right instead of a left at the end and go through a door with a wired window in it. And then suddenly, I am standing by the front desk as my cuffs are being removed.

Tom stands there too, awkwardly, his hand fiddling nervously with his keys in his pants pocket.

The guard says, "The charges have been dropped. Your things will be at the front desk in just a minute, you'll need to go over them and sign a paper saying everything's there." My eyes meet hers for only a moment before she looks away. Maybe it's hard for them to make eye contact with us after we're free.

She disappears behind the door again, leaving us alone in the cramped waiting room, the woman who works the front desk presumably off rummaging for the box containing my clothes, my shoes, my purse with the book on Byron and landscape, still half read, tucked inside it. I'm suddenly overwhelmed with a craving to finish it.

"Maxwell confessed," Tom says. "Apparently he was on psych meds—for schizoaffective something or other. But they didn't know that at the hospital, so he didn't get any there, and before they could figure out what was wrong, he started talking to God about his—sins."

"Bet Judge Crofford didn't know about the meds."

"No one did. Not even his top advisers. The drugs kept the worst symptoms under control, but—" He looks down. "Seven more victims have come forward."

Seven. And those are just the ones willing to talk to the police.

"Thanks for coming," I say.

"There wasn't time to schedule a call," he says. "I guess once the charges are dropped, they're eager to get you off the taxpayers' dime."

"That makes sense."

We stand in silence under the fluorescent lights.

"Anna," he says.

"It's okay," I say.

"I'm sorry."

"It's not your fault," I say. "I wasn't there. I checked out."

"I shouldn't have let you," he says.

"You're a good man," I say, too weary for this. "You always have to be helping someone. I didn't want your help, so you gave it to someone else."

"If I could take it back—"

"Don't say that," I interrupt. "Someone got her daughter back because of you. You wouldn't change that, so don't say you would because you think it'll please me. It won't."

He looks stricken, and I soften despite myself. "Honestly, Tom?" I say. "It's a relief to know that you're not an angel. It's a standard I could never live up to."

I don't tell him how much it hurts to see him tumble from his pedestal. This is why people need God—because people are awful, even the good ones. I've always prided myself on being so rational, so unafflicted by spiritual yearnings, not realizing my personal gods were Tom and Julie, the good people. But nobody ever gets to be good except on the terms the world hands them.

Finally, the front-desk matron emerges with a plastic bag holding my clothes and purse. I poke through the bag and sign the papers. Then I take everything into a visitors' restroom, change back into my street clothes, fold the blue prison scrubs neatly in a pile. I reemerge looking something like myself again.

Tom smiles.

As I set the stack of prison pajamas on the front desk, I wonder if this is it for Tom and me. If he can smile this easily at the sight of me looking like I did before, before all this happened, if he can so quickly forget the image of me as a prisoner, then he is always going to misunderstand who I am and what I am.

We exit into the bright sunlight. The sun is beating down on the Commerce Street port, and the air is scalding hot.

"Do you think Janie will come home?" I ask, thinking of her first date with the guy on the kickball team. I haven't heard how it went. I resisted telling her to meet at a public place, to let a friend know where they were going.

Tom looks uncomfortable. "She's staying up there for a while longer, Anna. She really wants to get back on track, finish all those incompletes and show her professors she can tough it out." He sighs. "I'm sorry. You know Janie."

I do know Janie. The incompletes were nothing more than a cry for attention, but she has terrible timing. Jane functions well under duress, gravitates toward drama, and can be generous as long as no one expects her to be. Then, when the waters still and her dramatics would be entertaining, she's back to her own world. I think of all the journals. "Wait for it. She'll switch her major to creative writing before the year is out."

"Why do you say that?"

"She'll want to start working on her memoirs."

Tom laughs, still a little uneasy, as we get into the SUV. We make our way to I-10, the churning of the air conditioner at full blast filling the silence. It's a little past six, and the rush from downtown has mostly cleared, but when we hit Loop 610, the backup begins. The lowering sun, undaunted by our visors, beats down through the windshield, and the tinting in the back windows only seems to trap the heat. As we slow almost to a standstill somewhere around the Voss exit, the air conditioner, losing velocity from the incoming wind, thumps down a notch in intensity and gives a faint rattle. I wonder if this is going to be the summer the A/C gives out on us. This is the stretch of road where that type of thing always happens.

Suddenly, I say, "Pull the car over."

"We're getting off at the next exit."

"Pull over now!"

He puts on his blinker. Traffic is sluggish, but he cuts across three lanes, nosing over and waving his hand like a flag in front of the rearview mirror. As soon as the tires thunk onto the shoulder, I open the door and Tom slams on the brakes as I stumble out. My stomach heaves up into my mouth and out onto the pavement.

There's not a lot in there, I've barely been eating, but I heave and heave. My vision goes red in the heat, and then black, and then Tom is there, on his knees behind me, with his big arms around me, supporting me. Waves of heat that reek of gasoline and vomit are coming up off the pavement, each one bringing a fresh wave of spasms with it, but his hands on me are warmer still. After a moment, I sink back into him like an armchair, and he settles down under my weight, and we sit together on the gravel at the side of the freeway.

"She left us, Tom," I say, but my voice disappears in the roadside symphony of honking horns and Doppler effects. He continues to smooth my hair back over my sweating temple, but now, despite the heat, I am shivering, cold and hot at the same time. I pull away from him, turn toward his face. I say it louder, but he shakes his head, still not hearing. Finally, I lean toward him and force my mouth to open wide and I yell at the top of my lungs, "*Julie left!*"

This time he understands, but shakes his head back and forth in response. "Come on!" he shouts, and starts to make his way to standing, holding out one hand to me and gesturing toward the car with the other.

But yelling has freed something in me that was pressed into the dingy little cage of a jail cell for the past week. Julie's deposition is still banging around inside me, and if I don't let it out, it will punch holes in my lungs, and I'll drown. "*Tom!*" I yell. "She *left!*"

"I know!" he shouts back.

"How can you be so calm?" I demand.

"Come on, Anna, get in the car!"

But it's easier to scream out here, and this is something I want to scream. "What kind of mother am I, Tom? I didn't know her at all!"

"What do you want me to do about it?" he yells back. "I didn't either!"

"But I'm the *mother!*"

"Yes, you're the mother!" he yells. "You're the mother, and she needs you right now. So let's get in the car, for God's sake, and go home and yell it at *her!*"

The adrenaline drains out of me, and I follow him to the Range

Rover and get in, feeling the car shudder as the traffic going past starts to pick up. The quiet when we shut the doors feels profound.

"You read the deposition?" I say in a voice that is only slightly hoarse.

"I didn't need to read it. I was there to hear most of it."

"How could I have been so blind? How could I have missed all that? It's like I didn't know her at all." I can't let the tears prickle up one more time today, so I press them down. "I know I've been broken since it happened. I know I've been awful with Jane. But I thought—before that, I mean—I thought everything was good. I thought I was a good mother."

There's a long silence. Then he says, "I think it would have been good enough, Anna. But we'll never know now. None of us know who we would have been. He took that away from us."

Tom starts the engine, puts on his blinker, and forces the car out into the Houston traffic. He's a wonderfully aggressive driver.

When we're moving again, he says, "Can I confess something?" I wait. "I wish it had been me who shot Maxwell."

I picture Tom the night Julie had her miscarriage, standing with the gun in his hand as I punched my fist through the bathroom door to get to my daughter. Then I lean over and take his hand.

There's a car parked outside our house, and when we walk in the door, Julie is sitting at the kitchen table with an African American man in a T-shirt and jeans. As soon as we walk in the door, he stands up.

"Mom, Dad, this is Cal," Julie says.

"Mr. Whitaker." Cal extends a hand to Tom, who takes it, though he looks a bit bewildered. Cal is almost a head shorter than Tom, but he doesn't seem as if he's craning his neck up to meet Tom's gaze. "Glad to meet you," says Tom, and I can see Cal scoping me out from the corner of his eye before turning to me.

"Dr. Davalos," he says. Julie must have schooled him in how to address me.

"I understand you helped Julie out of a tough situation," I say to Cal.

"You did too," he says, simply and warmly.

I wonder, *Is this the rest of my life? Are all of Julie's men going to have to live up to me? And do any of them know she was poised with her gun, ready to kill? Do they know what I really saved her from?*

People have a lack of imagination about women like Julie and what they're capable of. I was guilty of it myself once. I know better now, of course. But I would never disabuse the men in her life, the Toms and Cals, of the notion that Julie needs protecting. Fostering that illusion is part of how she's survived this long. To take away that coping mechanism before it has outlived its usefulness would be cruel.

Cal looks to be older than her, though it's hard to tell how much since his skin is unwrinkled everywhere but around his eyes when he smiles. I wonder if he will be with her on the day she outgrows the useful illusion of her frailty and how he will react if he's still around. It might be a long time before that happens, a lifetime, even. I may not live to see it myself.

Meanwhile, it'll be our secret.

"It's very nice to meet you, Cal. Now, would you and Tom mind if I talked to Julie for a few minutes?" I ask. "Alone."

Tom says, "I was just going to run up to the grocery store and get some stuff for dinner. Why don't you come along, Cal. We can get to know each other."

"Sure," Cal says after a backward glance at Julie, who nods. The two men walk out of the kitchen.

When they have been gone for a full thirty seconds, I look at my daughter. I don't know what I'm expecting. A revelation? To find out what color her eyes are, once and for all? I see the same woman I've been looking at for the past month, as much of a mystery to me as ever.

"Why didn't you come back?" I ask. "After you escaped from Maxwell. Why didn't you come home?"

There's a long pause. "I wanted to. I was going to. But it seemed like once he—did that to me, nothing went the way it was supposed to. Things kept happening."

I know some of the things she is talking about, and I don't want her to have to repeat them. At the same time, I don't want to shut her down, ever again. So I wait patiently, and after a moment, she goes on, giving me a strange look that I can't really interpret. "Besides, I didn't know whether you'd want me back."

I choke on my next words. "How can you say that?"

"I thought you'd be mad," she says with a weird smile. "I hated Julie. She was stupid and gullible. And she left you."

"You were only a child. He took you."

"He took me," she agrees. "But to me, it felt like I was leaving on my own."

"That's what he wanted you to think."

"And there was Charlotte. She was dead, and I was scared it was my fault."

"He wanted you to think that too."

"Well, he was good at it. Or I was good at believing it." She shrugs, giving up. "Anyway, I'm not sure it makes me feel any better if I didn't have a choice. If that's true, if I was just a random victim, then my life was ruined for no reason at all."

That, of course, is what I have always believed. I don't say it, but she can see me thinking it.

"You've never believed in God. I don't think Jane does either. Maybe Dad doesn't care either way. But it was different for me; I wanted to find something out there. I still do, I just don't know the word for it."

"Transcendence?" I say. "There's no such thing."

"But maybe there is," she says. "I don't know. Think of all those people at the Gate."

"I'd rather not."

"But you have to," she says. "You have to. What are they looking for? Why are they so happy there? Where else could they find that kind of happiness?"

"Poetry," I say. "Music. Art."

"That's not enough for everyone. It wasn't enough for me."

Her face looks sad and eager at the same time, and I suddenly recognize a glimmer of an expression I remember from her childhood. I never knew what it was before. It reminds me of something.

"'Not in entire forgetfulness, / And not in utter nakedness, / But trailing clouds of glory do we come.'" I almost stop there, but for Julie's sake, I finish: "'From God, who is our home.' Wordsworth."

"Why do you have to put quotation marks around it to understand it?"

"All I have is other people's words, Julie."

They are, at present, failing me. After another long moment

of silence, it occurs to me to that I have nothing to lose by just asking. "You came back for Maxwell, because you saw that magazine profile, okay. But you didn't have to come back as Julie. If you were worried about being blamed for what happened with Charlotte, why didn't you just leave an anonymous tip for the police and let them take care of it? Why did you come back to us after so long when you knew you would have to lie?" I take a deep breath. "Was it the money? It's okay if it was."

She looks up, startled, with china-blue eyes. "I missed you," she says.

The worst doesn't unhappen, but just like that, I am home.

Acknowledgments

The love and support of friends and family made this book possible. I'd like to extend special thanks to the members of my extraordinarily talented and committed writing group, Alissa Zachary, Linden Kueck, Victoria Rossi, Dan Solomon, and Paul Stinson; to Martin Kohout and his late wife, Heather Kohout, for the time I spent working on this novel at Madroño Ranch in Medina, Texas; to my agent, Sharon Pelletier at Dystel & Goderich Literary Management, for her infectious enthusiasm for this project; to Lauren Abramo at DGLM for tirelessly representing me overseas; and to Tim Mudie, my editor at Houghton Mifflin Harcourt, for guiding me patiently and insightfully through the exciting process of turning my words into a book. We did it! Biggest and best thanks are reserved for my husband, Curtis Luciani, for encouraging me to write a novel in the first place, believing in me when I didn't think I could do it, and always making sure I had coffee in the morning and a room of my own.